JESSICA LOST HER WOBBLE

J. Schlenker

Cover Photo Designed on www.canva.com
Bike at Beach
By IOFOTO

This is a work of fiction. All names, characters, locales and incidents are products of the author's imagination, and any resemblance to actual people, places or events is coincidental or fictionalized.

ISBN:692600655
ISBN-13:9780692600658

Binka Publishing

DEDICATION

To my husband, Chris, who continuously encourages me to write.

PROLOGUE

HE PLACED THE receiver back on the hook. How odd. Could it be a prank? No, the phone call was too official. Besides, none of his friends played jokes. No one he could think of knew about his past with Jessie. The call was definitely legitimate.

But why would a doctor contact him about Jessie? It had been decades since he last saw her. The doctor's tone was serious, and he simply stated that the matter concerned his ex-wife, asking if they could talk.

After all this time, he owed nothing to Jessie. He was sure they had settled what had been between them long ago. He was happy and content with his new life, and he wished the same for Jessie. He had no way of knowing if this were the case, though. He had lost track of her not long after they had parted ways. Maybe she had remarried. If so, why was she still using his last name? He struggled with whether to go or just to ignore the call. But his curious nature was getting the better of him.

Should he tell his wife about the call? Carol knew that he had once been married to Jessie. He kept no secrets from her. No, he would go and see what it was about and then tell her. That wouldn't be keeping a secret if he told her after the fact. He reasoned he would have more to relate to her if he waited until after the visit. Telling her beforehand would only cause her to worry. The whole matter might be nothing. He let out a sigh. The appointment was tomorrow. He would sleep on it.

The glow of the moon that night came through the bedroom window and lit up Carol's face. Over the years she had aged little. What few lines she had, dissolved into childlike innocence with her retreat into sleep. He wondered if time had been so kind to Jessie. He was deluding himself. He knew it hadn't been. A pang of guilt shot through him as he wrapped his arm around his wife's curved belly. Usually after making love he would pass out, but tonight was different. Instead of sleep he counted his blessings, one by one. But Jessie kept creeping into the picture. All the possible scenarios he could think of played over and over in his mind before exhaustion won out.

CHAPTER 1

JESSIE GRABBED her usual chocolate bar and cola and set them on the wooden counter. Its indented surface had seen better days. Day after day, people placed their customary purchases on this aged, worn structure. The oak, long ago absent of grain, had absorbed into its essence an ever so faint odor that came from every hand throughout the years that had ever stroked its exterior. It was not an unpleasant smell. It was a scent that said, *I know each one of you and what you will slide across my surface. I have ingested you into my skin. I know the routine.* You *are routine.*

If nothing else, Jessie exemplified dull routine habits — bad ones. The junk food was the least of it. For the zillionth time, she told herself it was time to give up her sorry habits, her old life, and start anew. That had been the plan all along in coming to the island. That was three years ago, not that it mattered. Time stood still here

It was a day like any other, yet there was a taste of change in the air. Today would be the beginning of a breakthrough. Jessie knew it as well as she knew her own name.

The owner of the store, Mr. Roberts, was in the back helping Mrs. Gibbons. Like the wooden counter, Mrs. Gibbons, too, had seen better days. Jessie looked back and smiled at Mrs. Gibbons and tried not to show impatience. No one on the island showed impatience or annoyance of any kind. It was one of those unspoken rules of paradise. That was the kind of place the island was, a paradise — a fantasy of the mind. Each resident made it into what they wanted.

Mrs. Gibbons personified the definition of whimsical. Short and boxlike in stature, she looked like something out of a cartoon. Gold-rimmed, sparkly glasses teetered on the tip of her nose. She painted her lips red in the center like a porcelain doll. When she smiled back at Jessie, the pale ends of her lips curving upward were nearly invisible. Mrs. Gibbons raised her eyelids, which didn't even come close to the umber penciled on eyebrows. She wore one of those typical brightly colored, flowered shirts that one finds on an island. Force of gravity and a thin shirt indicated she had forgotten to wear a bra. It was a blessing to the viewer she wasn't well endowed. Mrs. Gibbons finished her fashion repertoire off with neon red shorts, exhibiting knobby knees. The low-heeled ochre sandals she wore displayed chipped crimson toenails which matched her shorts. And as for Mrs. Gibbons' leathery tanned blue veined legs, well, you had to give her credit. Jessie wished for such a blithe attitude. She gave Mrs. Gibbons another smile, for good measure.

It was easy to forgive the fashion transgressions of a woman of eighty-something years, who had recently lost her husband. There was a lot of forgiveness on the island. Other than the paradise factor, to forgive, to be forgiven, and mainly to forget was why people came here. There were a lot of inhabitants like Mrs. Gibbons. Everyone referred to them as locals. Jessie fit somewhere in the void, between local and tourist.

Before the island, Jessie had lived in New York City. Aggravation was a way of life there. She could relate to Mrs. Gibbons and creatures like her having been on the wrong end of the aggravation and pity stick before moving here. Jessie saw Mrs. Gibbons and other misfits of society as kindred spirits and sympathized.

Annoyance, aggravation, criticism, or irritation of any kind was unfathomable, behaviors you left behind when you came here. Such attributes were akin to hitting a child. Even before Jessie came to the island, she never let such sentiments surface. She showed few emotions. It was the professional opinion of Dr. Linn, her therapist, that Jessie needed to emote.

Jessie had replied that she didn't know how. The doctor had interpreted it as she didn't know the meaning of the word and looked at her like she was stupid. That's how Jessie perceived it. Even though, he was from somewhere in Asia, he had a better command of the English language than she did. Jessie didn't know how to show emotion, at least in public. To Jessie, two or more people meant public. She let it go. Why explain? Explaining would only create those emotions she was uncomfortable with.

While Jessie hovered over the counter, she fingered over the packs of gum. It passed the time while she waited. She never purchased gum. She wasn't a gum chewer. Her ex had a habit of chewing it after he smoked, Juicy Fruit if her memory was correct. She remembered. Why pretend that she didn't remember even the tiniest little thing he did? There were big irritations and small irritations. His smoking was a big irritation. The gum chewing was minor.

Mr. Roberts smiled and looked her way. "Jessie, I'll be with you in a moment."

"No hurry," she replied as she scanned the magazines. Jessie had time. All she had these days was time. Like Mrs. Gibbons, it was becoming more about comfort and taking life at a slow pace.

For Mrs. Gibbons, the comfort thing happened after her husband's funeral. *What a cute couple they were* had become a cliché on the island. The bra had been for Mr. Gibbons. It just wasn't necessary anymore.

That was how Jessie felt now — unnecessary. She should ditch her bras. What a peculiar way to describe one's life — unnecessary. That was something she could remember her mother saying. Or was that her imagination? No, she remembered her mother saying, "I feel so unnecessary today."

While Mr. Roberts was in back assisting Mrs. Gibbons, a young blonde girl, wearing a pink shirt and jeans, entered the store.

Jessie's mother loved the color pink. Pink roses were her mother's favorite flower. She had a garden full of every variety of pink rose. Jessie did her best to hold onto the pleasant memories.

Jessie felt the young girl's eyes on her. She envied the girl's youthfulness but more so her straight hair. Every strand was in place falling in a perfect pattern down her back. Jessie pushed her own defiant caramel curl that fell over her right eye behind her ear. The move was counterproductive since it exposed more freckles. Jessie preferred to call them freckles. God forbid they were the age spots her aunt had warned her about. Aunt Agatha had been a big proponent of skin as white as a pearl and warned against too much sun; advice Jessie disregarded. Maybe she imagined the spots — just something her aunt had put in her mind. The impression had lingered there, the way her mother's feeling, of being unnecessary, had somehow lodged in her brain.

Jessie looked down at the magazine. The word UNNECESSARY glared out at her in big bold letters. Startled, she let out a small shriek, catching the attention of Mr. Roberts and the girl. Mrs. Gibbons was oblivious. Jessie looked up and said, "Sorry." She looked back down at the magazine. She refocused. It said in big, bold letters, "Necessary Items for Every Woman's Closet." It was just her imagination.

It was the same with the age spots — just her imagination. Besides, she had to push her nose up against the mirror to see them. Maybe they weren't there at all. Maybe she should ditch the mirror with the bras.

Funny, how all the negative thoughts of others took up permanent residence in her psyche. Jessie chanted a silent mantra, *think only pleasant thoughts*. It was her new exercise in changing her life, in breaking those bad habits. She had read a magazine article about how to change your life with positive thoughts. After reading the article, she decided that was to be her new mantra, think only positive thoughts.

She looked back at the blonde. What must the young girl be thinking? She had to be in her early twenties, maybe her daughter's age. Jessie was now pushing the mid-forty envelope. People had always thought her younger, but those days were getting further apart. There had been a lot of days when she had seen young guys looking at her, some even flirting. She chalked up no flirtations to little, if any, new guys on the island. The tourist season would bring them back. That was a positive thought.

Now, she was Mrs. or ma'am. Ma'am was a turning point that every woman dreaded. She still wore a ring. She didn't mind being a Mrs.

There had been no reason to take the ring off. Jessie had lost weight since coming to the island. She didn't own a scale, but her clothes were looser. She reasoned that when her finger got skinny enough, the gold band would just fall off. That would save her the trouble of the momentous decision to remove it.

Eating wasn't a big pastime on the island, except for fish fries. Jessie remembered all those late night dinners she had in New York. On the island, she often skipped dinner. Usually, she was in bed an hour after sunset, turning the pages of a magazine or a mystery novel until she fell asleep. She avoided romance novels. They were fantasy, something Dr. Linn had told her to get over. Dr. Linn was big on facing reality.

The blonde's quick stare penetrated Jessie's very soul.

Only pleasant thoughts, she told herself. Jessie knew everything the blonde was thinking. *She admired Jessie's carefree hair, natural curl with different streaks of colors running through it. It had touches of the rainbow — crimson and tinges of blonde from the sun. The blonde thought Jessie a natural island being, a legged mermaid, and wanted to emulate her.*

The blonde had worked at the makeup counter in a department store in New York. It started out as a summer job, but her boss kept asking her to stay. What she lacked in makeup skills, she made up for with an outgoing personality. Her supervisor had said that she had a way of making women feel good about themselves after their makeovers. Her customers felt on top of the world and wanted to exploit this new sense of well-being. That caused them to buy more makeup. Before coming to the island, she promised her boss one more month. She didn't want a makeup counter to be her career.

The blonde thought some women just looked good without makeup. On some days, she just wanted to tell them so. Even though she was a talker, she did her best not to let errant thoughts slip to customers as she worked on commission and therefore, needed to sell the make-up.

Island life was different. It had taken an hour just for her hair, and another for her makeup to get it just right so it wouldn't be over or under done. Then the breeze and negative ions coming from the ocean disintegrated all her hard work. She planned on putting makeup behind her when her samples ran out. It was just one of those customs she still adhered to for the moment.

She was young, and her moments had become wherever the wind took her. Before her alias as a makeup technician, she had subscribed to the beatnik scene, which required no makeup. She was a creature of extremes. Her father had suggested some time at the island as a place of transition and reflection. Her father had a yogic way of thinking. Behind the make-up counter, it was all about image. Even at her young age, she realized it was mere facade. Here, the makeup had to become a part of you, something that people didn't notice. So why wear it at all?

She looked over at Mrs. Gibbons. She thought how adorable she was while contemplating how to tone her down. She was midway through the makeover process before she commanded her mind to halt. She reasoned it would be sacrilege to take away her old lady island charm. She had been here two days. It was like entering an alien world. She could feel transition in the sea air already.

The blonde looked back at the woman at the counter. What was her age? Early thirties she thought. She saw her look back. All that natural beauty, and yet, there was a sadness about her. She felt like reaching out to her. She didn't know why.

Mr. Roberts, after attending to Mrs. Gibbons, made his way over and rang up Jessie's purchases.

"So, how have you been Jessie? Haven't seen you in a while," he asked.

"I'm fine, and how is your family?"

"Everyone is as well as could be expected. Cork will be home from college on Thanksgiving. Myra and I are looking forward to that."

He didn't bother to look at the prices. He knew them by heart. Just a month ago, Cork would have waited on her before making his way back to school. Jessie put a dollar bill down and took her change, declaring a bag wasn't necessary.

Mr. Roberts had known her for over a decade. He had known her children. His was a generational store, one of the first stores on the island, a landmark, to which everyone came. She had remembered old Mr. Roberts behind the counter on their first summers here. She knew old Mr. Roberts name was Carl. His son, the one waiting on her, was Carl, Jr. Jessie guessed him to be maybe ten years older than herself. He had reminded her plenty of times to call him Carl, but she just couldn't kick the habit of calling him Mr. Roberts.

Before making her way out of the store, she looked up, giving a less than confident smile to both Mr. Roberts and the girl who was now trying on sunglasses. If Jessie emoted anything, it was not having confidence.

The girl must have been visiting a relative since it was off-season. They got few tourists this time of year. Jessie had heard nothing. She had been such a hermit as of late. It had been two weeks since she did any grocery shopping. Nor, had she been to the laundromat for a good bit either. That was the place to hear the latest gossip. Even paradises had to have some excitement. She listened to the gossip but didn't gossip herself. She never knew any gossip to contribute, and even if she did, she didn't like making judgments. That didn't apply in her case. Jessie indulged in self-criticism. It was something that Dr. Linn had pointed out to her. She didn't need a therapist to tell her that. Jessie feared she was the topic of conversation at the laundromat, or maybe they found her boring. She pushed it out of her mind. She tried to leave the judgment back in New York.

Mr. Roberts would have filled Jessie in if the girl had not been within earshot. He knew all the comings and goings. Jessie and Mr. Roberts had an unspoken bond. Mrs. Gibbons might have also told her, although her information was rather unreliable these days.

The wooden door whined, and the bell rang as Jessie departed the store. Everything in the old store groaned, especially the wide-planked oak floor. The morning air was crisp and fresh as she stepped out onto the sidewalk. She felt the sea breeze and smelled the dogs and their owners before they approached, but the fish store down the street overpowered them all.

It was early and not too many people were out, except for the dog walkers carrying their morning cups of coffee. It reminded her of Central Park.

She sniffed the aroma coming from one of the coffee shops as she passed by. The locals referred to it as a hole in the wall, but of all the coffee shops on the island, it was the chosen one. Mugs covered one entire wall. Some belonged to the coffee shop. Etched names in a childlike scroll adorned the others. Most were bad examples of pottery class gone awry. They didn't need names. The wall of cups, as it was called, was a tourist fascination. Like Mr. Robert's store, it was an island landmark. Jessie thought if perhaps she could hold each one in her hands, she could sense the life of the person it belonged to.

Jessie preferred tea. Her husband was a coffee drinker. Both her son and daughter had followed in his footsteps. Josh sometimes had tea, but Gina never touched the stuff. Jessie had never felt the need for coffee or for a dog. Coffee had a bitter taste, and dogs were just too much work, like washing her hair. But after three years on the island, she was considering a dog, for company. Her daughter was on her second Scottish terrier. The first one died at eight years of age. Gina was eight when she got him. Annabelle, her second Scottish terrier, was named after a doll she had when she was little. Jessie would give the idea of owning a dog more thought. She didn't want to rush into anything.

Jessie was aloof by nature, and dogs were the opposite, just not a good match. It was the same with her and her husband. Not a good match. Her daughter had inherited the aloof trait from her. Gina was reserved around Jessie. She was different around different people, like a chameleon. Josh was a different story. He got along with everyone. He was exactly as he appeared, no pretense.

Could a mother love one child more than the other? No, she told herself. She loved them in an equal manner, yet in a different way if that made any sense. Sometimes it took a little more work to spread out the equality. Josh drew people to him like bees to honey. His life was cut too short. How many times did she hear the good die young? Still, it was not fair.

There had been several dogs on the estate she had grown up on, sheepdogs and watchdogs, all running free. On the island, where there was a leash law, the islanders treated their dogs like they were their children. They took them to the vet and talked about their people diseases. Jessie listened in all politeness as the pet owners told their stories. The world of pets spoke a foreign language she wasn't yet privy to.

Her mind wandered. She was too self-absorbed, another one of those bad habits or character flaws she hoped to abandon. She had known people that could meet someone new, talk to them for fifteen minutes, and have enough information for a book. Jessie was lucky to catch their name. Possibly she was just going senile like poor old Mrs. Gibbons.

Dogs had always come up to Josh. Her son hadn't had a dog but was as good with animals as he was with people. Animals had sensed the goodness in him. Jessie didn't know how to relate to people or animals. She attributed it to growing up without a mother.

Jessie's mother had died when she was young. She overheard the doctor talking about complications from female issues. Her father, who was much older than her mother, had never elaborated on the cause of death. He was too old school to speak openly about such matters. She gave up asking about her mother because it had caused her father great distress. That convinced her of her father's great love for her mother. The memories she had were shaky and inaccurate. Still, Jessie relied on any memories she could grasp, made up or not. Her father wasn't a big talker. Jessie must have taken after him in that respect.

After the funeral, her father gave her a locket, instructing her to treat it as a precious piece of jewelry. It was, and still is, her most precious and only piece of jewelry aside from her wedding band. It held an ink drawing of her mother. A tear rolled down her father's cheek as he placed it around her neck. Her father had never shown the least interest in remarrying. He had died before Jessie reached adulthood. His sister, Aunt Agatha, took charge of her. Aunt Agatha passed away not too long after Father. There was no one to tell her if her memories were correct. Jessie left the estate, all the furniture covered in white sheets to await the next owner. She took a page from her father's book and learned to leave things behind.

In retrospect, she concluded her father was afraid if he talked about her mother, a flood wall of emotions would break through. That's what might happen to her if she weren't careful. Jessie's father had been unapproachable when it came to her mother. He had been more than kind to Jessie and affectionate, in every other way. Any form of discipline just wasn't in his nature. He hadn't believed in striking a child, probably why she never spanked Josh or Gina.

So many things changed after her father's death. That was why she was on the beach in a small cottage by herself, no children, no dogs, no husband. She was leaving things behind. Emotions couldn't surface without reminders. Maybe she was running away. Jessie had no choice. She had to accept what was and try to make the best of what life had given her.

She wasn't alone. It was as if half the people on the island were in a self-check in witness protection plan. And, it was during this time of year she felt most exposed. There was little sun to rejoice in and few tourists to hide behind in October. The islanders used the dogs as their shield against life's adversities. They needed the dogs to sense the goodness in them. Maybe Gina needed the same. Jessie needed it now.

Gina was to make an appearance soon. Jessie, in her excitement, placed a dog mat, water bowl, and food bowl in the kitchen. The mere fact that Gina named the dog after her favorite doll made Jessie think that childhood couldn't have been all that bleak for Gina.

Gina's visit didn't come. She hadn't visited since Jessie came to live on the island. It was always the same excuse, a new boyfriend, not a good time to leave. Gina changed lovers with the seasons. She started college twice, but each time she dropped out. Jessie had once attempted a surprise visit back to New York to see Gina. It did not go well. Jessie hadn't mustered the courage to revisit that situation.

Mr. Roberts quit asking about her daughter. It was a

small island. Everyone knew everyone else's pain. He never asked about her husband, either. Jessie sensed that Mr. Roberts didn't like her husband, but maybe he failed to remember him. Mr. Roberts had never brought him up, even after her son's death.

Mr. Roberts was born and bred on the island. Most of the residents hadn't been. They made their way here hoping the ocean air would absorb their pain — physical, mental, or emotional. A lot ended up staying. That was the way it was with her. She just stayed. A summer escape turned into home. The island held many of the good memories, where her children had played on the beach. She had brought Josh and Gina here during the summers when they were just toddlers. Her husband came at first, but after a few years, he made work-related excuses to stay behind.

Even with all that had transpired in her life, she still found the ocean to be a hopeful place. Jessie didn't associate her husband with the island. She sat on the beach and imagined the troubles drifting out with the tide. But on some days, no matter how hard she tried to leave things behind, the tide would just bring them back in. This was one of those days. Everything was surfacing. It was her time of the month and a full moon to boot. She blamed it on that. Jessie knew that some women her age were already in the menopausal stages. Jessie had always been as regular as clockwork from age thirteen. That was when Aunt Agatha moved in with her and father.

She skipped breakfast. It was too early for a cola. So she put it in the fridge for later. She rarely drank alcohol. There were plenty on the island who did. A little wine in the afternoon helped the inhabitants deal with their misfortunes. Lack of money wasn't one of their difficulties. Most here had money, or they wouldn't be living here, including her. Money was not a template for happiness.

The thought of wine in the afternoon had more than once entered Jessie's mind. But drinking alcohol so early, or even a bottle of soda, was too akin to an addiction. Besides, she didn't even like wine that much. Nor did she own wine glasses. She already had enough addictions, mild ones. Drinking alone was more hard-core, a realm she hoped she hadn't reached yet or would never reach. A pot of tea met her requirements.

She struck a match, lit the burner and put the teakettle on to boil. She went through her array of blends, ninety percent herbal. Herbal was for company, not that there ever was any. Herbal also sounded like she had her life altogether, which she didn't. She was saving the herbal tea for her enlightenment period or for company, whichever came first. If she became enlightened first, then more than likely, she wouldn't have the need for company. She would be complete unto herself. That was how she envisioned enlightenment.

She chose the familiar oolong, a bag. Loose tea was for when she was feeling better about herself and felt like making the effort. She might as well stay in sync with the situation. Today was all about taking the easy route, like foregoing makeup.

She rolled back the wrapper on the candy bar she had purchased at Mr. Robert's store. It wasn't too early for chocolate, especially dark. Dark chocolate was better for you. It relieved depression. Jessie had read it in a magazine. After all, people ate chocolate donuts for breakfast. Was there a difference? What was a donut? It was flour and sugar laden chocolate, covered with sprinkles and powdered sugar. She was sure that science could make the case that a solid chunk of dark chocolate was healthier. She had long ago given up milk chocolate. She preferred white chocolate, although it wasn't chocolate at all. It was just cocoa butter, a by-product of chocolate, milk and sugar, another fact she had picked up in the same magazine article.

Jessie placed her new "used" book on the table. She had acquired the book a few weeks ago in the island's lone bookstore. Along with dogs, reading was a big pastime on the island. The book was about yogis.

The book reminded her of the day she was sitting in the hole-in-the-wall coffee shop, when a group of shiny bald monks dressed in orange robes sauntered in. It took a lot to ruffle the locals. This did. There were polite stares and raised eyebrows. That was the extent of their disturbance. At any rate, the locals were pillars of control. If a hurricane were to ever hit the island, Jessie knew she would be in good hands. The monks' presence on the island, even with all the wacky tourists one might see, was a rare appearance. Their manifestation made the locals take a brief reverential pause.

The five monks struck a chord with Jessie. All had herbal tea but one. He had coffee, black, the leader, no doubt. They were a jovial bunch, taking life in stride, as if they were experiencing a dream. What if it was all a dream, like the song, "Row, Row, Row Your Boat?" She had become philosophical since her son's death and since her divorce. Those things made most people reflect on life or step out of it altogether. Jessie was somewhere in the middle. She saw their appearance on the island as some kind of sign and later asked the bookstore owner if there were any books on monks. Myrtle, the owner, went to the back of the store and pulled out a worn cardboard box. She reached in pulling out one that was a little tattered around the edges. Today was the day she would read it.

Josh, like the monks, had taken life in stride. Jessie had dealt with the pain of his death in her usual manner, aloofness. On most days, she felt his presence; on other days, she felt she was dreaming his presence. When Jessie observed something good in life, she attributed it to Josh watching over her. Each day she made it a point to witness good or at least humor. Otherwise, she would go insane.

She made up games in her mind about the Islanders. They were like dolls in a house, put there for her entertainment. One day, she would write about them. It would be a best-selling novel. Her book would have a prominent spot on Myrtle's front table and be in the windows of all the New York bookstores. People excused authors for aloofness or detachment from life. Jessie decided from this point forward to delve more into the lives of the locals. She would have to find out more than names when she talked with them, but if it was a dream, couldn't she just imagine their stories?

Jessie wasn't so distant from life, not any more than most. She was just the center of her own universe as were other humans. She would get her book published. Those who branded her as aloof and remote would boast of her genius saying they knew it all along.

Or maybe she would just take up art. Every other island resident was an amateur or hobby artist. On any sunny day, one had to maneuver through the easels and their owners lining the boardwalk. Ocean scenes filled the local art galleries, shops, restaurants, and cafes. Paintings hung in the most incongruous places. She once saw one in a gas station. They were always a side item sold on commission. More often than not, the owner's wife or niece had painted them. Maybe the blonde girl was a budding artist who had come here to paint.

No, she would opt for being a novelist since that would set her apart. She knew no writers on the island, only readers. The oil painting market along with seashell sculptures was already too flooded. And besides she would have to join one of the artist groups or guilds on the island. They were all in competition with each other. There were groups for most things on the island. She wasn't a joiner. Most writers weren't.

Enough of this self-pity, she told herself. No, it wasn't self-pity. It was a plan. The chocolate had invigorated her to try something new. The book she was reading would give her inspiration. She would find some books on writing, but she couldn't show her face in the bookstore without at least starting this one. Without a doubt, Myrtle would ask her opinion of it. Myrtle was one of those outgoing sorts with an inquisitive nature. She always knew what everyone was reading even if they hadn't purchased it in her shop. Maybe the bookstore was just a front. In secret, Myrtle was writing her own book about the island natives. Jessie would have to get the jump on her.

The book in her hands had belonged to some professor. Two weeks after his funeral, his daughter had brought his entire collection in for a small pittance. He had been a physics professor by day and a closet esoteric by night. There had been books on Carl Jung, Emerson,

Thoreau, books on Gnosticism, and physics textbooks. Myrtle had given Jessie the easiest read. The box was dusty and Myrtle gave the book a quick wipe before depositing it in the bag. Myrtle told Jessie she had browsed the contents of the box upon its arrival and had not bothered to empty it since the books weren't the usual reads of the islanders. Jessie surmised that would be romance novels, fishing books, books on how to best catch them or cook them, or something having to do with dogs.

Jessie understood little about yoga or yogis. There were always art fairs during the summer along the boardwalk. The closest she ever got to a yoga practitioner was while visiting one of the weaving booths, three years ago. She didn't understand why there would be over one weaving booth since rugs would just be a collection pool for sand. Everything had traces of sand, one of the pitfalls of island life.

The hippie couple that had come to the booth was intense in their investigation of a thick white rug. The girl wanted the rug for a yoga mat. It was critical that it be white. White represented purity.

As far as vendors went, hippie or beatnik types were the norm. Jessie observed how the couple and vendor related to each other. The girl's boyfriend had a beard and tattoos, a vest, no shirt, and a macramé wristband resembling a dog's chew toy, grime embedded into its fibers. Other than cutting it off, there was no way to remove it from his wrist. Showers didn't seem to be a high priority.

His girlfriend had a neck-load of beads and scant clothing, revealing prominently the areas of her body that hadn't seen a razor. Nor, like Mrs. Gibbons, did the hippie girl feel the necessity of a bra. One could make the argument she didn't need one, except for those extra chilly days. Flat breasts had to be a plus for yoga. Ample endowments might get in the way or throw off one's balance. Balance was key in yoga. Balance was key in life. Jessie didn't have too much of it.

The booth had no cover, and the sun blistered down on them. Jessie's olfactory sense told her that deodorant also wasn't a high priority. *Be kind and not judgmental*, she told herself. She thought of the laundromat ladies. She was becoming one of them. Jessie resolved to become more compassionate in her observance of the couple. She reasoned over in her mind all the possibilities for the yoga couple's plight. There was no shower or bathtub for shaving, more than likely just a lake for bathing. The couple called a tent or Volkswagen van home. There was no money for impermanent items such as bras or deodorant. After psychoanalyzing the couple, Jessie's summation of them bordered on undying admiration. Maybe shaving was the next ritual she would drop. Whom was she shaving for, anyway? Bathing was different. She couldn't do without hot baths. A hot bath gave her a bit of peace and helped her sleep at night.

The official garb of vendors boiled down to tie-dye, jeans, loose fitting dresses, and an ample amount of beads and other handmade jewelry. An unwritten code of conduct and procedure applied. Trading was a crucial part of the art fair unwritten constitution. The food vendors were no exception. Jessie had spotted some pottery a few booths down, sitting on the side shelf of the funnel cake makers. No money changed hands. There was enough to be had from the island patrons and tourists flocking the boardwalk. Some of the vendors read books during the GrimaldisGrimaldisbetween customers. She knew her book about yogis and not a romance novel would be the book of choice by a vendor during a slow wave of customers. Their lack of worldly goods made Jessie conclude that *yoga couple* had already read it and were practicing its teachings. Jessie just wasn't there yet. She mentally added yoga to her list, right after dog.

Jessie finished the tea and candy bar and then tied her hair back away from her face. She donned her sunglasses and hat and grabbed her beach chair along with her book and walked along the wooden steps over the dune. She situated herself a few yards back from the ocean. She looked intently at the picture of the dark skinned Indian man with piercing brown eyes on the cover for a moment before opening the book. Chapter One.

CHAPTER 2

A STINGING wind blew off the ocean. Jessie's tolerance for the least bit of cold was decreasing year by year. She wrapped the blanket around her to form a cocoon and settled in for a yogic adventure. Upon closer inspection of the cover, she found that unlike the bald monks she had encountered in the coffee shop, this one had plenty of hair, like Samson.

Morning walkers passed, but Jessie ignored them. Likewise, both the tourists and locals ignored her. The locals, mostly elderly, were on their morning beach walks, only breaking stride to examine shells. On the island, forty-five was young. There was still time for her, or was there? She had accepted her fate of slowly transforming into one of the quirky old inhabitants. Or was she already there? Could the metamorphosis have already happened without her even knowing it?

She turned the page. She became engrossed in the book, shutting out her surroundings. Water tickling her toes brought her back to reality. Like the yogis, she had entered that no time zone. She had quit wearing a watch long ago. This new world of mystical yogis fascinated her. Some could transcend time and space. Some yogis could travel with the aid of their mind.

She looked up to find herself alone on the beach. Where was everyone? It was lunchtime. There was a schedule that everyone adhered to during six months of the year. That plan stayed intact until tourists flocked in. Only then did the island come out of its hibernation. That moment awakened subtly by some mystical wave of a wand.

Musicians carried their instruments along the boardwalk. Bands and orchestras increased at a steady pace at the pavilion. Dancing shoes stepped out of their boxes for that new coat of polish. Children and adults on bicycles covered the boardwalk. The odor of horses blended with the scent of dogs as carriages made their way over the streets.

The horses, like the locals, rested for six months of the year and came alive in spring. Jessie didn't even know where they kept the horses this time of year. The animals emerged out of winter hiding only one other time, during the holidays for an encore presentation. From Thanksgiving until Christmas, the island yawned and woke for a short while from its slumber. The carriages and horses adorned with sleigh bells would have looked so marvelous in the snow although she had never seen snow here. The laundromat ladies told her that the white stuff had come a few times.

For the last two hours, the island had all but disappeared from her mind. Her third eye had put her somewhere in the Himalayas. She conjured up different images of India. Colorful silk saris swept through crowded streets. Women in awkward squats pounded flour into flat breads. Bearded saints with unwavering eyes looked toward the Ganges. People shouted in a language she didn't understand. Heads bobbed from left to right indicating yes. It was the opposite side of the world, after all. A craving for mangoes and curry overpowered her senses. The world was magical. It was like New York City in some aspects. A sea gull landing in front of her jolted her back to the pastel shades of the island. She breathed in the sea air and decided she liked where she was. She picked up her chair, folded her blanket, and headed back to her cottage. This was her world.

She must face one of her toughest decisions of the day, lunch. The other one was dinner. Sometimes to make matters easier, she skipped dinner altogether. She shook the sand off, threw her blanket over the railing, and entered through the back screen door. It wasn't locked. There was no need. There were no crimes on the island.

She looked through the fridge. It was bare except for limp carrots and celery, cottage cheese, and a jar of mayonnaise. Another even more pressing decision popped up, when to break down and go to the store. She checked the cottage cheese for mold. It appeared to be okay. She looked through the cupboard. No fruit cocktail left. She must get some real fruit. What she wouldn't give for that mango just now. Did the island grocers even have fresh mangoes? Pineapples, yes. That was about as exotic as it got here.

Back in New York, they had anything you could imagine and more that you couldn't. Anything in question took the local shop boy to fill you in since the store owners often spoke in broken English. They relied on their children to get by. It was that way when she had first moved to New York. The kids grew up speaking English. Some of them didn't even speak their parent's native tongue. They understood them well enough unless it was to their disadvantage. They grew up with street smarts. Her ex had been a product of that environment. She looked in the cupboard. She opted for the easy bag of chips. Her eating habits were atrocious. She resolved to do better. Tomorrow. It was always tomorrow. She put on the teakettle and pulled out her dependable box of oolong.

She sat at the kitchen table, teacup in one hand, and the book in the other. Many of the yogis lived their life in silence. She did too, in a way, but not in the same meaningful way as they did. Some might call her a hermit. Many of the people on the island lived in the same manner. Maybe this is where the newest hermits came to roost. The vastness of the ocean, that primordial pool of souls, acted like a homing beacon to all the wandering hermit souls. She theorized the already reincarnated hermits were either born here on the island or in India. Hermit or not, everyone here was a bit crazy or eccentric.

Reincarnation, that was a new term for her. Well, not new, just hidden in the back of her mind somewhere, ready to leap out. It both intrigued her and made sense to her. It was like yoga. She knew about yoga, somewhere in the deepest recesses of her mind. She also knew from actual experience — if you could call seeing the hairy couple picking out a yoga mat actual experience. She had never tried any yogic poses. At forty-five, her body might break. If she did it alone in her cottage, how long might it be until someone found her? Unlike the dogs on the estate, the dogs here weren't trained for anything such as sniffing out injured people.

She just wasn't ready for yoga, and she knew of no one to teach her. Attempting it on her own was out of the question. She had never been athletic, except for walking great distances if one could call that athletic. Cars were rare on the island. Most walked or rode bicycles.

She had walked plenty in New York. She hated the subway. The bicycle she had brought to the island with her, she never rode. It needed a good de-rusting should she decide to try again. Riding a bicycle all over the island had been one of her goals. When she was young, she was all over the estate on her bike, on dirt roads as well as those bumpy cobblestones. In her younger days, her bicycle was an extension of her body. She didn't think her body would be able to handle those bumps anymore. She wasn't sure if she could even ride a bicycle at this stage of her life. It had been years. No, decades. Her legs were just too wobbly now. Her self-confidence was wobbly. She had lost too much in life. Why couldn't Dr. Linn understand that?

Maybe the blonde girl had brought a bicycle to the island. The girl looked about her daughter's age. They looked nothing alike, though. Her daughter had an Audrey Hepburn kind of look and was just as beautiful. Gina had inherited her father's straight hair. Josh's was caramel colored with a pinch of wave, like her own.

She found her note pad, and made out a grocery list. There wasn't that much to choose from on the island. There was fish, crabs, lobster, shrimp, and more fish. Seafood took up one whole side of the market. Crackers, for fish dips and spreads, ran a close second. Back in New York ethnic stores lined the streets. The island did have a farmer's market. She planned a separate trip for that on Saturday. It was late in the season, but still you could get some good things. Maybe she would even try to cook something Indian. Her one-time experience with Indian food had been in New York. She had insisted on something different. Her husband took her to the Indian section of town. They stood out like sore thumbs. A lady in a sari came to their table and welcomed them. Jessie assumed she was the owner or the owner's wife. Jessie suffered from heartburn all night. Her husband lay snoring beside her. He had a stomach of cast iron. She had been up several times during the night reaching for the bicarbonate of soda.

The next day, someone had told her she didn't know how to order. She should have started out mild. Jessie loved the tea and could have sipped on it all day long. The waiter called it chai. Her favorite island coffee shop also offered a wide variety of teas, one of which was chai tea. That was how it read on the menu — chai tea. That always sounded weird to her. Chai was the name that Indians gave to tea, so in essence, wouldn't the translation be tea tea? Jessie mentioned that once to the server, but the remark had been lost on her. The server had just given her a funny stare.

Was her love of tea from an Indian incarnation or a British incarnation or just from being born British? After a few chapters of the book, she was eager for a past life regression. Maybe delving back into another time could explain her situation in this life. Would she need to remarry her ex to set things straight? How many lifetimes had she and Gino spent together? That thought plunged her elevated mood into a downward spiral. She would need a book on self-hypnosis. Myrtle might think her odd. What did it matter? Life was definitely different here. Back in New York, she wouldn't have cared what the clerk at the bookstore might think of her choice, and he wouldn't have cared in the least. She suspected most clerks looked at porn under the counter while customers browsed. Jessie missed the New York bookstores. Like the produce stands, they overflowed with variety.

She looked down at the yellow blue-lined pad and penciled in curry. Might as well stop by the bookstore on the way. She had no clue how to even use curry and was going to need a cookbook. She had now read enough of the yoga book to give Myrtle a decent opinion. Maybe she would suggest the book as the local book club book pick.

The book club met twice monthly, and she hadn't attended in at least six weeks. When she was there last, the book discussed was "On The Road," by Jack Kerouac. It had come out a couple of years ago, hailed as a masterpiece. Jessie just didn't get it. Maybe her literary skills needed refining. Maybe she was just more into reading about yogis than beatniks, even though she could see some similarities.

Jessie had joined the book club as a way to meet new, interesting people, a way to shed some of her aloofness. It didn't happen. The majority were women over sixty. Being a minority of one, Jessie found it all a bit boring. Was she deluding herself into thinking she was in the book club for the books? Was she actually hoping to meet a tall, dark eligible bachelor at one of the meetings? Maybe. And while she was facing her subconscious yearnings, make that tall and blonde. Gino, her ex, was dark and short.

The next strike against the book club was that the women were all such gourmet bakers. Jessie was a little underwhelming in that area, too. Sometimes she thought the book discussion was just an excuse for a culinary competition. There was no way she could win if that were the case, so she opted not to return, as her turn to bring the refreshments was coming up. Molded cottage cheese and chips just wouldn't cut it. She envisioned Mrs. Gibbons and the others snickering behind her back. Maybe she could evoke sympathy if she just told them the truth. She grew up in England, and everyone knows England's reputation for food. She grew up without a mother, having no one to teach her even bad English cooking. She only had servants to cook food. No, it was better to leave that part out. She married young into an Italian family. Her mother-in-law wouldn't let her near the kitchen, lest she somehow curse what the Italians deemed as holy. Within twenty-four hours, they would all be taking turns bringing covered dishes to her cottage.

If only the professor were still alive. His attendance might make for an interesting, more insightful book club. She imagined him to be like the tall, graying blonde hair man she used to see in the park. He wore a colorful bow tie and radiated distinction. Jessie never saw him wear the same bow tie twice. She imagined them lining one whole side of his bedroom like the mugs at the coffee shop.

A séance to summon the professor was an idea, but

then mediums scared her, as did Ouija boards. Sylvia, her best girlfriend in boarding school, had one. Jessie suspected Sylvia of pushing the letters around to spell out the boyfriend she wanted. Even though it was just a game to the both of them, still, she feared they invoked evil spirits. She didn't need to add evil spirits to her life. There was enough in her past haunting her already. If she called upon the spirit of anyone it would be Jesus, Mother Mary, or the saints of India.

Jessie ran a comb through her hair. By mid afternoon, it was definitely due. She didn't bother to apply makeup. Why break her streak? She grabbed a fresh pair of pedal pushers, as the other ones still had some sand in them. If she did stop shaving she thought, she would have to wear longer pants, as she was not yet so carefree as *yoga girl.* Maybe she would just pluck the hairs off the tops of her toes to be safe. She once heard a man in a New York cafe proclaim one of the reasons he couldn't love a particular woman was because she had hairy toes. Jessie didn't want hairy toes to keep her from finding true love if there was such a thing and still possible for her. A bow-tied, gray-haired professor couldn't care less about hairy toes. Jessie thought of Josh. Hairy toes would not have stood between him and true love. He was the least shallow of any person she had ever known.

She headed out the front door, still not bothering to lock it or even carry keys. She had tucked her keys away in a drawer. That is where they stayed. The one precious thing, other than the locket that she had worth stealing lay in a metal box in her bedroom closet. A thief would take neither.

Jessie entered the bookstore. Myrtle was still eating her

lunch. Customers had interrupted it briefly, but now they were leaving with their books. Myrtle returned to her crab salad and asparagus. Jessie admired Myrtle. She was not only eating something healthy, but Myrtle struck her as having a last quarter of life plan. Well, maybe it was the last half of life plan. Myrtle had a healthy lifestyle and proper attitude. Who is to say that she wouldn't live as long as the yogurt eaters in the Caucasus Mountains? Jessie had thought she had read something about that in Life Magazine.

Myrtle's dress was immaculate. She could have worn one of those loose fitting hippie style dresses and no one would have thought the worse of her. Myrtle came here to be by the ocean after her husband died. She was born on the island but met and married one of the tourists and returned with him to Pittsburgh. It was after his death that she returned to the island.

Myrtle worked in a bookstore there, as well. Books were her life. Not only did she love what was inside the pages, but also she loved the smell and texture of the paper. She had a whole section of different notepaper and cards. Stationery did a nifty business on its own. Most people living here had ample time to write cards and letters. It was always Myrtle's dream to own a bookstore herself, rather than just work in one. It was the first full fledge bookstore on the island.

Up until Myrtle's appearance, there was a limited selection of books and magazines on the island. Her husband's investments made it possible. Myrtle sank it all into her dream. She could have just lived off the residue of his earnings by the seaside. But she didn't want to spend listless days on the ocean watching the tide roll in and out. Myrtle wanted interaction with books and the people like herself who loved them. She was also one of those gourmet cooks that stole the refreshment show at the book club meetings. She had to give Myrtle credit for being humble about her superb culinary skills.

Myrtle's husband, Walter, had been an avid reader himself, his favorites being the classics. His ashes sat in the back of the store in a Greco-Roman type urn. The works of Socrates and Plato and other philosophers whom her husband had loved to read surrounded the urn. Jessie had to admit it was an admirable way to remember her dear departed, but a bit on the quirky side at the same time. Everyone on the island had his or her quirks, even the most stable ones. For all she knew the laundromat ladies regarded her as the lead eccentric quirk of the island. Oh, how they loved to gossip.

Jessie was browsing through the cooking section when she looked up to see the blonde girl running a feather duster along the top of the books.

"Hi, I'm Amelia, but just call me Amy. Do you need any help?"

Jessie knew since it was a small island that she would run into her again but didn't think it would be so soon.

"I'm Jessica, but just call me Jessie. You work here?"

"Oh, I'm here visiting my grandmother and helping out," replied Amy. Jessie looked over at Myrtle. That made sense. Jessie could now see the family resemblance as well as the likeness in family traits. They both had this neatness about them.

Amy talked with the speed of a race car. She was taking a year break from college, just to get her head together she said.

“Most of these books aren’t my cup of tea, but Grandma orders what the customers want.”

“You like tea?” Jessie asked.

“That was just an expression, but yeah, I like tea.”

“I was looking for a book on Indian cooking.”

Amy perused through the shelves, “Hmm, seafood, seafood, chowder, ….no, no Indian, but we could order one. Are you looking to make curry? The secret to good Indian cooking is in the spices. I could teach you if you want. Until we get a book in, that is, if you do want to order. I learned from my mother. She loved Indian cooking. So does my dad. If you don’t want to order, I could just teach you. But if you did want to order, my grandmother is looking to expand and add some different titles to the bookstore.”

“That would be great. Sure you could order me what you think best. In the meantime, you could teach me. I was on my way to the market. What would I need?”

“Spices. Plenty of spices. Coriander, turmeric, cumin, ginger, cardamom, red pepper. Curry boils down to spices. We could make some chai. You said you like tea. Well, you didn’t say you liked it. You asked me if I liked it. I just assumed.”

“Yes, I love tea. I would love to make chai. I won’t say chai tea, as that would be tea tea.”

Amy laughed.

“You get that?”

“Yeah, why wouldn’t I? It was funny.”

“Oh, never mind.”

“I could tag along to the grocery store if you don’t mind.”

"That would be great, but aren't you on the clock?" Jessie asked.

"Oh, no, my grandmother is pretty lenient. She won't mind. I'm not actually getting paid, just a commission on any books I sell to customers. And, I just sold one, didn't I?"

"In that case maybe you ought to order me a couple of cookbooks. I could use all the help I could get."

Amy smiled and put down her feather duster. "Grandma, I'll be back in a bit."

Myrtle just nodded and continued her lunch.

They began their trek to the market. It was less than a mile away. It gave them plenty of time to talk. The faster they walked, the faster Amy spoke. Amy told Jessie she was an art major and philosophy minor. She took after her grandfather in a lot of respects as well as her mom. But she didn't have a business head like her grandfather, nor did her mother. Her mom was a sculptor. Her mom had been thinking about doing one of the summer art shows here, which would double as a visit to Grandmother, but she died last year. She had been sick for a year. Not so much ill, just weak. Her heart had given out. Thus, Amy was taking a break to get her head together and help her grandmother. Amy's father, Myrtle's son, was still back on Long Island. He would join them for Christmas, or maybe even for Thanksgiving if he could take time off from work.

Underneath the primness and properness, both Amy and her grandmother had a real Bohemian streak running through them. Amy had been going to Columbia University. That is where her mother and father both went, where they met. She would have entered college about the same time Jessie had moved here permanently or was the move actually permanent? Jessie was still up in the air about that one. Was anything really permanent? Her life had already told her anything but. Could they have run into each other before in New York? Could Amy have crossed paths with her daughter? Not likely to both questions. New York was a big place. They could have passed each other on the Brooklyn Bridge. Everyone passed at some point on the Brooklyn Bridge.

They were almost there. Jessie hadn't contributed much to the conversation, just a lot of head nods. Amy talked enough for the both of them. It was just as well. Jessie was still having difficulty talking about her life in general. In fact, she hadn't talked about it at all, except for the few mumblings she made to the therapist. Dr. Linn had told her she was refusing to move forward. He continued to tell her things she already knew. Heck, she wasn't even facing forward for that matter.

More than a therapist, she needed a friend she could confide in. Clare was the closest thing she had to a confidante, but she found it hard to tell Clare everything. There was Gina, but she felt saying the most ubiquitous things would be like asking her to choose sides. Jessie didn't believe in making children choose sides. Gina saw all, anyway, and if it came to choosing sides Gina was old enough to make that decision. Jessie wanted Gina to have a good relationship with both of her parents. Maybe her biggest fear was that she would choose her father and push her completely out of the picture. That was the root of their relationship difficulty now, or so she thought. She didn't have a clue what went on inside her daughter's head. This girl she had just met, Amy, was an open book.

Jessie grinned, fitting since the family business was a bookstore.

They walked along, all this chitchat bouncing back and forth through Jessie's head, as she compared lives. Amy was half her age and so much more advanced compared to herself. If only Jessie had taken a year off to find her own self. What would she take a year off from? Marriage? She hadn't gone to college. She married way too young. In her day, girls didn't have careers. They married. Girls were more liberated today. After all, it was the cusp of 1960. Now at almost forty-five, Jessie was taking that year off. But that year off had turned into three, and still she hadn't found herself. How could she find herself when so many pieces were scattered and just plain missing?

Amy kept the conversation going until they reached the double doors of the market. The grocery store was the most modern building on the island. Jessie reached for a carrying cart. Jessie was so used to holding things in and keeping a distance from people. It was a wonder this girl was talking to her at all. She had now wished that she had put a dab of makeup on. She had once read in a magazine that women wore makeup to impress and compete with other women, not to attract men. She could resonate with that.

Jessie gave little concern to her appearance until one day when she thought she met her husband's mistress. A tall, angular woman in a red clingy dress was walking up the street toward her. Her black eyelashes were long enough to brush against passers-by if she chose to turn her head. But the woman's eyes were directed toward Jessie. Jessie had seen the woman once with some people her husband knew. The woman slowed down in her stride as she gave Jessie a once over. Make that a twice over. Jessie pulled the brim of her hat down trying to avoid eye contact. The woman continued on as if Jessie wasn't worth the trouble. A strong aroma of perfume lingered in her absence. The woman was so chic and model tall, unlike herself. Jessie didn't dare look back. She walked fast and ducked into the nearest department store, Bergdorf's, and asked for a makeover.

She hadn't been a big frequenter of Bergdorf's or Macy's. The lady at the makeup counter guided her through everything, and she was happy to do so, considering she worked on a commission. Afterward, Jessie went to the beauty parlor. Jessie wore her hair long but let the beautician take three inches off. The beautician did some straightening in the back, leaving curls down the sides. She told her she could pass for an auburn Lauren Bacall.

At home, Jessie sat stiffly on a chair determined not to let a strand of hair move from the spot the beautician had put it in. She waited patiently for her husband. He came in and asked why she wasn't making dinner. She ran to their room crying, shutting the door behind her. Several hours later she came out, with the kink back in her hair, eyes and cheeks all black with mascara, only to find her husband gone. She assumed he went to the tall, angular woman. It was months later that she found out she wasn't his mistress at all, just a friend of the other man. And, the chic tall lady wasn't even a woman. If she had looked down she might have seen the size eleven high heels. Jessie was totally blindsided. Makeup and new hairstyles didn't seem so important anymore.

She and Amy meandered down the spice aisle. Lots of Old Bay. They pulled out all the spices suitable for Indian cooking. There was curry, a bit of dust on the lid. Jessie started to put it in the cart, but Amy stopped her, saying that was cheating. She said they would start from scratch. That's what makes a good curry. There was no fresh ginger, so they opted for the jar. They did find fresh sticks of cinnamon. They got everything they would need for chai as well. Amy said they would need some black tea, the loose variety. Jessie assured her she had that, thinking she would finally be pulling out the loose tea for company.

CHAPTER 3

THE WALK back went by even faster than the walk there. They both wanted to dismiss their sandals and walk along the beach, but the sand and the heaviness of the bags would have been like walking in quicksand so they opted for the boardwalk. They had walked along the street side on the way there. Unique stores and quaint little cottages, some clapboard, some brick, lined the streets. Jessie's own cottage had shake shingles. All the houses had picket fences. She wondered why. Maybe it was something decided by the city fathers and mothers, like the dog leash law. Her fence could use a coat of paint, though.

On the way back Amy's conversation centered on her boyfriend, ex-boyfriend that is. Life was full of exes, even for the young. Gina had certainly left a string behind her. The way Amy put it was they were both leaving their options open at this point, especially in light of Amy's extended leave of absence. Jessie concluded Amy's ex was of the beatnik variety. She envisioned him much like the guy in the weaving booth but not to the extreme of the characters in "On the Road." Instead of yoga her boyfriend had concentrated on poetry and philosophy. He also dabbled in sculpture, an existential style. Amy had met him in philosophy class.

Jessie gathered Amy wasn't a virgin. But then, what girl in her early twenties was, especially in this day and time. Or, for that matter, in her own day and time, living in New York City, if you had any kind of date life at all. Virginity or at least the façade of virginity was a tradition upheld only in the South and in certain foreign countries. At one time, America was the foreign country to her. Now England was.

At age sixteen, Jessie left England never to return. There was no one or no place to go back to. As far as a string of boys went, well she never got the chance to find out since in England she had gone to an all girls school. Jessie experienced the opposite sex at the customary social functions and dances. Those dances proved awkward for her. She married the first boy she ever dated. She wasn't even sure if she could technically refer to it as dating. The whole thing was reminiscent of an arranged marriage. Except parents weren't involved.

Aunt Agatha was to be the designated fact of life giver when Jessie reached the proper age, but that plan went awry. What little she knew came from Clare and Sylvia. Sylvia was as clueless as herself. The real enlightenment as far as the sexual act, or lack thereof, came from her husband on her wedding night.

England was so far away now. Any trace of an accent was long gone. Amy, nor anyone else could never have guessed from where she originated. When Jessie did open her mouth to speak, she sounded like she was from nowhere. Nowhere was sort of like being unnecessary. At any rate, England was a different life ago. Jessie felt she had lived a multitude of lives in this one lifetime. She divided her life into segments.

Amy's father hadn't approved of Dave, the ex-boyfriend. Still, he was one of those parents who gave his daughter plenty of leeway after she entered college. She saw the respect Amy had for both her parents and her grandmother. It was evident they raised Amy to think like an adult. Jessie saw Amy as having her head together. Most girls do until it comes to matters of the heart. Jessie's intuitive instinct told her that Amy didn't love Dave. Rather she loved the Bohemian spirit of Dave, seeing something of her mother's nature in him. Maybe that is why Amy still had her head together. She had never fallen in love. Dave was an attempt to hold onto her mother. Amy had seen him as a free spirit like her mother.

Again, she was analyzing. People told Jessie she was too serious, always analyzing everything over in her mind. She had a real problem just letting go and going with the flow. Again, analyzing — herself this time.

Jessie did have a sense of humor, a dry one, one that went over most people's heads. So, the fact that she had any sense of humor at all wasn't evident. They often looked at her as the server in the coffee shop did when she remarked about "tea tea." Her husband understood her sense of humor but chose to ignore it or regard it in his usual way, with sarcasm. Jessie often wondered where her own people were [illegible] on some other planet most likely. Josh must be there now. He was in a mystical place, definitely a higher plane, looking down on her.

Amy was so open. If only her own daughter were this open with her. But then, most daughters weren't that open with their own mothers. Jessie sensed that Amy was open with her mother and envied it. Jessie could relax around Amy. The time flew by. Five minutes with Gina could be excruciating. Maybe it was because with Gina, Jessie was putting too many demands on herself. Jessie longed for a good relationship with Gina but didn't have a clue how to make it happen. She was always trying so hard that she pushed it away. She was at the point of giving up on it.

Gina imagined that she was judging her every decision. Or maybe Jessie just imagined that Gina imagined that. Gina was hard to read most of the time. Gina was adaptable to most situations and most people but not to her own mother.

Gina was a born actress going back and forth between roles. Maybe Gina was aloof around her because Jessie, herself, was reserved. That was the chameleon in her. Jessie wasn't judging Gina. Unlike most mothers, she didn't tell her what she should or shouldn't do. Jessie wondered if Gina was this way with her father since the divorce. Gina never brought up her father, and Jessie never asked. She didn't want to be one of those divorcees that used the child to find out about the ex-husband. Maybe she would have been one of those women if she had even given a damn what her ex-husband did. But she did care about Gina's relationship with him. Did she just say the word damn? That so wasn't in her vocabulary. Was she finally emoting? Amy used it a couple of times. It must have rubbed off. Amy's language was far from vulgar. She was honest.

Was Amy helping her to get to the root of something here? Could this be the breakthrough Dr. Linn had hoped for? She hadn't had any progress in three months of weekly therapy sessions in New York. She couldn't even get mad. Maybe she just wasn't ready then. Everything was still so fresh, the death, the divorce. The divorce came after the death or at least the separation. The actual official divorce came a year later. There was no point in continuing the pretense of marriage any longer. A good part of her therapy appointments were spent in silence. Her ex was footing the bill, a fact he reminded her of at every opportunity. He only agreed because he cared about what others thought. It began with couple's therapy. He needed to show he wasn't the party at fault, and that he was doing everything in his power to hold the marriage together. He told Dr. Linn that he was all for continuing with the marriage, but it was she who no longer had any interest in it. Jessie never once disputed him or said anything to the contrary. What could she say? It was true. Gino's whole life was pretense. Somewhere underneath it all there had to be a real person. Jessie never knew that person.

Jessie abandoned therapy after moving to the island. It was more convenient not to continue. It wasn't helping and looking for a doctor on her own was too complicated. Gino had chosen Dr. Linn. The only therapists were on the mainland. The island didn't need therapists. Who needed therapists when you had the sea air? Gino, in one of their rare moments of continuity, agreed that sea air was all she needed. That was after he had said her feelings didn't matter. He washed his hands of the matter and refused to pay any more bills. It was just as well since she wanted to avoid any dealings with him. This was the second time he said her feelings didn't matter. The first time was early in the marriage when she dared to put herself above his mother. Jessie knew he meant her feelings didn't matter with regard to everything and not just with regard to his mother. There were other times when he got down on his hands and knees and pleaded undying love for her. It was a roller coaster ride, and Jessie wanted off.

Jessie could never call him anything but Gino. After Josh's death, he changed it to Gene. She was so stupid to have married so young and to have married him, but then out of her stupidity came Josh and Gina. So all was not lost.

His temper erupted like Vesuvius when she announced she was pregnant with Josh. The baby would come almost nine months to the date after the wedding.

All was well for a while when his mother found out she would be a grandmother. Four years later, after tiring of the withdrawal method, Gina would come along. The announcement caused no blowout as she chose to keep this pregnancy from him. Jessie picked Josh's name. It was short for Joshua. Gino insisted on an Italian name when his daughter arrived. Gino didn't get too involved with the children, though. She had the children; he had his business and whatever else he may have been up to. Jessie rarely questioned him about his business or anything else.

Jessie lost interest in his comings and goings long before the marriage ended. Losing interest and the aloofness was her way of remaining sane. The only thing she couldn't avoid was the fighting. There was no way around it, nowhere to hide. He insisted on them. He was like a vampire sucking blood. What he couldn't take out on the world he took out on her. If she tried to leave, he blocked the door. Jessie endured the bi-weekly ritual, and it was a ritual. She tried everything to abate them. She cried. That didn't work. She fought back. That didn't work. She tried listening and giving advice. That didn't work. She tried sitting like a zombie. That did work to some extent. He needed a reaction. Maybe if she had tried love, but love, if ever they had it in their relationship, had disappeared long ago.

Was she so cold she couldn't love? In front of others, he called her a prude. As usual she took it. Would love have worked with him? Do men and women have different feelings, different needs? She had failed as a wife. Volatility was just a big part of his nature. It was like an explosion that had to erupt within him, and she was his target. After his erupting lava drenched every part of her psyche he would be okay and could even laugh, as if it never happened. Jessie couldn't heal the scars. This part of their marriage stayed behind closed doors. But the children knew, and they suffered. He kept up a front. Like she knew his nature, he knew her nature and knew she would never confide in anyone. It was one of her many failings. Confiding could have helped, but she was afraid of the judgment. Her father had always said, *"You make your own bed, you lie in it."* Or was that Aunt Agatha. They both said it. Jessie took that to heart. But times were changing, and she had lain in that bed far too long. If she had a head on her like Amy, she would have never lain in it to begin with. Jessie blamed no one for her predicament but herself.

Amy and Jessie approached the cottage, entering through the back screen door.

"My grandmother doesn't lock her door either. A lot different from New York, huh?"

"Just make yourself at home while I put this stuff away." Jessie saw a cobweb out of the corner of her eye. She felt relieved Amy couldn't see her inner cobwebs. She pushed the stack of papers and book over to lay the bags on the table. She vowed to herself to clean before Amy's next visit. Jessie was already planning on a next visit. Amy was a breath of fresh air.

"This is one of my favorites," Amy said, reaching for the book.

CHAPTER 4

"MY PARENTS met him once."

"Met who?"

"The yogi on the cover."

"This same guy who wrote the book?" An instant regret registered in Jessie's head as she asked that. Calling this saint a guy somehow sounded irreverent. From what she had read thus far, he surpassed any ordinary being. But Amy didn't seem repulsed by her statement. She didn't think too much surprised Amy.

"Yeah, it was before I was born, and conceived, for that matter. They were in California on their honeymoon. They went on a wine tour and the following day, went to one of his lectures. He told the crowd to be spiritual alcoholics. I thought my dad was joking when he told me, but he wasn't. Makes you wonder if he singled them out knowing they were drinking their fill of wine the previous day. They said he could do things like that."

"But you never met him yourself?"

"No, but his writings were permanent fixtures in our house. My parents practiced yoga and were off and on vegetarians, especially after my mom got sick. They were strict for the last year of her life. It did help her. I'm sure of it. You wouldn't know anything was wrong with her until the final year of her life and even then, not always. She was born with a weak heart but didn't find out about it until after my birth. That was when it got weaker. That's why they never had any more children. But she still insisted on being active. Maybe she would have lived a lot longer if she hadn't have been. But she said that was no way to live life, so weak heart or not, she didn't slow down. Maybe it was the good diet, or maybe it was just the way she grabbed onto life and squeezed every ounce of juice out of it. That's what my dad said."

Amy had yogic qualities. She knew what you were thinking. She anticipated your next question and just answered it.

"Will your grandmother be expecting you for dinner?" Jessie asked.

"No, she'll be all wrapped up in one of her shows, Lawrence Welk or Jack Benny. But, if you don't mind, I'll make a quick call just to let her know I'll be home later."

They munched on the celery and carrots they had picked up at the store. They added peanut butter and jelly sandwiches to the mix. That was dinner.

They agreed to save the curry dinner for another time. They did make chai, the Indian way. Jessie wasn't sure she could remember the process. It was a little more complicated than putting water on to boil and pulling out a tea bag. Jessie had decided that she had gotten into a rut as far as food. She needed to add a little complication into the mix. Amy didn't seem to find anything too complicated but then she was young.

Gina would consider this whole thing time-consuming. But then she lived in New York amidst a plethora of ethnic restaurants. All was at her fingertips. And, she ate and hung out with her theater crowd. There was no time for such things as cooking from scratch. Jessie had time — a little too much, and she was squandering it away.

They sat at the kitchen table, Amy, talking about this and that. She had moved on to college life now and about her job experiences. She worked at different jobs on her college breaks. She related funny stories about giving women makeovers in the cosmetics department. Jessie told Amy about her Bergdorf makeover but not the aftermath. Nor did she say what prompted her into getting the makeover.

The sun was going down. Amy exited through the kitchen door. Her grandmother lived only a few blocks away. Everything on the island was within a few blocks.

Jessie was glad they had decided to forego the curry undertaking until after the farmer's market trip. The day had been out of the norm, both exhilarating and tiring. Amy was a ball of energy, and it was contagious. Jessie made a plan for tomorrow morning to run a dust rag through the house and suck up the excess sand with the vacuum cleaner. That Amy had ventured no further than the hall outside the kitchen where the phone was, was a relief to Jessie. All the talking up to this point had been about Amy's life. If they had gone into the front room, Amy would have seen the pictures of her son and daughter. That would have brought up questions.

Jessie doubted her ability to express herself with regard to her family in actual verbal tones. Her whole summary of the situation had been in her head. Jessie mustered few words in Dr. Linn's presence. At this point, she didn't even know what might come out of her mouth if she tried to speak about the past. Could she bring up her son's death? Could she talk about her exile from her daughter or her divorce? Had Amy noticed she wore a wedding band? She didn't wear it out of love. It was just a fixture like the sand. It was also a protection mechanism. Jessie abhorred the title of 'the divorcee'. The one time she took it off just added to her troubles. So she put it back on.

Jessie went to sleep practicing actual dialog out loud. She did it the way she remembered Gina practicing lines before a play. She prayed that answers to relieve her miseries would come in her dreams. Jessie feared a breakdown, at the least, tears. She hadn't shed tears since Josh's funeral. So what if she cried? Did she care what anyone thought? Not Dr. Linn. Did she care what Amy thought? To be honest with herself, yes she did. She definitely cared what Amy thought, even though she had just met her today.

She saw in Amy what she wanted to be. Amy was open with her feelings. She didn't hide behind anything or anyone. She didn't let her pain destroy her. Already at her age, she had plenty of pain. She had lost her mother. But she turned the pain into something good. She transcended the pain. Amy was fresh life. Jessie needed Amy. This island needed Amy.

Jessie talked until her voice became hoarse and until her words slurred. She drifted off to sleep during her recitations.

CHAPTER 5

JESSIE AWOKE at 7 AM feeling rested. She couldn't remember any miraculous answers coming during her sleep, nor any dreams for that matter. She usually remembered her dreams. Yesterday was one of the few times since coming to the island that her waking hours had been more active than her dreaming hours. She always felt more rested when she didn't remember them.

Still dressed in pajamas, she opened the back screen door, walked outside, and sat on her back porch waiting for the sun to rise. Something in her felt like a fresh start. She sat there for an hour, part of the time with her eyes closed, just soaking in the warmth. She listened to the pounding of the waves and the squawk of the seagulls. The moment she opened her eyes, she saw a dolphin in the distance. Was it a sign? Dolphins with those ever-present smiles on their faces, reminded her of the Buddha.

Was this the beginning of meditation for her? No, she wasn't sitting correctly. Did you have to sit in a yogic pose to make it happen? She was on her back porch rocking chair. Could you meditate in a rocking chair? She wanted a swing. Jessie loved swings and could sit on a swing in a cross-legged meditation pose. It was movement, back and forth, back and forth, like the waves. In England, her father put a swing in the garden area. She remembered sitting there with her mother. After her mother's death, her father never came there. Jessie made it her private place. It was where her mother's pink rose bushes grew. This porch facing the ocean was her new private place. A swing would make it complete. She would talk to Jackson about one.

Jackson was the jack-of-all-trades on the island. He did all sorts of odd jobs for people. He made things happen. She made a mental note to ask him about a swing the next time she saw him. He was usually somewhere on a ladder with a hammer or paint bucket at someone's cottage.

Jackson had the keys to the island, so to speak. He watched most people's cottages while they were away and did repairs during the off-season. He did anything that needed attended to. She needed to talk to him about painting her fence, too. Jackson did some gardening work for her in the past. Jessie loved flowers and any kind of garden, but she didn't keep it up. A green thumb wasn't her forte. That expertise belonged to her mother and Clare. Jessie reflected back on the beautiful gardens on the estate. The estate employed a gardener, but her mother oversaw it. Myrtle's garden took the prize on the island.

How did she find the time to do it all? And how did she have the energy at her age? Amy took after Myrtle in the energy department.

Jessie left the porch and walked out farther onto the sand, closer to the ocean. She maneuvered her legs into a meditation pose. She clasped her hands in front, not knowing how to position them. She began in earnest this time trying to remove all thoughts from her mind. The more she tried, the more they came. They were memories, memories of herself and her children when they were young, out on the beach. Josh busied himself building sand castles and a whole series of canals. If he had lived, he might have been an engineer. He also loved trains. He had a magnificent train set. Gino brought it home for this eighth birthday. He wanted to play with it on the sand. Jessie hadn't let him for fear of ruining it. He had cried, and she regretted that now.

Gina only showed interest in her doll, which she referred to as her little girl. She took it everywhere until it fell apart. She made up wild stories. Everyone loved Gina's imagination. She once had to use ninety-nine band-aids on her little girl, Annabelle, because a shark had bitten her. They were good memories. Maybe meditation was about good memories. Gina loved make-believe and play-acting. She still does. Jessie had every faith in Gina's acting ability.

Most parents would dissuade their children from going into acting. Jessie believed in letting her children follow their dreams. That especially held true for Gina, being a girl. Girls could dream just as big as guys. Both Gina and Amy were proof of that. Well, she didn't know exactly what Amy's dreams were. But whatever they were,

Jessie had complete faith that Amy would make them happen.

Jessie almost fell asleep. A sea gull, once again, brought her back to reality. She made her way back to the kitchen and looked through the pantry. She pulled out grits, better than her habitual chocolate and cola. She put on the teakettle. Maybe she would go through the process of chai in the afternoon. Afternoon tea was a custom, one she had kept up all her life. During her last couple of years in England, Aunt Agatha had moved in with them when her husband had died. Aunt Agatha was old or seemed so at the time. She was older than Father. Aunt Agatha was a strict traditionalist, and afternoon tea was one of those traditions she was relentless about following.

Agatha was more old school than even Jessie's father. Her father tended to indulge to some degree. When she thought about it, she had to admit her father spoiled her a lot. He never discouraged her tomboyish traits and let her run wild most of the time. Maybe it was just guilt or pity due to the lack of a mother. When Aunt Agatha volunteered to replace that mother figure, Father was only too eager to hand over the responsibility.

Aunt Agatha often referred to Jessie as Tarzana. It was a not so affectionate term Aunt made up after seeing the silent film, "Tarzan." Jessie overheard Aunt Agatha lecturing on how Jessica needed some refinement. Aunt Agatha told Father that it was time she became a young woman and quit running around the estate like a young ape. Aunt Agatha was keen on lectures, especially when it concerned Jessie. Aunt Agatha had told father if he didn't feel inclined to marry again, then she would have to take on the responsibility of turning Jessica into something respectable. Relieved, Father handed the responsibility over to her. Jessie knew that part of the reason Agatha volunteered was also to be with Father as she was lonely after Uncle's death. In a more compassionate lecture, she told Jessie that her father also needed someone to take care of him.

Agatha began the uphill battle determined to see that Jessica grew into a proper lady. She scrubbed Jessie until her skin hurt. Even though, Aunt said she was only trying to get off all the dirt and germs, Jessie knew she was attempting to eradicate her freckles. Jessie had once overheard her mention them to her father. Aunt said she didn't know how Jessica would attract a proper husband with such a complexion. Aunt Agatha always called her Jessica. Jessie was unladylike, and a boy's name according to Aunt. She was there to erase all traces of Jessie being a tomboy and of being improper. Aunt was all about properness. She would faint dead away if she could see her now.

Agatha wore out brushes on Jessie's hair. With each brush stroke, Aunt Agatha shook her head and rolled her eyes at Jessie's hair's unruliness. Jessie remembered Aunt saying many a time, "Jessica, we've been brushing for a good half hour and have made no progress that anyone could see." Aunt always liked to say 'we' to something Jessie wanted no part in. Jessie could still see Aunt Agatha vividly in her mind.

Aunt's eyes were half open, half closed as if she was in constant thought. She did a lot of thinking with her eyes. They were a blue gray that matched her hair. One side of her lip was always positioned higher than the other, stretched up, no doubt, by the tight little knot of a bun crowning her head. At other times, her lips looked ready to move as if she were going to dispel her thoughts at any moment. Sometimes they quit in mid-quiver. More often than not, though, she did spill her mind. For Aunt Agatha to hold in a thought or opinion would be like every strand of Jessie's hair to suddenly fall into place.

For such a small whiff of a woman, Aunt had a commanding presence. On most days, she wore a starched lace collar against a navy dress with pearl buttons that matched her skin. On special occasions, she removed the lace and substituted real pearls. Jessie gave those pearls to Gina on her sixteenth birthday.

Aunt did have a sense of humor. Like Jessie's, it was dry. Jessie inherited it from her, or maybe she learned it from her. Behind Agatha's back, Father referred to her as Aggie, giving Jessie a little secretive wink each time he said it. Jessie liked the fact that she and father had secrets. There was nothing dry about Father's humor.

Jessie surmised that Agatha had been a tomboy much like herself and had to be whipped into fashion by her own mother. It worked. Aunt Agatha married into wealth and respectability. It didn't hurt that she came from it herself. But her life was more than wealth and respectability. She had a genuine loving marriage. Maybe her uncle had loved her own tomboyishness and dry sense of humor. Maybe he fell in love with her heart.

Jessie remembered her uncle being a robust man with a heavy laugh that bounced across the room. Opposites attract. Aunt Agatha, underneath it all had a heart of gold.

The freckles, Jessie must have inherited from her mother. Maybe Father had fell in love with her mother's freckles. The way her father broke down at her memory, Jessie knew her mother must have had a heart of gold as well.

When Jessie was fourteen, Aunt Agatha talked father into a sort of coming out for her. She said it was time for her presentation into society. Jessie was a little more developed in the physical sense than most girls her age, and Aunt Agatha was getting up in years and feared she couldn't wait any longer for a coming out. It would be in the form of an ocean cruise to America. Sometime after their return, a proper party would take place in Jessica's honor. Father was reluctant, but Aggie usually had her way with him. She argued that progress, towards Jessica's developing into a lady, was going much too slow. Extra measures must be taken if Jessica was to grow into proper womanhood.

Aunt had once before been across the big pond to America. It was her most unforgettable experience, and she thought Jessie should have it as well. She would act as Jessic's chaperone, accompanied by one servant. Agatha picked a twenty-year-old girl named Clare. The world of servants — that was also so long ago. Servants were something Jessie took for granted growing up. Some were like family. Clare would become so.

Agatha made that first ocean cruise in 1913. It was often a source of conversation for her. She and Uncle boarded a ship owned by The White Star Line, which also owned the Titanic. People would ask her if she was the least bit worried. She would often joke it didn't concern her in the least since lightning didn't strike twice in the same place. To Aunt's relief, their Atlantic journey was uneventful with regard to icebergs or lightning striking.

Father took care of the arrangements for both Jessie and Aunt Agatha. Shortly after, Father became critically ill. It was a massive stroke. One side of Father's face and body caved into gravity. He lasted only a few days after that. He lay on his bed sometimes trying to talk. Words came out slower and slurred. Speech was hard for him. Recognition was too. He mistook Jessie for her mother. He called Aunt Agatha Aggie to her face. Aunt only smiled at him and grasped his hand firmer. He drifted in and out of different times in his life. Agatha and Jessie sat by his bedside, along with a nurse, in silence until his last breath. The English weren't given to showing affection in public. It wasn't proper. The addition of the nurse made the gathering public.

Jessie went to her room and broke down in tears after they took the body away. She suspected that Aunt Agatha had done the same. On the day of Father's death, there was heavy rain and lightning. It also rained the day of the funeral. Agatha now dedicated her every breath to Jessie. Agatha left it to Father's attorney to settle all estate matters. Jessie was the sole heir with Agatha has the guardian. Aunt Agatha had plenty of her own money.

They needed the trip now more than ever. They went on with the plans, and in June, along with Clare, three large trunks and various smaller boxes, they boarded the ship.

Agatha would have normally kept a strict eye on Jessie, but with Father's passing, her health was waning, putting a damper on her all-seeing eyes. One might attribute it to the constant churning of the ocean. Agatha's stomach had not held up as well this time as on her first crossing. This would be Agatha's last transcontinental trip, not that she was planning on any more.

Jessie's father left her well off, making Jessie easy prey in America, the land of opportunity. Jessie wasn't what one might consider attractive. Her unruly hair and freckles were only made worse by the Atlantic winds. Jessie was also quite shy and suffered from a queasy stomach around boys. That put her even more at a disadvantage with the opposite sex. A girl's school hadn't prepared her for what she was about to encounter.

Her intimidation around the opposite sex was her saving grace in that it kept her virginity intact until her wedding night. Boys her own age scared her. She was most comfortable around older men. It was what she was used to, having mostly been around Father, his business associates, and servants.

They put down anchor in New York. The first thing to catch Jessie's eye was the giant green lady she recognized as Lady Liberty. The second thing or person rather, was a dockworker. He looked straight at Jessie and winked as they descended the ship's ramp. He had the darkest hair and the most perfect olive complexion. Agatha was too flustered at the time managing their paperwork to notice. But Clare noticed. She didn't let on. Jessie looked back to find him still ogling. He tipped his flat tweed hat. Jessie knew her freckles had turned red. No matter, it was a one-time encounter she was sure. Jessie would be turning fifteen in a couple of weeks but was still too young for a suitor. Jessie didn't dare look his way again. Agatha would have had a stroke herself if she had seen what had transpired.

Clare was a sturdy, big bosomed girl, all prim and

proper, showing the humblest respect in front of Aunt. This gave Aunt grounds to rely on Clare more and more as each day went by. Clare had a whole different approach to life when Aunt wasn't looking. Clare covertly snuck off below deck partying as wildly as any man after Aunt fell asleep at night. Jessie had kept her secret. Maybe that is why Clare didn't say anything about the boy who winked.

Porters took their trunks, strapping them onto the back of a cab before making their way to a hotel. All three were in amazement of the splendor of this city. Jessie had never seen so many people congregated in one place except in London, but it wasn't the same. The people here were of all different varieties. They yelled out in a jumble of languages. The different tongues melded together like drops of water forming one big ocean. Horses and carts lined the curbs. Everyone had something to sell. Cars and pedestrians zigzagged around each other. Horns honked without a break. A plethora of sounds merged into some universal language, making Jessie want to cover her ears and take it all in at the same time. She would eventually learn to adapt.

Jessie tilted her head upward to transcend what was happening on the ground level. She blinked to adjust to a vertical landscape rising above her. New York struck her as not knowing in which direction to grow or in which language to communicate. There were cranes and scaffolding reaching to the clouds. Workers were everywhere. Some wore hard hats. Others wore tweed flat caps like the one boy who had winked at her. Businessmen wore black or brown fedoras. Everyone wore hats, even the women. It was 1929 and little did they know it was all on the cusp of coming to an abrupt halt. It was early summer, a few months before Black Tuesday.

They arrived at their hotel, The Biltmore. As they entered upper Manhattan, the scene changed. There were still just as many workmen scurrying around. But the language was predominantly English and the dress more refined and elegant. People walked as if they were in some frantic hurry to get somewhere. The women wore stockings with seams, and all the men wore suits and ties.

Agatha and Uncle had stayed at the Biltmore on her previous trip. Agatha told Father this trip was for Jessie, but Jessie found Aunt Agatha reawakening her own past glorious recollections. Aunt Agatha's eyes darted in all directions as she pointed out familiar reference points she remembered on her previous trip, sixteen years earlier.

They would be there for the duration of the summer, returning just in time for the start of boarding school. There was much to explore. And explore they did. They visited the shops, the restaurants, and Central Park. The park was Jessie's favorite.

They watched as workers laid the foundation for what was to be the tallest building in the world. It was to be the Empire State Building. Anywhere else they might have never left the confines of their hotel as it offered all they needed. But as marvelous as their hotel was, the actual city itself was more so.

Nearing eighty, the trip had been quite strenuous on Aunt Agatha, but she wasn't one to let age stop her, slow her down maybe, but not stop her. After lunch, Agatha was given to afternoon naps. Jessie caught up on her reading and correspondence during that time. She had promised almost all the girls in her boarding school class postcards. She promised Sylvia letters. Aunt's naps became longer. The trip being harder this time around, Agatha was prone to staying within the boundaries of the hotel a good portion of the day. Aunt turned over the reins of the chaperoning responsibility to Clare. That was the first mistake.

Jessie reflected. There were so many mistakes in her life. While she was supposed to be clearing her mind and centering herself in the present, she was reliving her past. Is this what happened during meditation? Maybe she needed to revisit the past and put it into the proper perspective before beginning anew.

She couldn't feel her legs any longer as she had sat cross-legged for so long, but she did feel a slight pinch on her toe. She opened her eyes to look up and saw Amy.

CHAPTER 6

"I WAS walking down to the pier. Do you want to walk along with me?" Amy asked.

"Sure, let me ditch the blanket and grab some flip flops."

They walked along the shoreline maneuvering through the fishermen and their lines.

"I told you yesterday why I was here. You never told me why you are on the island. I could have asked Grandma, but I thought if you wanted to talk about, it you would, and you don't have to if you don't want."

"I don't know. I wouldn't know where to start. And, I doubt if your Grandmother knows all that much."

"Grandma knows an awful lot about the people on this island. It's a good thing she has a liberal attitude."

"Well, the parts she doesn't know might be too risqué

for your young ears."

"You don't really believe that do you? And do you think I'm that young?"

Jessie smiled. "No, I don't, on both counts. You ARE young, but I believe you are wise beyond your years."

They passed the colored beach. There was no one there, just the sign. They gave each other uncomfortable looks. They both knew there were no colored people on the island. The ones who did use the beach came from the mainland.

"Like you, I lived in New York before I came here," Jessie began. "My ex-husband is Italian. There were a lot of prejudices. Still is, I guess. Certainly not to the extent that colored people have it, but it hurt just the same. I hurt for him. I hurt for myself. There was hardly a day when we didn't hear "wop" or "greaser" or something else. Being Italian excluded us from a lot of things. But still there was opportunity for him. It's different for colored people. He was always trying to both improve himself and prove himself. There were a lot of days I think I was part of the plan to prove himself to the world."

"You said ex. You still wear a ring."

"I guess I more or less wear it for protection of some sort. Taking it off would leave me exposed somehow."

"I thought maybe you still loved him."

"I married so young. I wasn't mature enough to know what love was. I didn't have any examples to go by. I was alone in the world. He was the only boy I knew. He was older and seemed like a man who knew the world. He was only 19. That seemed old at the time. I was just turning 15. He knew so much more of the world than me, or at least he talked like he did. He could maneuver New York like he had lived there all his life. In fact, he had only come there a year before I first met him. At the time, he seemed like my savior. I desperately wanted to love and to be loved. I fantasized about love. But then what girl that age doesn't? God knows I said the words enough to him, most of the time thinking I really meant them. It just became a habit saying them. And then one day, the practice just stopped. Anyway, that is the condensed version of what happened."

Amy after some reflection said, "I guess a lot of marriages are like that on the inside. I'm fortunate my parents were one of the happy ones. You came to America pretty young then?"

"Yes, you don't know how fortunate. Like I said, I was just turning fifteen the first time. My aunt had brought me over on a cruise. It was a different era then."

"I can just imagine. I would love to be older. Those times seem much more romantic."

"Oh no, don't wish your life away. The past always seems more romantic. It was exciting. In a lot of ways, it was harder. You don't notice at the time. It's just life happening. There was the war, but then there is always a war. Besides, if you had been born earlier, you would have missed a lot of conveniences and the great parents you were born to."

"Yes, you're right. You see, I'm not such a wise soul, after all. Luckily, my dad missed the war. He was a little bit older and missed the draft. Things might have been different if that weren't the case. I might not have even been born."

"I'm glad you were. Yes, same with my husband. He also missed the selective service."

"What was your husband's name?"

"Gino, but everyone called him Gene. That is, he changed it to Gene. Of course, not his mother. And not his Italian friends. And, I still call him Gino."

"Certainly sounds Italian."

"Definitely Italian."

"You said you were fifteen the first time you came over. When did you come to America for good? When did you marry Gino or Gene?"

"The first time, we had stayed the summer here, in New York, that is. That is when I met Gino. Everyone called him Gino when I first met him. He didn't change his name until later. It was to gain more acceptance and to help him better move up in the world. I believe there were other reasons as well. He still looked Italian, but his name didn't sound so.

"He seriously wooed me. It was behind my aunt's back, of course. Everything was so prim and proper back then. It was especially so for English girls who came from money and lived on English estates. My aunt was old, and the trip hadn't agreed with her, so she spent a good deal of the time in the hotel room. Our servant attended to me. She was only twenty at the time. She was so excited about America herself that I got left on my own a good deal. Her name was Clare. Clare and I sort of had an understanding. I wouldn't tell what she was doing if she didn't divulge my meetings with Gino to Aunt Agatha. It was an unspoken agreement between us. Aunt had initially picked an older woman to make the trip with us, but she backed out at the last minute. Clare was too young for Aunt's tastes but was next in line."

"Agatha, that is a proper English name if ever there

was one. I guess Jessica is too."

"Yes, I guess, but my mother's maiden name was Jessie. Thus, my name."

"And, you had servants, wow!"

"Yes, even one of those big country estates. At the time, I just thought it was normal. I went from country life, a secluded life if you don't count pigs and sheep, to New York City. It was overwhelming."

"How secluded? How many servants do people have on country estates?"

"We had a cook and a couple of maids. There were more farm workers than anything else. There was a stable guy, and people that took care of the cows, the sheep, and and the gardens. The property and animals needed maintenance. I used to ride my bicycle all over the estate. All the workers sort of looked after me."

"I need to get a bicycle. We could ride bikes on the island like everyone else."

"It has been so long since I've been on a bike. I have one here but only attempted to ride it once. I was so unsteady on it, so out of practice. I'm afraid it's rusted now and needs some repairs."

"Were there other kids on the estate?"

"Not really. A couple of caretakers lived on the estate. One had grown children. The other had a couple of boys about my age. I saw them some during the summer but didn't know them too well. They stayed busy helping their father. I was shy. Other workers went home to their families at night. The cook lived with us, but she had never married. I had a nanny until boarding school. I started boarding school at twelve."

"What about your parents? I find this all so

fascinating. Am I asking too many questions?"

"No, I think it does me good to talk about it. I hadn't thought much about the distant past until just recently. England was another lifetime. I've never really talked about it to anyone. Gino never seemed too interested in my childhood. My mother died when I was four. I remember so little about her. And, maybe what I do remember I'm just making up in my mind. My father died shortly before my Aunt and I came to America the first time."

"Sorry, I sidetracked you with all my inquisitiveness. So, when did you come over for good? You apparently met up with Gino again."

"Yes, after we returned to England, my aunt continued to live with me as my guardian. Clare continued to work for us. I went back to boarding school, which was less than an hour away. So, I was always home on the weekends. Gino wrote at least one letter a week, sometimes two. Of course, I wrote back. My aunt was already in declining health. It would have declined even more so had she known about the letters. But Clare intercepted the mail and saved the letters for me until I came home on the weekends. I dare say I would not have come home every weekend except in anticipation of the letters."

"It all does sound so romantic, an overseas love affair."

"The other girls at the boarding school thought so, too. I took the letters back to school and read selected parts to them. It was an all girls' school. I think a few of them looked forward to them as much as I did. They sort of held me with a new respect. A few were uppity and looked down their nose at me because he was Italian and not a proper Englishman. But then, he was also American, living in New York City. That added to the glamour and intrigue of it all and made up for the fact that his roots were Italian."

"I'm certainly intrigued. You could write a book about this."

Jessie smiled. "Well, after another year at boarding school and a summer on the estate, I turned sixteen. Aunt Agatha threw a big coming out party. There were my aunt's friends and distant relatives. There were a lot of the boarding school girls, that is the ones living close enough to make it and some of their parents. My trust also came due then. My aunt, along with my father's estate lawyer, was handling my trust."

"You had a trust?"

"Yes, still do, at least for a little while longer. It will run out soon."

"Wow, that speaks of wealth! Do you have plans for when it runs out?"

"Not great wealth, just enough to live comfortably on. It has greatly diminished with inflation, but still, I'm not complaining. It's what I call my own money. And, no I don't have plans. I'll cross that bridge when I come to it."

They had arrived at the pier and each bought a cola. They walked out to the end, sitting far enough from the fishermen where the ocean would drown out their conversation. Jackson was on the other side of the pier replacing some boards. Jessie smiled and waved at him. She thought she would try to catch him before they left, to see about that porch swing.

"So back to the story, I mean your life," Amy said spellbound.

"Some of the girls stayed over at the party, and stayed up all night talking. All boy talk, of course. They thought I was so experienced. But the most I had ever done was kiss Gino. Or rather, Gino kissed me. I had no idea if I even did it right. I didn't let on. They considered Gino and I secretly engaged. I guess in a sense we were, although he had never officially proposed. The way he worded his letters implied marriage in the future. So the girls just assumed. They all thought Gino was so worldly. He was already talking of business pursuits. He was still a dockworker but was moving up in the world. I conveniently left the dockworker parts out of the letters I read to them.

"A lot of his letters were just him bragging. Gino did that a lot, but at the time, I believed it and so did the girls. He was a hustler of sorts, so part of it was true. Shortly after we had met, I let it slip about my trust fund. Maybe that was the sole reason he wrote and respected my virginity. I'll never know. God knows I questioned him about it plenty of times later on, but he always denied that is why he married me.

"A few weeks after the party, Aunt Agatha slipped and fell, breaking her hip. She took to her bed. She didn't last long. Her health wasn't great, but I expected she would be around for a good while longer. The doctor said she had a fracture of the sort that was risky for a woman of her age. There was no one after that. She wasn't blessed with children. A cousin whom I hardly knew helped me with the funeral, as did my father's lawyer. Clare was also a great help to me. The trust was now completely mine to do with as I pleased. Father's lawyer thought it best to take it out in monthly stipends and let it accrue interest in a bank. I followed his advice, and now I'm glad I did.

"Gino urged me to come to America, now that my aunt was gone. Clare urged me to, as well. Of course, she would make the trip with me. Clare was closer to me than anyone at that time.

"I loved getting Gino's letters and his attention, but I didn't feel in love. I just felt excited that I had a boyfriend. He was a world away. I thought I would eventually meet someone in my own country when the time was right. I would forget all about Gino, marry, and raise my own children on the estate. My aunt dying so suddenly changed everything.

"I panicked. I succumbed to Gino and Clare and to the girls at the boarding school. It was my own fault for building everything up to more than it was. I backed myself into a corner. I made Gino into some kind of superhero in their eyes. Like I said, I let them think we were getting married eventually anyway. Now, they were pressing hard. Father's lawyer set the trip up. I was only planning on staying a few weeks to get my head clear, maybe with Gino's help. Clare was of the opinion that it would help. I can't say it was entirely selfish on Clare's part. Her heart was in the right place. Clare would be there in later years on many occasions.

"Father's lawyer was quite impartial in the whole matter and looked at everything through the eyes of business. Maybe if he had daughters of his own, he might have stepped in with some fatherly advice and told me to stay put, but he didn't.

"I said my farewells to my school friends. A whole group saw Clare and me off as we boarded a ship.

"This time, I got sick while we were traveling. Clare

attributed it to nerves. After everything that had happened to me, I knew she was right. I spent almost the whole time in my cabin. I have to admit, Clare played the mother role well. She stayed with me most of the time, even at night. She didn't go off partying this time. We only had each other at this point. She nursed me back to health.

"When we reached New York, Gino was waiting for me. He said he had missed me so, and that we should get married right away. I don't think he wanted me to have time to change my mind. He already had two wedding bands.

"We went straight to a justice of the peace. One of his friends met us there. He and Clare acted as our witnesses. It all happened so fast. We spent our honeymoon night at The Biltmore, where my Aunt and I had stayed before. The room was reserved, so why waste it? Clare was next door. The next day, he kissed me bye and went off to work. We stayed at the hotel for a week. Then he took me to meet his mother."

The disappointment was apparent on Amy's face. "No great romantic wedding night. You sort of skipped over that."

"Not at all. In fact, it was rather disappointing. I had no idea what to expect. I was incredibly nervous and still feeling ill. I was so tight down there that the marriage never got consummated. He was frustrated and angry at the same time. I thought there was something wrong with me. He didn't want anyone to know. How could any pureblooded Italian live that one down? Nor did I tell Clare. The whole thing was just too embarrassing. I can't believe I'm telling you this."

Amy smiled.

"At the end of the week, he took me to meet his mother. She was cordial but not overly friendly. I think I bashed her hopes of Gino marrying a nice Italian girl. If she had known we hadn't consummated yet, she would have gone straight to a Catholic priest and had the marriage annulled.

"Rosa, his mother, was a strong presence in Gino's life. Even to this day. His father more or less did her bidding, as did the rest of the family. They still do. There were younger sisters and brothers, all, but one married, now with big Italian families. I was the outcast."

"So, when did you consummate? I'm assuming you didn't live your marriage in celibacy." Amy's eyes widened, "Or did you?"

Jessie laughed. "No, I didn't. I mean live in celibacy. Actual penetration happened a couple of weeks into the marriage. Nothing spectacular. A lot of soreness, but mostly, just a feeling of relief. I had a child almost nine months later. I still can't believe I'm telling this to a young girl my daughter's age whom I only met yesterday."

"People say I'm easy to talk to. You have children? You hadn't mentioned anything about children until now. I wasn't thinking in that direction just yet but was getting there."

"I have a daughter almost your age. Have you ever thought about being a reporter or better yet, a therapist?"

Just then the sky grew dark and drops of rain started pounding down. Beach weather could be so unpredictable. The fishermen began gathering up their paraphernalia. Jessie saw Jackson packing up his toolbox. Jackson yelled over, offering a ride.

They scooted into the pickup's cab next to him.

"Amy, meet Jackson. Jackson, meet Amy. She is here staying with Myrtle, her grandmother."

Jackson smiled. "Yeah, I've seen you around. Pleased to meet you, Amy."

Amy said, "Nice to meet you, too. If you don't mind, drop me at the bookstore. I promised Grandma I would have lunch with her, almost that time now, and also, that I would help out this afternoon and give her a break. It should get busy with the rain spoiling the beach for people."

They arrived at Jessie's cottage first. She hopped out. "Thanks for the ride Jackson." Before closing the door, "Amy, do you want to go to the market together this Saturday? Oh, and Jackson, I want to talk to you about a possible porch swing." Jessie didn't mention the picket fence. The porch swing was higher on her list.

"Yes, great, will see you Saturday, if not before," Amy said.

"Jessie, I'll see what I can do," Jackson replied.

They drove off, leaving Jessie feeling both lighter and exhausted. She had said more to this young girl in a few hours than she had spoken in three months of therapy. She fell asleep on the couch to the sound of the rain.

CHAPTER 7

JESSIE SLEPT like a log all through the night. What was that? Eighteen hours of sleep? No dreams? She felt groggy but recharged. She also felt hungry. It was still raining, just drizzling though. It looked like it might keep it up all day. She put on the teakettle. This morning it would be grits and cheese and shrimp, the works. She grabbed a banana after she got everything started on the stovetop. A banana was at least a step in the right direction. She laughed out loud, remembering the chimp in Tarzan and about Aunt Agatha referring to her as Tarzana.

During the next couple of days, she settled into the comfort and coziness of her cottage and became all wrapped up in her book with the sound of rain in the background. It was that time of year. A fire in the fireplace would be nice, but she hadn't bothered to have firewood delivered. It wasn't that cold. It was just the idea of reading her book in front of a fireplace. It was so English. She made a mental note to herself to call Jackson.

That was another one of his roles, dropping off bundles of wood to the local residents. Upon reflection, she thought about how Jackson almost singlehandedly kept the island functioning. He came and went in his invisible cloak. He consulted, did his job, and before you knew it, he was gone again. He was a mild mannered Clark Kent without the glasses. He was always in a good mood, and he had a ruggedness about him. Unlike Clark Kent or Superman, Jessie had never seen him smoothly shaven. His face always had a hint of stubble as if he had misplaced his razor that morning. With those steel blue eyes and those curly locks, one curl usually hanging over one of his eyes, he could have been on a cover of a romance novel. He was more than just a good body — a good body, which was much too young for her. He undertook his projects in all seriousness as if he were working out great mathematical equations. There wasn't much small talk with him, and since Jessie wasn't one to make too many inquiries, he would just have to remain a mystery.

Perhaps he could be the subject of that book she was going to write. It could be something like Clark Kent by day, Superman by night, or maybe mild mannered Clark Kent turns into a vampire at night. She didn't remember ever seeing him at night, but sometimes she would see a light coming from his garage; therefore, he couldn't be a vampire.

Saturday rolled around. Luckily, the rain had stopped. It was a great day to go to the farmer's market. She and Amy hadn't bothered to set a time. But it was nearing nine and still no Amy. Maybe Amy didn't realize you had to get there early to get the best produce. Since Jessie lived closer to the market, she figured Amy would just stop by. Maybe she should call? Maybe Amy was already there. Jessie decided to go by the bookstore first. She could ask Myrtle about those cookbooks she ordered. She knew it was too soon, but it was the excuse she needed. It was only a little out of the way. In case she might miss Amy, she left a note tucked in the back screen door, the usual point of entry.

Myrtle was alone in the bookstore. She looked up as Jessie came in. "I thought you and Amy were going to the market this morning?"

"Yes, I did too."

"Well, she headed that way bright and early. I thought you might be having an early breakfast together first. You probably just missed her. You've been spending a lot of time together. I'm glad. Amy could use someone like you right now to get her mind off all that mess."

"You mean because of the loss of her mother?"

"That has been hard enough, but I was referring to all that other stuff."

"Other stuff?"

Myrtle placed her hand over her mouth as if she was trying to stop some sort of secret from escaping. Then almost in a whisper, she asked, "Amy hasn't mentioned anything?"

Myrtle hesitated as if she was thinking of something to say to change the subject. So, Jessie picked up the ball and just threw it out there towards Myrtle. "Do you mean all that stuff about her ex-boyfriend?"

Jessie was proud of herself for plowing right in there with a question. She felt she had scored a three-pointer.

Myrtle just shook her head in disgust. "We can hope an ex. We can hope we never see him again, not that I've ever seen him myself. That's not likely. He doesn't know where she is, but he could find out. I only know what her father has told me about him. Amy doesn't elaborate, at least not with me, and besides I guess she doesn't want to talk about it, and I can't blame her. I only know the state she was in when she arrived here. But she seems to have cheered up since she's been here. I could attribute it to the fresh sea air, but I know you have helped her get her head turned around, and I'm grateful to you."

"No, honestly, nothing to thank me for. I think Amy has a pretty good sense about things and a good head on her shoulders. Amy has been a Godsend to me as well."

That last statement evoked a look of motherly love from Myrtle. Myrtle had known about the loss of her son. Jessie got those looks a lot on the island. Most of the locals knew, but no one said anything. Jessie sensed how uncomfortable people were about approaching the subject with her. Most were careful to avoid anything that even could relate to it. Everyone just assumed he had died while serving in Korea. The last picture she had of him was in his uniform. It sat in her living room on a table along with the photo of Gina and Annabelle. When people saw the picture and inquired, she merely said he had died. People naturally assumed he had died in Korea. She let them assume. Mr. Roberts even thought that, or so she thought that is what he thought. His own son had served there but was alive and well working on the mainland. That was the bond between her and Mr. Roberts. They both had sons that had served in Korea.

"Well, Amy has perked up during the last couple of

days even with all this rain," Myrtle said. "So whatever you have been doing, I still can't help but to give you my immense praise."

Jessie thought about the last two days? Where had Amy been spending her time? It certainly wasn't with her. If this beatnik boyfriend of hers was so horrid, then she couldn't have been in such good spirits. Or could she? Maybe they got in touch somehow and reconciled. She knew how that could be. Her own relationship with Gino had been a roller coaster ride. There were so many ups and downs, elation one moment and near suicidal thoughts the next. Could Amy be in one of those moments of elation? Relationships could be so complicated.

With that, Jessie thought it best to take leave. She didn't want to alarm Myrtle. Jessie put on a cheerful face. "Well, bye for now, Myrtle. I'll just head on over to the market before all the good stuff is gone. I'm sure I'll catch Amy there. Oh, and I love the book on the yogi."

CHAPTER 8

JESSIE REMEMBERED that she had forgotten her bag. She always took her own with her. So, she stopped at the cottage on the way back to pick it up. Maybe Amy would be waiting there. She entered through the gate of the picket fence that fronted her cottage. She still hadn't asked Jackson about painting it.

She checked the back door. The note was as she had left it, still tucked in the door. She put a pen on the table by the door in case Amy might want to write something should Jessie continue to miss her.

At the market, Jessie wandered down the single lane of booths. It was short in comparison to the farmer's markets back in New York. They went on for blocks. You could hardly shuffle through the crowd there. At the island's market, you saw everyone. It was a gathering place for the locals, but it was getting late. The crowd had thinned down.

No Amy. She could have asked around if anyone had seen her but thought that not wise. She didn't want people forming a search party. After all, she could be back at the bookstore with Myrtle all ready. It was too early to cause alarm.

Jessie tried to block the worrisome thoughts. She selected vegetables for the curry. Without Amy's guidance she had no idea, so got one or two of almost everything. She chose broccoli, potatoes, cabbage, onions, carrots, eggplant, and an artichoke. None of the merchants had mangoes. Somehow an artichoke didn't sound Indian, but she loved artichokes and would eat it anyway, so it didn't matter.

She walked back to her cottage at a turtle's pace in hopes that she might see Amy along the way. That didn't happen. The note and pen were still there. She began to put the produce in the fridge.

Was Amy in any sort of danger? She thought about the boyfriend. She thought about Gino. Gino started out at the beginning of their relationship as a safety net for her. She didn't realize she was flirting with danger in his supposedly safe arms. In looking back at it now, she hadn't married for love at all but for comfort and refuge. Gino saw America as the land of opportunity, and it was. Not all of that opportunity was above board. And some of it was dangerous.

Her life with Gino started out exciting enough. She had to give him that. Unfortunately, his kind of excitement often struck a chord of terror in her. After the initial honeymoon, there were many sleepless nights. On some mornings, she woke up drenched in sweat and twisted covers from the nightmares. Gino slept through it, on the nights he was there.

Gino was full of contradictions. Life with him was complicated. If she should ever look for another relationship, it would be one without complications. The one time she did seek something of that nature also turned out to be full of difficulties. But that came much later in the marriage. Was that possible, a relationship without complications?

They spent their wedding night at one of the most luxurious hotels in New York. Gino loved the idea of luxury, but the actual details of it intimidated him. After the rushed wedding, she was content to have dinner in the hotel's dining room. The day had already been enough to exhaust anyone, but her new husband had a better idea. It was something called pizza.

The bellboy took both her and Clare's luggage up to their eighth floor room. Clare had the room next door. To her surprise, Gino grabbed her and carried her over the threshold. The whole act was awkward. Still, Jessie found the attempt romantic. Everything happened so fast.

Gino had his best suit on. At the time, she didn't know it was his only suit. He came to the boat prepared. He always acted with confidence. A confident appearance was something he worked hard at. He brought a small bag with his personal items. He placed his toiletries, consisting of a toothbrush, hair cream, and razor in the bathroom. With equal precision, he hid away a fresh pair of underwear, socks, work trousers and a shirt in the bureau drawer. Gino looked at his watch. He gave Jessie little time to freshen up before whisking her back down the elevator and through the lobby. He nodded to the doorman, and once again they were out on the city streets.

They walked into this pizza place, and immediately several men at one of the tables shouted out to her new husband. The place was bustling with activity. He didn't introduce her, just yelled back to them. "Boys, my new wife. We could use some privacy if you know what I mean." The men gave some approving wolf-like calls and went back to their pizza eating and business.

Gino called them pies, and you could order them as individual slices or whole. Jessic only wanted an individual one, as her stomach was still questionable, but Gino insisted on the entire pie. She was sure that was to impress his friends. There was something about the whole scenario that flattered Jessie. She knew he was definitely showing her off to his buddies.

She suspected Gino knew his friends would be here at this particular time of evening. Later, she knew it had been a set-up, a term she would hear Gino use plenty of times during their marriage. The attention made her feel pretty, although Gino had never told her she was pretty. He had never told her in his letters or in person that she was beautiful or pretty.

She later learned Gino had a reason for everything and the proper timing for everything. It was just like he knew when his friends, or rather business associates she would find out later, would be there. She had to admit the pizza was great. It was her first time eating pizza. She and her aunt hadn't experienced this on the prior trip. Aunt Agatha had introduced her to the culture of New York, the museums and such. Her aunt would not even have understood the concept of why one might even want to eat pizza. Jessie was sure that Clare had experienced this kind of nightlife — places like Grimaldi's. Jessie's favorite thing about New York remained Central Park. She felt at home there. It reminded her of the estate.

There was the long walk back to the hotel. The sky was lit up with stars. They took several detours. It was just as well. The night air and a long walk diminished her tension and invigorated her. They went past the East River. He told her about the dead bodies somewhere on the bottom. She tensed back up and pulled closer to him. In retrospect, it wasn't exactly the romantic talk of young lovers. She had no expectations of what a honeymoon should be. Gino had big dreams. His talk resounded of his letters. It was her honeymoon night, and instead of feeling deeply in love, she felt kind of lost. It made her cling to him even more.

Back at the room, he stripped down to just his pants. He began undressing her and kissing her and then removed his own last bit of clothes, and that is when the frustration started. They finally decided to call it a night. There was always tomorrow, he said. She sensed the fact that there being no question of her virginity greatly pleased him. He got over the failed attempt quickly, flopped down onto the bed, completely naked, and began a small snore. All the hard work apparently wore him out.

Jessie went into the bathroom and stared into the mirror for the longest time. She wondered who she was, who he was, and what this new life was going to be all about. Then she donned her nightgown and crawled like a schoolgirl into bed beside him. She lay there for hours staring out the window at the lights of the city, contemplating if marriage got any better. Was this what happened in all marriages? Everything felt so strange.

The next morning, he rose early, putting on his work clothes as if nothing the night before had happened and kissed her bye. It was Friday. Typically, he worked on Saturdays as well, but he told her he had gotten it off for a short honeymoon. She would spend her first full day of married life with Clare.

Clare was all smiles, looking at her slyly. Jessie didn't want to burst her bubble so acted timid about the night before. That was easy enough. Besides, maybe what happened was normal. If she had any intuition about what was coming when she stepped off the boat, she would have brought along a copy of "Lady Chatterley's Lover" to read on the ship. She doubted that Clare had read it or read any books for that matter. She also doubted if Clare was a virgin. Clare could shed some insight on the situation, but Jessie couldn't bring herself to ask. Clare was more inquisitive about future plans as they concerned her than about Jessie's sex life. Jessie assured her she wouldn't abandon her.

Gino and Jessie spent most of the weekend at Coney Island. On Saturday, she tried a hot dog. On Sunday, she tried a corn dog. She found she liked pizza and hotdogs, not so much corn dogs. Gino had brought her into a different world. Jessie loved the beach at Coney Island. Her father had taken her to a beach a couple of times. Once she and Aunt Agatha had gone. They spent the whole time sheltered under a tent. Aunt Agatha complained about the sun, refusing to let Jessie stick a toe outside the shaded area. Still, she loved all beach experiences. The beaches in England were quite different from those in America. They were rougher and rockier, more romantic.

They stayed at the hotel for a couple of weeks. Consummation had almost happened the last night there. She felt some hope. But the pain became excruciating, and she tensed up. There was blood, quite a lot, and not from her period. It wasn't time for it, not for another couple of weeks.

The sight of her blood scared Gino limp. She imagined him envisioning having to wrap her body and get it out of the hotel and down to the river undetected. She would be just another body piled up on top of all the others. Clare would go to the police, but it would all be in vain. Only Gino, and maybe his cronies, would ever know what had happened to her.

After two weeks, they checked out of the hotel, Clare included. The luggage was strapped to the back of a taxi. They stopped by a boarding house in Brooklyn on route to his family's home where they arranged for Clare to stay. Jessie paid and gave her an allowance for food and other necessities and said she would check back in with her before month's end.

They went to Rosa's, Gino's mother. Gino's whole family was crowded into this tiny house: father, brothers and sisters. It was clear his mother ruled the roost. She was quite intimidating. Any tension that had lessened during their first two weeks of marriage returned after meeting her. This was not going to help with the completion of the consummation if that was ever to happen.

No matter how hard she tried, Jessie couldn't do anything right around Rosa. Jessie didn't know the proper way to eat spaghetti, an unforgivable sin. Rosa just shook her head, giving her pitying glances. There were words of Italian she didn't understand. Were they talking about her? Gino's father ate his meal in silence, not even bothering to look up. The brothers talked back and forth, in English, all the while nudging and kidding Gino. Since they spoke in English Jessie knew the conversation was meant for her ears too.

The girls hardly took their eyes off of her, especially Bella, the youngest. She was eight. Jessie felt she might have an ally in the family. Bella's idolization of her was short lived as Rosa reprimanded Bella more than once not to stare. After the meal was over, Rosa sent her off to play.

Jessie wasn't accustomed to wine at meals. Nor could she handle it, another unforgivable sin in an Italian family. She had to admit it did help with the tension. She was dizzy after a few sips, though.

Their appearance had caused a total disruption in the small house. Bedding arrangements were altered. With the help of the wine, inside the thin walls of his parent's bedroom, consummation was complete. Without the wine, after facing Rosa, Jessie's vagina, which she did not even know the name of at the time, would have probably clamped solidly shut for the remainder of her life.

Jessie knew the use of the bedroom was a one-time deal. Jessie insisted they use her money for a small, but comfortable, apartment. Gino did not complain, seeing how keeping her and Rosa under the same roof, a small one at that, was not an option.

The next day they found a cozy little brownstone a few blocks away. It was wedged tight between other brownstones as all houses were in Brooklyn. It had a small kitchen connected to the living room, bathroom, and one bedroom. It was adequate for a first home but more importantly private. They could have rented a room, something more applicable for the pay scale of a dockworker, but Jessie insisted. She insisted on using her own money for furnishings and everything they needed to get started. They opened an account the next day in a nearby bank.

Gino didn't make any attempts at sex for another three weeks. Since she didn't know what was usual in these circumstances, she tried not to concern herself. She was busy enough discovering the streets and shops around them. She dedicated herself to the job of making them a new home and learning to cook spaghetti and anything else that was easy. She retrieved Clare during the daytime to help her out.

Jessie's period didn't come in the two week allotted time. Nor did it come in the following two weeks. If there was any question in her mind that she had actually had sex, it vanished. If she were pregnant, which she was almost ninety-nine percent certain she was, she would go to a doctor while Gino was at work. She would confirm her one percent doubt before telling him.

She heard a knock on the screen door. It was Amy. Relief. And she was with Jackson?

CHAPTER 9

AMY CRINGED with a look of guilt on her face that quickly turned into a smile. "I'm so sorry. I'm so sorry. But we have a surprise for you!"

This whole scenario brought back memories of Gina not showing up when she was supposed to. It was always because of a boy. She was always apologizing, never meaning it, at least never meaning it as the years progressed. The difference was she was sure Amy meant it. Amy was an adult now, just like Gina. Since Amy was not her daughter, Jessie didn't have the right to reprimand. Still, she did.

"Amy, I was worried. I sound like a mother, don't I? Have you talked with your grandmother? I saw her this morning at the bookstore. She thought you were with me these last couple of days. I didn't want to say anything to make her worry. I let her think everything was all right and told her I would catch you at the market."

"Yeah, we checked in with her before coming here, but onto the surprise. We'll be right back."

They went out to Jackson's pickup and came back carrying a swing.

"You said you wanted a swing, so we picked one up, along with the hardware. Jackson is going to install it for you while we do the curry. Is that okay? Tell us where you want it."

Jessie was amazed and felt a little ashamed, "Yes, that's great, more than okay! Well, let's see, I was thinking on the back porch on the end if it will work there."

"I'm sure Jackson can make it work." Amy smiled over at him, and he back. "Did you know he has an engineering degree?"

Jessie was fascinated with this whole new development."No, I didn't know that."

Jackson hadn't said anything up to this point. "Well, Jessie, I'll go out to the truck and get my toolbox and get started on the swing. Maybe you and Amy can get started on that curry. I'm famished. We skipped lunch, trying to get back in time."

"Sure, we'll get right on that."

Amy followed her into the kitchen. Jessie opened the fridge, showing Amy the vegetables. "Hope these are okay."

"They'll be okay. A lot of Indian cooking is just a hodgepodge anyway. The secret is in the curry. And there are so many different kinds it might shock you, maybe into the hundreds."

"So, what's going on with you and Jackson? And, where have you been? How old is he anyway? Around early thirties, I'm guessing?"

"He's thirty-three, and I think I'm in love."

Jessie's eyes grew big, and her eyebrows rose as high as Mrs. Gibbon's. "That was quick." Jessie thought back to Gina's petite love sagas.

"I know, but we have spent the last few days talking and finding out all about each other. That's all, just talking, well, some kissing, but no more than that. He's either shy or just respects me. I can't tell yet."

"Amy, try not to put any sudden moves on him." She and Amy must have been together in a past life. Talking to her like this just seemed natural, and Amy got Jessie's humor. Jessie continued, "Where have you been all this time your grandmother thought you were with me?"

Amy peeked through the kitchen curtain at Jackson. He looked up towards the window and winked at her. She let the curtain drop back down. "Isn't he so handsome?"

"Yes, I would say handsome in a rugged sort of way." This whole conversation reminded Jessie of when Gina had her first crush and couldn't stop talking about the boy.

She had just entered high school, and they were both in ninth grade. He was Irish, and his name was Eugene. He walked her home and carried her books. He was also ruggedly handsome if you can say a fourteen-year-old boy is ruggedly handsome. It was the sandy curls and Irish rogue that endeared him to Gina. It didn't hurt that he was also the tallest boy in their class. She was the envy of all the girls, because she was the only one who had a steady boyfriend. All the girls in her class looked up to her. Their courtship lasted through all of ninth grade. By summer break, they both moved on. Gina outgrew him. That was the longest relationship she ever had. She outgrew each new beau at an exponentially faster rate after that.

Jessie laid out the vegetables and handed Amy a cutting board and knife. She got out the rice and put a large pot on the stovetop. She thought they better put the whole bag on. Jessie figured Jackson might have a hearty appetite. Plus they needed to feed all that ruggedness.

"This morning we got up super early, with the fishermen, and caught the ferry going to the mainland. We had breakfast at this little coffee shop that had art on the walls. Well, everything around here has art on the walls, doesn't it? But this wasn't your typical ocean and seashell art. It was all portraits, something like the work of Picasso. It was all so romantic. Jackson said one of them reminded him of me.

"Then we happened across the swing at a yard sale. We thought we would get back in time for the market, but one thing led to another. We went into this new shop. A young couple ran it. It was out of a house, but it had the coolest things. There were lots of candles, which they made themselves. She did the candles. He did pottery. The pottery operation was in back. They sort of had a little courtyard with a kiln at the edge. He was in the middle of unloading it. So, we had to watch. Jackson bought me one of his teapots. He couldn't afford the painting that reminded him of me. But, I love the teapot, my first gift from him.

"The couple that ran the shop is also heavy into yoga. We have to go together soon. You and I. I can't wait for you to see it. Anyway, we talked to them for the longest time. And before we knew it, we had missed the ferry and had to wait for the next one, which didn't come until one. And, of course, that was another hour. But now, here we are."

"Yes, here you are, you and Jackson. I'm still trying to wrap my head around all this, but life is constantly taking different turns, and this one seems like a good one. You say he has an engineering degree? So, why is he working odd jobs on the island?"

Amy gave her that kind of duh look. "Why is anyone on the island? He has stuff, too. He just had to get away for a while. And, he likes island life. He likes doing his own thing, being his own boss. Did you know he has all these projects going on in his garage? He makes things. He's great at woodworking. He does some furniture, but mostly small things that require a good deal of engineering. He loves making clocks with all wooden parts, with all the inner workings exposed. He's meticulous with his creations. He thought he might do next summer's art fair.

He just started taking his work to the mainland to sell in a shop over there, and he's already getting some orders."

"That's great. I would love to see his work." Jessie started getting out the spices.

"Oh, we need to soak the rice first, just fifteen minutes. Sorry, I'm getting all flustered over Jackson."

"Yes, I noticed. Remember I'm a novice at this."

Jessie found the whole experience of cooking with Amy fun. She felt good vibes going into the food. That was important. She used to have heartburn so bad during those years with Gino. It was all those bad vibes Rosa was stirring up in the sauce. At first, she attributed it to her pregnancy. Gino said so too. The doctor had told her that was common, and with the birth it would disappear, but it didn't.

Heartburn was rare since she moved to the island. Jessie had tried to learn to cook the way Rosa did, to please Gino, but she learned that was never going to be possible. Rosa had attempted to teach her. Each attempt was more like a lesson in teaching her how she would never be the good Italian daughter-in-law that she had hoped for. Both Jessie and Rosa gave up after a while.

Besides heartburn, during her first pregnancy, she suffered from morning sickness. Maybe that wouldn't have been so bad, but the sickness lasted all day. Was it a coincidence that the sickness didn't start until she finally told Gino that she was pregnant? He didn't take it well.

They had never had time to discuss the aspect of having children. Maybe he was just unprepared, but he was greatly agitated that she was with child. He had quite the outburst. She ended up crying in bed most of the day. Later, he apologized and said that would never happen again. To make it up to her, he fixed ravioli for dinner.

There had been a lot of outbursts and make-ups during their time together. Gino took over the evening meals during that time. He loved to do it. Or maybe he just liked to hold the fact over her that he did it. He was always saying, "Look how much I do for you." She thought he felt guilty that her money was paying for their living expenses. Gino started needing more of his own paycheck for investments. He never elaborated what those investments were. She learned not to question him too much. Whatever they were, they paid off.

After she had moved to the island, she hadn't touched Italian food. She had a pizza now and then, but she always ordered it without the tomato sauce. More than once she had to repeat the order, or they would forget and put the sauce on.

In spite of all the pregnancy sickness and heartburn, Josh was born and turned out just fine. He was a little small, only six pounds, one ounce, but he quickly gained weight. Rosa was so thrilled with her first grandson, even though he looked more like Jessie than Gino.

Josh was such a lovable child. He could melt the hardest heart. He grew up being the peacemaker in the family. Once when she and Gino were fighting he went up to them and placed Gino's hand over hers. She had felt so ashamed.

Two years later, she became pregnant again, or so she thought. There wasn't any scientific proof of it since she didn't go to the doctor. But her period was over a month late, and she just had that mother's instinct that she was pregnant again. Remembering Gino's promise that he would never react that way again, she told him before verifying it.

She had taken Josh to spend some time with Clare to have some alone time with her husband. Jessie had visions of him hugging and kissing her and telling her how happy he was. Maybe he would even take her out to celebrate, even if it was only for pizza. She had obviously been in some kind of denial over how their marriage actually worked and how bad of a temper that he could sometimes have.

Once again, she ran to bed, crying most of the night. When she finally got up to go to the bathroom, she found that her period had started. She could never know for sure, but felt this baby did not want to come into this situation, and she couldn't blame it. Gino would later deny that she had even been pregnant. But a mother knows in her heart.

She had to give Gino credit though. Even though he was so reluctant to have a child, he was a downright decent father. He spent as much time as possible with Josh. And, Josh looked up to him.

Two years later, she became pregnant again. She never said a thing. It was five months before she showed enough that Gino suspected. He said, "You're putting on some weight. You're not pregnant are you?" She gave him a puzzled look and continued reading "The Cat in the Hat" to Josh.

Jessie never got sick during this pregnancy. So, there was no tell-tell signs. There was never even any more mention of it, even though it became quite apparent she was definitely pregnant as more time passed. Once Rosa had guessed, it was no longer an issue for Gino. His mother's approval was all it took. If she ever got pregnant again, she decided she would just tell Rosa, bypassing Gino altogether.

Her weight, pregnant or not, was never an issue with Gino, too skinny, too fat. He didn't seem to care one way or the other, just like he hadn't cared about her makeup or hairdo. One day he came home from work to find Clare and the midwife there. She never knew him to raise his voice around other people, just the immediate family, meaning her and Josh. He acted so happy when he saw what was happening. He became a part of the whole scene like he was the greatest husband that ever was and had been supporting her the whole time. Most people believed them to be the perfect couple. She let everyone believe that. It was that thing about making your bed and lying in it.

The curry was simmering. Amy was adding the veggies. The rice was almost done. Jackson had come in and asked if he could do anything. Jessie showed him where the dishes were and asked him to set the table while she got out the loose leaf tea and put the teakettle on to boil. Jessie realized that this was her first official dinner party, even if she wasn't doing a great deal of the cooking. It was definitely time for the loose-leaf tea. Enlightenment was sure to follow.

Jessie put a candle on the table and lit it, and they all sat down to eat. It was the perfect evening. The food tasted great. All those good vibes coming from it were overwhelming.

She had never heard Jackson talk so much. He was quite intelligent. He would have to be to have majored in engineering. She could see what Amy saw in him and thought it was a good match. He was easy going but at the same time serious and grounded. Amy was kind of the opposite. They complimented each other. Jessie saw him reach for Amy's hand during the dinner more than once.

Afterward, they all tried out the swing. When they left, Amy said she would teach her how to fix some Indian dessert next, some rice pudding, something called, kheer. It sounded like rice overkill to Jessie, but she wanted the full Indian experience.

Jessie quit worrying about Amy, knowing she had Jackson now. She could tell by the way he looked at her that it wasn't a fling. She also thought if the beatnik boyfriend should show up, Jackson would protect her.

Jessie slept soundly that night.

CHAPTER 10

THE NEXT day Jessie went out to buy wine and wine glasses. The next time she had guests, who would more than likely be Amy and Jackson, she would entertain with a little style. Who knows? Maybe she could move up to hosting a book club meeting.

She also purchased some cheese and crackers, just in case she wanted to keep it light and informal.

Jessie usually only drank on special occasions. Wine was a way of life in Gino's family. She didn't question on that first night that she had dinner at Rosa's that wine was served during prohibition. She knew that Gino had procured it. What she didn't know at the time was that he procured it on a regular basis. She didn't know that he had something going on the side with the men she first encountered on their wedding night at the pizza place, either.

After Josh was born, Gino quit his job at the docks. Jessie was never sure what his new job was. She only knew he had more free time, coming and going as he pleased. He might come home in the middle of the day. He would go out at night on business, returning late or in the middle of the morning. On some days, after long nights, he slept in until noon, or until Josh or Gina, after she was born, woke him up.

He never was quite clear in explaining his new job to her. To sum it up he called it investing in different pursuits, and that, as a woman, she wouldn't understand it. She explained to him that her father had been a businessman and invested, but he wasn't gone all hours of the night. Gino replied that New York was different from England.

She questioned how they could be doing so well when the country was going through a depression. Gino told her there was always opportunity to be had in America. That is why his family came. Gino had never talked about his family's roots and what it was like back in Italy. But then, she never told him much about England either. He never asked. Sometimes, she longed to go back. She wondered how different life might be rearing the children on a country estate. Gino would be bored pretty quickly. Gino rarely went to Central Park. Nature wasn't his thing.

He began bringing home gifts. It was always something different. It could be anything from a turkey or ham for holidays or for just no occasion. Sometimes it was jewelry, something she almost never wore, or toys for the children. On other days, he would bring her flowers. They always seemed a little wilted. He called them added benefits of the job. He also began dressing nicer. His closet was now full of suits. Sometimes, he would give her a hundred dollar bill and tell her to take a taxi to Manhattan and pick him out a nice suit. He said Clare could keep the kids. Clare did love to babysit the kids. He would add, "And if you want a nice dress for yourself, that is fine." He always carried a wallet full of cash.

On some trips, she would take Clare along. Clare married a clergyman, of all people. Jessie would never have guessed that one in a million years. Clare had become a devout Presbyterian. She, Gino, and the kids went to her wedding, a big church affair. Josh was the ring bearer.

Clare and Graham didn't have any children. Clare confided that they wanted them, but when nothing happened, she went to the doctor. To her dismay, the doctor confirmed she couldn't have children. So, they contented themselves with their church life. To fill the void, Clare often babysat for various parishioners as well as Jessie. She loved being around children. On most Sunday mornings, she stayed in the church nursery. She helped Jessie most of all. She was a Godsend in that respect. On days when Jessie wanted to go to a museum or just shopping, Clare would go along as a nanny. Clare started out as a servant to Jessie, but now, they were best friends. Josh loved Clare and called her Care.

When Gina was two, Gino decided it was time for a bigger place. He insisted that they stay in Brooklyn to be close to his parents, even though more and more of his business was taking him into Manhattan.

Out of Rosa's family, Bella was the only one still at home. The others were married and starting their own families. Rosa still ruled the family like the queen of the hive, and she loved having gobs of grandchildren. Whenever they were all gathered at once, you couldn't move without bumping into someone or tripping over a child. Twice a month they all met at the queen bee's cramped house for a big family dinner. It was one of those unspoken mandatory functions. Jessie didn't dare protest. The good thing was that now with so many added members, Jessie could disappear into the background.

Gino was Rosa's favorite. Not so with Leo. Leo, Gino's father, was hard to read. There was something behind Leo's glass exterior that Jessie didn't quite understand. She asked Gino once, to no avail. He only gave vague generalities about his growing up years in Italy.

Gino was the oldest. Even though Rosa had a definite hold on him, Gino knew how to sweet talk his mama, and whatever he was up to, she turned a blind eye. Jessie was often jealous of her. He always put his mama's wants and needs over hers. There were times when Jessie thought Rosa flaunted this. It became an unspoken competition that Jessie couldn't win.

Jessie had suspected for some time that he might have a mistress. After all, what business did a married man have out at all hours of the night?

Clare started seeing Gino in a different light after she got religion, and Jessie confided to Clare about seeing the lady who she thought was his mistress on the streets of Manhattan. That's when Clare pulled a double whammy on her and told her that one day, she saw him coming out of a bathhouse on 28th Street. Jessie was in shock. That explained a lot to Jessie, his disinterest in sex with her, for one.

So much about their marriage had been a ruse for

him to keep up appearances. Sometimes Jessie thought it was all an act just to please his mama. But why choose her, if he only wanted to please Rosa? He could have pleased her more with a nice Italian girl.

Jessie never broached the subject with Gino. She wouldn't know how to start and was afraid he might lose it. There was no purpose in adding more salt to her wound, the wound, which just kept getting bigger with each passing year. Jessie used all her energy these days just to avoid arguments with him. She had the children to think about.

Maybe a vacation was the answer, one away from New York City, a lovely beach somewhere — something other than Coney Island. Maybe it could revive something in their marriage, the something that was never there.

They had never had a proper vacation. Jessie brought it up to Gino, and he shrugged her off, saying it wasn't a good time, maybe when Gina got older. But this time, she wasn't going to be ignored. She had done her research and presented brochures for him to look at. She placed the flyers before him. He lit up his cigarette and acted disinterested. The next thing she knew, she heard words coming out of her mouth that were most uncharacteristic. She looked at him sternly. Without blinking, she said in her most serious manner as if giving him an ultimatum, "Consider it an investment."

He gave in much too quickly. Somehow, she suspected that he knew she knew. Maybe he knew Clare had seen him. Perhaps he had been waiting for this day and expected it to go much more badly. They rented a car and headed for the island cottage she had picked out.

CHAPTER 11

A COUPLE of weeks had passed, and Jessie hadn't even caught a glimpse of Amy. She respected her love life and understood, though she wished she had one of her own, an uncomplicated one like Amy and Jackson had. Then one morning Amy showed up wanting Jessie to go to the mainland to see the shop that she and Jackson had visited. At last, she thought, some more adventure with Amy.

She took a quick shower and got dressed while Amy enjoyed the swing. Luckily, it was still warm for late October. Jessie was still able to wear her sandals and pedal pushers. They took off, walking towards the ferry. While they walked, Amy filled her in on what was going on with her and Jackson.

Their love was growing. That was good to hear. Any

spare time Amy had, she was spending at the bookstore. Grandma approved of her and Jackson. That was also good to hear. Now Amy wanted her father to meet him. He would be coming to the island for Thanksgiving, and they wanted Jessie to come as well. Having no place else to go, she accepted. If any other alternative came up, like being able to spend it with Gina she could always cancel. She could hope but thought it not in the realm of possibility.

Jessie always loved Thanksgiving until Josh's death. After that, everything fell apart. The holidays after his death were just like any other day. Until then, she loved most holidays, even though she had to spend them with the queen bee. There was always some festive event to celebrate holidays in New York City.

It was a ritual for the whole family, including Gino, to go to the Macy's Day Parade on Thanksgiving. She always took the kids to sit on Santa's lap at Christmas time. Josh accepted every fantasy without question. At age four, Gina had started to become cynical, questioning why there were so many Salvation Army Santas throughout the city.

Gina was always way more advanced than her years. When she was eight, she wrote a note to the tooth fairy, explaining she had some additional expenses and would need more money this time. She became quite spoiled. Her dad was always slipping her a dollar bill, sometimes five, here and there, way too much money for a child her age. Trying to explain fiscal responsibility to her was useless. Gino favored her. She had his looks, olive complexion, and dark hair. He loved showing her off, Daddy's little girl. Josh tried even harder to please him, but Josh was never jealous of Gina. If anything, he looked out for her, protecting her like a big brother would.

The first summer on the island, they stayed for two weeks and returned home. Gino was antsy the whole time and itching to get back to business. Josh loved the water and the sand, most of all the sand. It was perfect for his building projects. Gina loved the water. She was like a dolphin around the ocean. She had to be constantly watched. She was always running towards the waves, Annabelle in her arms.

She and Amy approached the ferry. The air was brisk. On the ferry ride, Jessie found out what Jackson's stuff was, the reason he was doing handyman work on the island. He had just started as a junior engineer for Boeing in Chicago. Everything was looking up. He was engaged to marry the daughter of one of the bosses there. But the relationship turned sour. They just wanted different things in life.

Jackson wasn't that success oriented and didn't like city life. His fiancé did. He had grown up on a small farm outside of Chicago. He loved the open air of the farm but hated cold Illinois winters. He especially dreaded all those cold mornings he had to get up at the break of dawn to feed the animals and milk the cows.

Jackson was good at tinkering, as his father put it, so he worked his way through college, earning an engineering degree. Jessie thought about Josh and how he might have been an engineer.

"After Jackson's breakup, he just wanted to get away to think. He just kept drifting until he ended up here." Amy said.

Okay, not that much material for a novel. The whole story had been written a zillion times. Boy meets girl. Boy and girl break up. Boy finds new girl, true love. Jessie hoped that Amy and Jackson had true love. Maybe the drifting part would be nice fodder for a novel. Who knows what he may have encountered along the way? Oh, but Jack Kerouac had already written about that one. And although critics found it novel worthy, she didn't.

They stepped off the ferry, Amy leading the way. The exterior of the shop was more or less what she expected. It boasted bold paint with various pottery sculptures adorning the front yard. Jessie observed birdbaths and some weird cylinder shapes piled on top of one another. She guessed them to be some new modernistic form of sculpture. Jessie looked around to see some wire contraptions and various other oddities. It was reminiscent of some of the Greenwich Village shops.

They entered the main room to the overwhelming fragrance of candles. Indian sitar music played in the background, adding to the ambience. A girl with long dark hair walked out, telling them to make themselves at home. The girl remembered Amy and asked where her boyfriend was. Amy told her he was home working on some of his own projects as their shop had inspired him. A man, her partner, covered in tattoos, with longish hair and a bandana tied around it, and an unkempt beard walked in.

Jessie wondered why they looked so familiar. Then she remembered. The art fair. This was *yoga couple.*

Jessie didn't say anything about seeing them a few years back. It was definitely them, no mistaking that. Amy introduced her and began talking a mile a minute to them, so Jessie browsed the pottery collection while they talked.

Jessie became enchanted by a tea set she saw. The guy's name was Bruce. He was the farthest thing from a

Bruce that Jessie could imagine. Bruce saw her admiring the tea set and asked if she wanted to see what he had just pulled from the kiln. The yield was still cooling down in the back.

"You have to see this whole kiln operation," Amy said. So, they walked out back. A low wooden fence surrounded the whole backyard. Amy was right; the fence, not that tall provided an excellent view of the island. The kiln was in one corner. In front of it sat tables covered in pottery, some of it only partially glazed.

Jessie's eyes moved around the yard. In one corner sat a claw foot bathtub. She remembered back to the art fair and how she had wondered if they took baths. Surely this was just part of the art décor and not where they bathed. They both smelled quite fresh this time. They smelled like their candles.

Jessie's eyes darted back to the tables of pottery. She liked one of the colors better that they had in the back and asked if it was the same price. Bruce said yes. So Jessie said she would take it. Bruce told her it would have to cool a bit before he could wrap it for her.

While they waited, they walked through a beaded entrance into another room. This was where the music was coming from. A record player was set up in the corner. Other than that, the room was almost empty, painted white, even the wooden floor. There were yoga mats, pillows and blankets piled into one corner. Jessie smiled at seeing the white rug from the art fair in the corner. On the way out of the yoga room, she saw a small restroom with a shower, apparently for customers as well as for the owners. There was a narrow set of stairs next to the restroom. Jessie gathered that led to their sleeping quarters. She envisioned a mattress on the floor.

Angela, the girl, said they had yoga classes there twice a week.

“This is really what I wanted you to come for," Amy said excitedly. "I was saving it as a surprise. We have to take a yoga class together.”

“Oh, I don’t know, Amy. Except for walking, my body is so inflexible. I’m almost forty-five. It could be the end of me.”

"Or it could be the beginning of you."

Angela laughed. “Amy is right. And, we wouldn't let you break. There are all different kinds of yoga. We have a beginner's class. A couple of women in their seventies come. And the group isn’t that big. As you can see, the room isn’t that large, and I would have guessed that you were in your thirties.”

Jessie melted hearing the compliment. “I don’t have a yoga mat.”

“We have them here as you can see, and if you should like yoga, which I think you will, we sell them. You have a body for yoga. I can tell.”

Feeling cornered and running out of excuses, Jessie quit resisting and let the excitement of a new adventure take over. “Okay, where do I sign up?”

When they were ready to leave, Bruce and Angela both placed their hands in a prayer position in front of their chest and bid them Namaste. Amy returned the gesture while Jessie did an awkward wave of her hand.

They left the shop, Jessie carrying the bag with the teapot, and Amy carrying the bag with the cups.

The talk on the way back was all about yoga. Amy enlightened her on different poses, showing her some on board the ferry, which drew a crowd of onlookers. Jessie felt intimidated by the various asanas, the name Amy gave the poses, even though she knew Amy was only doing the simplest ones in an effort, not to scare her off.

Every time she encountered Amy, there was something new. Isn't that why she came to the island, to begin a new life?

CHAPTER 12

JUST AS Amy and Jessie came up to the back door, she heard the phone ringing. It was an odd sound to her. She rushed in to pick it up, placing the bag of pottery on the table with a thud, at the same time thinking maybe she might have damaged it.

Jessie didn't know if the phone had been ringing long or had just started. Her immediate reaction was panic She so seldom got calls. Her next thought was Gina. Was she okay? Was it even her calling? She grabbed the phone, "Hello."

"Mom."

"Is everything all right?"

"Of course, why wouldn't it be?"

Jessie hesitated, starting to say, well, *you never call, so I just thought*….but held her tongue not wanting to ruin any good mood already established.

Amy, sensing the call was important, placed the bag of cups on the kitchen table and waved bye to her.

"Mom, I'm getting married! Do you want to come up to help with the wedding plans?"

"Of course I'll help you. Do you want to tell me about him?" Jessie said before Gina even got the words out. She didn't have a clue who Gina's latest boyfriend was and at this point, didn't even care. She was just so glad that Gina was reaching out to her and wanted to include her in her wedding plans. Jessie was elated, maybe more so than Gina if that were possible.

"Mom, don't get too excited. You'll meet him when you get here. It's not going to be anything all that elaborate. Fifty people in attendance, tops. Well, you can add another fifty to that when you include dad's family."

Hearing the words 'dad's family' put Jessie back into panic mode. She would have to see Gino, or Gene, as he was now called, again. But no, don't even think of that. Don't let Gina hear any panic in her voice. Look at the positive. Gina is talking to her and even wants her as a part of her wedding.

One of Jessie's biggest fears was that Gina would one day get married and have children, and she would find out through Clare. She would have grandchildren that wouldn't even know her.

The call could have been from Clare. Why had she not even thought of Clare when the phone rang? Jessie knew why. It was because Clare had given up on calling her. For the last year, they had just sent each other cards with short notes written within. Clare's would sometimes be long and require a separate piece of paper. Jessie's had become shorter and shorter. They said something like, "Hope you are having a wonderful Thanksgiving or Christmas or Easter." Jessie always followed with, "Hope you will come to the island for a visit soon! Love, Jessie." Jessie signed her notes to Clare with love. But she had never even picked up the phone to call Clare since she had been on the island. Clare had been there for her in the toughest times. She loved her like an older sister, sometimes like a mother.

"Gina, who is he, what's his name? How long have you been engaged?"

"His name is Chris. Just since last night. I've already told dad. I would have called you last night, but it was way too late. You know how dad is, always up at all hours of the night."

"What does he do?"

"He's an actor and an artist. He plays some bit parts in theater productions right now, but I know he's going to have a starring role someday. He's that good. He also does some artwork for sets. But I wanted to let you know we wanted to get married on Christmas. I know it's short notice. But, like I said, we are keeping it small. How soon can you come to New York?"

"That is quick! I'll call about flights just as soon as we get off the phone, and I'll call you back, when I know something."

"Thanks, Mom, and I love you."

"I love you, too, Gina."

Jessie put the phone back on the hook, tears forming in her eyes. It was great to hear such joy in Gina's voice. She would make the call for the airline in just a moment. She had to collect her nerves and savor the moment. Her daughter needed her. Her daughter even said she loved her. Right now, she was the happiest mom in the world.

She tried to breathe slowly and to meditate for a moment before calling the airline. No, best to call a travel agent, she thought. She didn't want any mishaps. She had to send out a prayer. Everything had to go well. Her relationship with Gina hung in the balance. More than anything she wanted a good, no make that great, relationship with Gina.

There was something about Amy. Maybe she was an angel who had come to help her turn her life around.

CHAPTER 13

THE NEXT day Jessie was up before daylight. She hardly slept a wink. So much to do. She could sleep on the plane.

She had called Gina yesterday telling her that she had reservations to fly out the day after tomorrow. She had one day to get packed and get everything in order, mainly the cottage. She didn't know how long she would be gone, or if she would even be back to the island before the wedding. More than likely she would stay in New York the whole time. Where would she stay? A hotel for all that time would be expensive. She might have to blow the rest of her trust on the wedding trip, but it would be worth it. There was no sense in worrying about it now. She would figure out arrangements when she got there. She could, after all, stay with Clare. Now she wished she had called her some or at least kept up the correspondence. Clare would never turn her away. That she was sure of. Gina might have other plans for her. She would see when she got there. Jessie wanted to be at Gina's complete disposal.

Had Gina already told Clare? Maybe Clare was already getting the spare room ready for her. Clare always kept a distant eye on Gina. She did it for Jessie, and she did it because she cared. In one respect, she helped raise Gina. Clare was Gina's godmother. Gino had wanted one of his thug friends to be the godparents, but Jessie had set her foot down, saying it had to be Clare and Graham. It was only right. It was one of the few times she spoke up to Gino. The thought of some of those people he hung out with being godparents to Gina was appalling.

They didn't even pick godparents for Josh. Being from England, Jessie had never thought of the concept of godparents. And Gino wasn't in that tight with his so-called friends at the time, although Jessie would hardly consider them friends. They could turn on you in an instant. She didn't want the children anywhere near them and forbade Gino to bring any of them into their home. She had to admit he was good about adhering to that request.

Clare was a great godmother to Gina. She was the daughter Clare never had. Clare was capable of watching someone incognito. She had done enough spying on Gino without Jessie even asking her to. She had kept a watchful eye on Gina ever since Jessie had come to the island. Jessie was so grateful to have Clare as a friend. Gina was mostly what Clare talked about in the correspondence that they did have. She knew that any news of Gina was what Jessie wanted to hear.

With Jessie's absence from New York, she knew Clare

would be there in a pinch for Gina. Clare would more than likely show up before Gino. She doubted Gina would go to her grandmother in case of an emergency. Gina had learned to be evasive when dealing with her grandmother, as she didn't want her interfering in her life. Rosa had a way of doing that if you let her. Gina had developed the same skills as her father in handling Queen Bee.

The yoga class. Jessie needed to cancel it. She would have Amy do that for her when she went, if she still went without her. She was sure she would. Maybe she could take Jackson in her place, or Myrtle. Myrtle was spry for her age. She was sure she could outdo those seventy-year-olds in the class.

Would Amy and Jackson take her to the airport? She was confident she could depend on them. She would tell Amy she might not make it back for Thanksgiving. She might not even make it back until after the New Year. Everything was up in the air at this point. Amy would understand.

Had she even told Amy she had a daughter? She remembered Amy broaching the subject once, but somehow they had gotten sidetracked, to her relief. Yes, she remembered she had said she had a daughter but got no further. It had been the day they were caught in the rain. So much had happened in such a short time.

The rain was a blessing. On that day, it would have been too painful to talk about Gina. What could she say? Jessie wasn't a part of Gina's life. And talking about Josh, well that was even harder.

Amy might think her a bad mother. She thought of herself that way, although she didn't know how she could have done anything differently. Maybe she didn't know how to be a mother because she grew up without one. Now all she wanted to do was tell Amy about Gina, the way Amy talked nonstop about Jackson.

She dialed the bookstore's number. Luckily Amy answered. She wasn't sure she would be there or off somewhere with Jackson. She asked Amy for the favor. Or rather she asked if both she and Jackson could drop everything to deliver her to the airport tomorrow morning. It would be bright and early, but she knew they were capable of getting up with the fishermen since they did it that one day.

She didn't tell Amy why. She just told her she would fill her in on the way. Amy said she would call Jackson right away and get back with her.

The answer was yes, which was a great load off her mind. She could get to the ferry easily enough, but now she wouldn't have to rent a taxi from the mainland. Amy and Jackson taking her made everything simpler.

She scanned her list and her luggage making sure she had everything. There wasn't all that much to go over as far as packing. She only owned casual clothes now, suitable for the island. She would have to buy whatever was appropriate when she got to New York.

She supposed she should lock the cottage door. She would give Amy the spare key. Jackson already had one. Jackson had a copy of most cottage keys. How did he ever keep them all straight? The one thing Jessie did have packed, tucked away in a safe cubbyhole of the suitcase was the locket of her mother. Other than what was in the metal box in her closet, the locket was the most precious thing she owned. She hoped Gina would wear it for something borrowed. Gina loved to look at it when she was a little girl. Jessie was always careful to hold it as her little fingers touched the sides so it wouldn't get damaged. Jessie always told Gina it would be hers one day. It was time.

Jessie positioned her luggage by the door. Her skirt and blouse were ironed and laid out ready to wear, along with the only pumps she kept since moving to the island. She also had stockings laid out. *Oh, God please don't let them have runs*. It had been so long since she had stockings on. She found an old bottle of clear nail polish and laid it on the dresser just in case.

Fortunately, the pumps had low heels for easy travel. It seemed like ages since she had worn heels. Could she even balance in them? Maybe it was like riding a bicycle. It would come back to her or so they said. She was afraid of wobbling all over the place in them.

The first time Jessie ever wore heels was when she boarded the ocean liner to come to America for the first time. Aunt Agatha had said it was time to shed her schoolgirl shoes for the proper shoes a lady would wear. Jessie remembered when she wore them along with silk stockings on the New York City streets. She adjusted, but she preferred comfort. The one good thing about the war if you could say there was a good thing was that she could take off her stockings. During the war, nylon was reserved for the manufacture of parachutes, and she wanted to do her part. It was more of an excuse not to wear them. She thought many women felt the same way. The whole thing of shaving your legs and wearing heels and stockings were for the pleasure of men, not women.

She had never had occasion to dress up on the island. It was one of those unspoken rules that went with plane travel. Flying was a model's runway for passengers, for both men and women. They might not let her board if her dress wasn't up to snuff. This was too important. She could take no chances. If she messed up, Gina might never forgive her. Then she would be back in the same boat she was in before the wedding announcement.

Wedding announcements. She thought over all the things that needed to be done and started to make a mental list. Then she decided to get a notepad and pen and start writing. She didn't want to forget anything. Maybe Gina already had a list.

Gina was sensible, something that Jessie lacked. Jessie had never planned a wedding before. She didn't know the first thing about it, except for what she had observed in Gino's family. Everyone in Gino's family was now married with the exception of Bella.

They feared Bella was going to be an old maid. Bella had been in attendance at all the family weddings, always the bridesmaid. Gina had been a flower girl more than once. Jessie had never been asked to take part in the weddings other than as a spectator. They did allow her to sit with the family, which was generous on Rosa's part. Maybe she was just too hard on Rosa. Italian weddings were all so festive. Italian weddings required lots of dancing and lots of wine. She didn't see Gina wanting that kind of wedding. She was sure Gina wouldn't want Rosa running the show, either.

Was there time for a bridal shower? Maybe one of her friends was already planning it. Everything was happening so fast. Why was everything happening so quickly? Could Gina be pregnant? She hadn't even thought of that.

Gina was so theatrical. Jessie assumed the man she

was marrying was too. Wouldn't they want some kind of big production? Maybe they were keeping it small because she was pregnant. Maybe they were so used to big productions that they just wanted to keep it quiet and simple, especially if Gina were pregnant. Quit thinking that Gina might be pregnant, she told herself. If she were, Jessie would be there for her. And she would have a grandchild, a grandchild that could come to the island and play on the beach. She was getting ahead of herself. They hadn't even had the wedding yet and she was thinking of grandchildren.

Jessie checked to make sure her outfit was laid out correctly. She didn't want to have to iron it again. The last time she wore this outfit was at the first book club meeting. She was out of place. They served wine and wore flip-flops. Jessie found the book club meetings to be ultra-casual. Most gatherings on the island were, even church, as far as she could tell, even though she didn't attend. On some Sundays, when she was out walking she saw people coming out of the building. The book club people came out, dressed in the same attire, carrying a Bible instead of a wine glass.

Jessie had been invited to attend church more than once, but there was never any pressure. No one ever showed up at her door and witnessed to her or told her she was going to hell. In New York, sometimes the Jehovah Witnesses or Mormons would knock on her door. She always used the children as an excuse, saying she needed to go check on them. She wasn't lying. Children of any age always needed checking on.

She would need to attend Clare's church at least once. It would hurt Clare's feelings if she didn't. Maybe that was where Gina wanted the wedding. It would be great if she did. It would be so much easier. It would be like having a person on the inside, so to speak.

Clare had never tried to save Jessie's soul. If anyone walked his or her talk, it was Clare. Her wild days were over when she said "I do". Everything seemed to change in that instance for Clare.

In retrospect, Clare hadn't been all that wild. Jessie had just been naïve. She still could be at times, as Gina so often reminded her. On some days, she thought Gina was raising her. Maybe Gina had been her mother in a past life.

There had been plenty of weddings at Clare's church. She would know how to plan one. Clare had a great voice and often sang solos at the church. Maybe Gina would ask her to sing.

The only thing to do now was to set the alarm and get some sleep, if that was possible. She didn't want to arrive in New York with bags under her eyes. She didn't know how soon she would see Gino, but she didn't want to look like she had deteriorated since he last saw her. She had her makeup all set out on the bathroom sink. She would get a do-over when in New York. It had been so long since she had one. But not at Bergdorf's. That had bad memories for her.

Why was she thinking of Gino? Why did she care what he thought? He never seemed to even notice her much when she lived with him. Long before she quit wanting him to touch her, she used to walk between the shower and the bedroom naked. She would pretend that she thought he wasn't there. It was all a ruse to get some kind of reaction out of him. He might as well have not been there. He didn't even look her way. He would just sit there and smoke his cigarette.

She needed to get what Gino thought out of her mind. He probably didn't think of her at all these days. Besides, for all she knew, he was completely bald now. It had been three years since she had last seen him, and his hair then was thinning and starting to turn gray. He blamed the gray on her.

Jessie was so nervous about everything. At this rate, she would be bald and gray herself before she even boarded the plane.

She told herself, *Meditate Jessie, Meditate*, as she finally laid down trying to go to sleep. She would definitely take up yoga when she got back. At this point, she was becoming desperate for some kind of yoga practice. The yoga couple was so serene. She wanted to be that way too, only with smooth legs and underarms. Maybe she could take a class or two in New York just to calm her nerves before the wedding. Somewhere amidst all the worrying, the next thing she heard was the alarm.

CHAPTER 14

THE ALARM sounded like a bomb going off, and Jessie felt her heart almost leap out of her chest. She reached over, turned it off, and staggered from the bed in a daze. It took a moment to realize why the alarm clock, something she rarely used, even sounded. Then in a flash, it all came back to her, and her heart once again did a flip flop.

Nerves seized her body as she remembered what a big day was ahead. She went to the bathroom, washed her hands, and began brushing her teeth. The rhythm helped calm her. She did an extra minute, all the while organizing in her mind her carefully laid out plan from the night before.

Systematically, she put her toothbrush and toothpaste in her suitcase. She stepped into the shower and stood under cold water to rinse away any remains of sleep. In an effort to remove bags from her eyes, she tilted her head letting the beads of water pelt against her closed eyes like tiny ice packs. Jessie moved the water temperature up a notch and shampooed and rinsed her hair twice just like on the directions. She would leave nothing to chance. She would have to blow dry. Normally, she let her hair dry on the beach, but there was no time for that. She shaved her legs, rinsed, and stepped out, giving herself the luxury of two towels, one wrapped around her head and one around her body.

She applied her makeup as close to a professional as possible. She should have asked Amy to spend the night. She could have used her expertise. Jessie donned her robe and blew her hair dry.

Another loud noise startled her. It was a rap on the back door. She tightened the belt on her robe and opened the door to be greeted by Amy's smiling face, Jackson at her side. "Hi, we didn't want to be late. We know it must be something important."

"Come in. Make yourself at home. I just have to get dressed. " Jessie looked around, "I think that's all." Was her nervousness showing?

They followed her as far as the living room. This had been the first time either of them had been any farther than the kitchen or dining area. Jackson sat down on the couch, but Amy, full of energy and fidgety, began an inspection of various objects in the room, stopping at the picture of Gina with her dog.

Jessie had forgotten about Gina's dog, Annabelle. Gina might want her to be a part of the wedding. That would be so like Gina. Amy shifted her stance and stared at the young sandy-haired boy in uniform. Jessie thought,

No, please don't bring up Josh right now, as she was afraid of tears ruining her makeup. Jessie hurried into the bedroom and finished dressing. In a few moments, she came out fully clothed and shut the bedroom door with a loud bang and shouted out, "I'm ready!"

Amy and Jackson stood in the middle of the room, coming out of an embrace.

"I can't thank you enough for doing this for me," Jessie said, grabbing her purse.

Jessie hadn't even thought of breakfast. She didn't want to dirty up the kitchen. She would grab something at the airport. She would have some time to kill. It was a lot earlier than she usually ate anyway. She hoped Amy and Jackson had already eaten or weren't hungry, as she didn't want to waste any time getting there. The ferry was usually reliable. *Please let it be so today.*

"So, why are you going to New York? Could it be because of one of those pictures on the mantle?"

Leave it to Amy to get right to the crux of the matter. "It's because of the one with the dog. That's Gina, my daughter. She is getting married. I'll tell you as much as I know on the trip." She went towards her luggage, acting distracted by travel plans so Amy wouldn't bring up the other picture. So far, it was working.

Jessie did a once over in every room of the cottage before giving Jackson her luggage to take out to the pickup. She was so glad it wasn't raining, not that it rained that much on the island. She locked her door as they headed out for good and handed Amy the extra key. Amy didn't act surprised.

"I'll look in from time to time if you want, although you know how safe the island is."

Jessie squeezed in the truck cab next to Amy. She checked her purse to make sure she had the ticket before they pulled out on the road. Then she remembered she was picking it up at the airport. She had never been this anxious about anything before, but everything had to go right. Well, that wasn't exactly the case. She was plenty anxious on her own wedding day, but it all happened so fast, she didn't have time to think about things in advance like now.

Jackson noticed her agitation and asked in a soothing voice if all was a-ok to go before stepping on the gas. She assured him she was fine, and it was okay to proceed. It was good to have both of them looking out for her. It was good they were together. They made a good team. Today, it was almost as if Amy and Jackson were the parents. It was like that even though Amy was close to Gina's age, and Jackson was closer to Josh's age, or what Josh's age would have been. Jessie hadn't thought of the age similarities until now.

Amy reached over and put her hand atop Jessie's and said, "Ok, we're off." She paused before saying, "So, you never talked about your children."

Jessie was a little cautious in replying. She hoped Amy would think it wasn't intentional. "Well, I believe you had asked me about children once when we first met, and I started to answer, but something sidetracked us. Oh, yes, it was the rain. We were running for cover. That's when you met Jackson. And anyway, I wanted to talk about you. I didn't want to be one of those mothers who talked non-stop about her children. I was afraid I might bore you to death."

"No, I love to hear about your life. I told Jackson a

little about what you already said. I hope you don't mind."

Jessie looked over at Jackson a little embarrassed.

Jackson quickly interjected, "Oh, no, Jessie. She didn't say anything that would lead me to think any differently than I already thought about you. I've always thought that you were a very nice woman, one of the nicest on the island, and certainly one of the youngest winter residents, besides Amy that is. I thought you were a lot younger than what Amy told me your age was." He stuttered during that last remark. "Uh oh, I probably wasn't supposed to know your age."

They pulled up to wait for the ferry. They were plenty early. It would be at least another twenty minutes before it returned to the island.

"So changing the subject, or getting to the topic at hand, tell me about Gina," Amy said. "Tell me about this wedding. Was that the urgent call you were on when we got back from the shop the other day?"

"That was Gina telling me she had just gotten engaged and needed me to come to New York as soon as possible to help plan the wedding. You know, planning a daughter's wedding is every mother's dream. That's why I booked the first plane to New York."

"Has Gina been engaged long? Have you met her fiancé?"

"No, it was all kind of sudden. I should meet him at the airport when they pick me up."

"I can tell you are so excited."

Jessie laughed. "Really, can you?"

"And nervous," Amy added.

"That, too," Jessie said.

Jessie noticed a sad expression on Amy's face, and she

watched her brush back a small tear. "What's wrong, Amy?"

"It just dawned on me that I don't have a mother to help me plan a wedding."

"Oh, Amy, I'm so sorry. You know it was the same with me. I was out there all alone for the most part on the day I got married. There was Clare, of course. I don't think I've ever told you what a great friend Clare has turned out to be over all these years. But, maybe one day I could help with your wedding. After this, I'll have experience. And you know Myrtle would go all out for your wedding."

Amy looked over at Jackson, who didn't act the least bit uncomfortable. For all Jessie knew, he might pop the question before the New Year. He was older and experienced, ready to settle down. Amy still needed to finish college, though. So, it might be a long engagement if they did decide to get married.

Amy's face brightened. "How elaborate will this affair be? Not to be indelicate, but you indicated you and your ex both had money. Oh, I just thought. I bet seeing him will be hard."

"Yes, but I guess it's a small price to pay for Gina's happiness, and I think we can both be civil towards each other. It's not like either of us will be bringing a new spouse or date to the wedding. At least I don't think he will. I know I won't. Clare will be there, I'm sure. She has always been my rock."

"What about your son, the one in the picture? He'll be there, too, won't he?"

Jessie grew silent. But she remained calm.

Amy and Jackson just looked at her as if frozen in

time.

Jessie finally said, "He died. I'll tell you both about it sometime, but not today. Everything has to be perfect today."

Amy, once again put her hand on Jessie's and squeezed it. Jessie was surprised a little when Jackson added his own hand to the mix.

Jessie felt some kind of relief, like something alien, had departed her body. Maybe this was what was meant by a chakra becoming unblocked. She felt a weight had been lifted and that she had come clean somehow with Amy. Maybe the island had given her a new life, or at least she was on the road to one. Perhaps in a few years, a grandchild would be playing in the sand by the cottage, just like Gina did when she was small.

The ferry's horn sounded. So far, everything was going according to schedule. Jackson waited his turn to drive his pickup on. There were few of them there this morning, mainly fishermen. The next ferry would be more crowded, taking those who worked on the mainland over. Most people car-pooled across the ferry. It would be senseless to take your car across the ferry every single day when so many worked on the mainland. Over the years, they had a system worked out, even though many worked at different places.

A couple of the men came over to talk to Jackson while they drifted over to the dock. They acknowledged Jessie and Amy, saying it was a great morning, the air was all crisp and clean. Jessie knew their faces but had forgotten their names. She was so bad at names. She would have to try hard to remember names at the wedding. It was only proper etiquette, and it would put her in a better light with Gina and her friends. Gino was a natural at remembering names.

They rode off the ferry's ramp and headed toward the airport, which was only about five miles. They had once talked about putting an airport on the island. It was voted down. The island fathers and mothers wanted to keep the island as pristine as possible. There was a small emergency landing strip to get planes in and out should any emergency actually arise. It hadn't gotten any use since she lived there.

The airport was small, nothing like LaGuardia, which she would be arriving at. Jackson parked in temporary parking, which was just a few cars down from long-term parking. The division was a joke.

He grabbed her luggage from the back of the pickup. They walked her in and up to the ticket desk and made sure she had everything she needed before saying their goodbyes. Jessie felt like a little child being seen off. They offered to wait with her, and she thought Amy wanted to, but Jessie insisted they had already gone well above the call of duty. They all hugged. She hugged Amy back especially hard.

"Promise you will call or write or send pictures. I know you will be so busy, but you might have a little time to drop a note before the New Year," Amy said.

Jessie promised, waved goodbye to both of them, and proceeded to check in. She watched them linger a few minutes longer until they knew she was all right. Jessie almost cried tears of joy at that point, thinking how great they had been.

An announcement came over the loudspeaker that Jessie's plane would be departing a little early. It wasn't long until Jessie had her seat on the plane. A man about her age was sitting next to her. He looked at her and asked, "Nervous about flying?"

She gave him a smile. "No, not nervous, just excited. Going to see my daughter. She's getting married."

"Congratulations!"

She closed her eyes after they were in the air and drifted off to sleep.

The next thing she knew, the announcement to fasten seat belts was made They were getting ready to land. Her stomach growled, and she realized she hadn't eaten anything at the airport as she had planned. Plus, she had slept through refreshments and the meal on the plane. She would offer to take Gina and Chris out to eat as soon as they collected her luggage. Someplace nice. Good restaurants were one of the things she missed about New York.

The man next to her let her out. "You had a pretty good nap there." He got her carry-on down for her and said, "Go ahead. You've got a wedding to get to."

She thanked him and wished him a good time in New York. She checked to make sure the purse she wasn't used to carrying was on her shoulder before making her way down the aisle.

She rushed out through the gate, looking over the crowd. There was Gina waving at her, not looking at all like a bride-to-be. And next to her was Gino. What was he doing here? She made her way through the crowd towards them.

Jessie lifted her hand to wave back. Seeing the gold band still on her finger caused her to flinch her hand backward. She had meant to take it off during the flight.

She wiggled it off into her pocket as she approached them.

After a cordial hello, she did her best to ignore Gino, who stood there fidgeting, not knowing what to do with himself. Jessie reached to hug Gina and felt her tenseness. Her eyes were puffy, and her makeup streaked from tears.

"Mom, there isn't going to be a wedding after all."

CHAPTER 15

JESSIE HELD tightly to Gina's tense body, in part to comfort her, and in part to steady herself. No food and the turn of events, along with Gino's presence, left her feeling faint. He stood like a lost child, lines etched against a grim face. One moment he gripped his hat in front of him like a shield. The next moment he twirled it nervously. Self-consciousness was uncharacteristic of Gino.

He hadn't uttered one word to her, even though she voiced a meek hello in his direction. It felt like they had been standing there for an eternity in rigid positions. Jessie imagined people were staring, but when she looked around she noted they had their own concerns, mostly happy reunions. Still, the three of them stood there, white-faced, like there was a death in the family. Gino finally said, "Let's get out of here."

The scenario was reminiscent of when she found out about Josh's death. Gino had the same nervous stance. He had never been her rock of Gibraltar. Clare had been.

She was at home, alone, when both the police and Gino came to the door to tell her about Josh. She tried to shake the whole eerie feeling off as they proceeded to baggage claim.

Gina still had her beautiful figure, something Jessie noticed as she walked out with her arm around her daughter's waist. Gino's bald spot glared at her as he walked several paces ahead.

An awkward silence permeated the air until Jessie pointed to her bag. Gino grabbed it walking towards the front of the airport, where he hailed a taxi. Even though it was a dreary day, Gina pulled a pair of sunglasses from her purse, no doubt to hide her red swollen eyes.

Jessie breathed a sigh of relief when Gino sat up front. The whole situation was uncomfortable enough. The thought of being squeezed in next to him repulsed her. Seeing him again made her whole former life with him seem surreal like a Dali painting.

The driver awaited instructions. Gino looked back at Jessie. "Where to?"

Jessie looked at Gina, but she was too shaken up to make decisions. So Jessie said, "I hadn't made any arrangements. I was going to wait until I got here. Can we go back to your apartment for now, Gina?"

"Mom, I moved in with dad." Gina said it as if it were a given, something she as a mom should have known.

"It's okay," Gino said. "We'll go back there until we decide what to do. Driver, Park Avenue."

Drops of rain splattered against the windshield. The rain and steady beat of the wipers drowned out the noise of the city, yet made the silence inside the taxi bearable. Jessie remembered reading in a magazine that a New York City woman had invented windshield wipers. Little bits of trivia always flooded her mind when she was nervous.

Gino and Jessie had taken an apartment in Manhattan before the divorce. Jessie wanted to get out of Brooklyn, that house, that neighborhood, where Josh's death occurred. For once, Gino hadn't argued with her. That was when he changed his name to Gene. It was also the same time he made a clean break from whatever it was he was doing, if anyone could truly ever make a clean break from it. It was a vague career path that she knew not to question.

There were a lot of changes around that time, but they came too late. He got a job as a pharmaceutical salesman or something like that, like a title on a business card gave his business pursuits credence. She knew it was his connections with his pizza friends that got him that position which allowed him the luxury of living on Park Avenue.

There were still lots of perks with this job. Gino put great stock into perks and added benefits. The industry was supposedly completely legitimate, and Gino got in on the ground floor. It was a fresh start for him after Josh's death.

Jessie had trouble calling him Gene. And, his mother, well calling him Gene was out of the question. Jessie doubted if Rosa even knew he was going by that name now. Gene just sounded better on Park Avenue.

The rain came down harder, and the wipers picked up

their pace. The airport wasn't the proper place to talk about what happened. Nor was the cab. She had hoped to get Gina alone, but now she would be in the apartment with Gino. What else could go wrong? She knew. Rosa could be waiting there.

Oh my God. What if Rosa was waiting in the apartment? This would be the nightmare that just kept getting worse. She was afraid to face Rosa after she had walked out on Gino. She was scared to face Rosa on most good days. But she doubted if Rosa was there. Rosa hardly traveled out of the confines of Brooklyn. She said Manhattan was too fancy for her.

Rosa had one of her queen bee moments when Gino announced they were moving. Jessie remembered the scene well. Jessie had just sat there, not speaking as she usually did with Rosa, but this time as she sat there, tears began flowing down her cheeks. Seeing Jessie this way baffled Rosa. Rosa regained her composure, placing her hand on Jessie's shoulder, and said, "Maybe it's for the best." She understood a mother's grief. It was the one moment she felt as if she was a daughter to Rosa.

The cab pulled up to the curb, next to the awning. Even though Jessie had only lived there three months, she remembered the apartment building well. Dave, the same doorman was there. Jessie wondered if he would remember her. Dave always knew everyone by name. That was the job of a good doorman.

Dave had once called her the sad lady. He knew she walked in the park every day. There was another woman who walked in the park every day, too, and Jessie always saw her. Jessie would watch her feed the pigeons. This woman was obsessed with them. At least Jessie hadn't turned into pigeon lady. She might have if she had stayed in New York. She made it a point not to feed the seagulls on the island. They could fend for themselves.

Dave always held the door open for her and said, "Have a nice walk in the park today." On rainy days, such as today, Jessie normally sat by the window and looked out at the park.

She was thankful Gino splurged for the park view. That was one of the few times in their time together that Gino practically said your wish is my command. She had been guilty of playing on his guilt.

She always suspected there was something more about Josh's death than she had been told. Maybe Gino was just sparing her from something she couldn't handle. Jessie always wondered why Gino was with the police that night if it was a hit and run. It was in the middle of the night. No one was out on the streets, and no one saw it. Why was Josh even out that time? That was so unlike him. Gino had said he just happened to be walking up the sidewalk when the police car drove up.

Gino assured her it was a random thing, a coincidence, and there wasn't any more to it than that. Part of her wanted to know if that was really the case, as nothing random ever happened with Gino. Every move was always well calculated. She never pursued it. She thought it best not to. What else could she do? If there were more to it, it wouldn't bring Josh back.

Gino had identified the body and taken care of all the funeral arrangements within twenty-four hours. The body was in bad shape, and she didn't need to see it, was his way of putting it. The casket was closed. She never questioned him as she had a difficult time coping with the death and wanted to leave it all behind. She didn't want to leave Josh or his memory behind, though. She just wanted to leave the whole business of the mystery and mess of his death behind. She had left so many things behind in her life. After all, could she change anything?

Dave greeted them at the cab door with an enormous black umbrella. Doormen are always prepared, especially Dave. He helped Gino with the bag. Gino slipped him a bill. Dave's eyes sparkled as he looked at Jessie and said, "Nice to have you back."

"Thank you, Dave." She didn't want to say that she wasn't back to stay. Nor, in all honesty could she say good to be back.

They continued up the elevator in silence.

Gino, not even bothering to remove his hat, carried her luggage toward their old bedroom. She detected sympathy coming from his dark brown eyes, which seemed deeper set than she remembered, upon seeing her panic. "Don't worry. I thought I would move out for a day or two. It will give you and Gina some alone time, until you figure out what you are going to do. I'm sure you have a lot to talk about with your daughter. There are fresh sheets in the hall closet. Well, I'm sure you remember where everything is. Nothing's changed."

Jessie breathed a sigh of relief and some of the tenseness left her body. Maybe the apartment hadn't changed, but Gino seemed to have. He was more docile. Nicer.

Gino didn't bother to pack a bag. Maybe he had clothes elsewhere. It wasn't any of her concern. She was just glad he was gone.

As they sat on the couch, Jessie reached over for

Gina's hand. "Are you going to tell me what happened?"

"Mom, you look pale."

She always looked pale compared to Gina. Even after living on the beach for three years, Jessie had only managed to expand her freckles. Gina had her father's beautiful olive complexion. Taller than both of them, she could easily have been a model.

"Don't worry about me. I'll just get some water. I'll be okay." Jessie headed toward the kitchen area, divided by a bar from the living area. Two bedrooms and a bath were down the hallway. It wasn't one of the roomier apartments in the building. In fact, it was one of the cheapest ones with a park view, and it was only on the sixth floor, just high enough to get a good view of the park. Cheap apartments on Park Avenue were still expensive. But even a cheap Park Avenue address was prestigious.

Jessie opened the refrigerator door and looked for some water. Instead, she found cola. She had almost given them up but reached for one, knowing it would help with her shakiness. "Do you want one?" she asked Gina.

Gina shook her head no. Jessie instinctively opened the drawer she knew would have the bottle opener.

Jessie returned to Gina's side, depositing the bottle on the coffee table beside an ashtray full of cigarette butts. On the other side was a lighter and an opened pack of Lucky Strikes. She had always detested his smoking habit. Next to the cigarettes was a pack of Juicy Fruit.

Fortunately Josh or Gina never followed suit with the smoking. At least Josh hadn't. That she was sure of. He abhorred the habit as much as she did. If Gina smoked, she never did in Jessie's presence. Possibly she hid it but if anything would make her reach for a cigarette, this would.

Jessie broke the silence. "So, Gina?"

"Mom, I would have called you to let you know. You wouldn't have had to make the trip. But it just happened this morning, and it was too late to reach you. Your plane had already taken off."

"Gina, I would have come anyway. You should know that."

Fresh tears streamed down Gina's face. Jessie fumbled through her purse and handed her a crumpled kleenex. "Mom, he just called it off. He didn't give me an explanation. The only thing he said was it's better to call it off now than to end up married and miserable and have to go through a divorce."

Jessie relished hearing the word mom roll from Gina's lips. She only wished the circumstances were different.

She held her, feeling rusty at the whole mom thing. "I'm here for you and will be for as long as you need me." Jessie paused and asked, "Is there anything else you need to tell me?"

"Like what?"

"Nothing. I'm here for you," she repeated. And then she hugged her some more.

After some silence, Jessie asked, "How long have you been living here with your father?"

"I don't live here. I just sort of come and go. I don't actually live anywhere. I was just coming and going, staying part time with Dad and part time with Chris in the village. I still have stuff there. I guess I'm going to have to go and get it. I guess I'll move in here for now. I have no place else to go."

"Gina, if you want me to go with you to get your stuff, I will."

"Better you than Dad. You know his temper."

She had never seen Gina this shaken up over a boy before. Gina had always been the one breaking the relationship off. Most of her relationships didn't even get to the breakup stage.

She had faith that Gina would get over it. She was strong. In that respect, she took after Rosa. This would only make her stronger, and hopefully wiser. She was already stronger and wiser than Jessie ever was at that age. By Gina's age, Jessie had had two children and still remained naïve about much of the world.

"Do you feel like going somewhere for dinner?" She couldn't believe it was that late. It had been one of the longest days ever. She doubted if Gina had eaten all day either.

Jessie went over to the window. "We could take a walk in the park. The rain has stopped. If you felt like it, we could see if we could get into Tavern on the Green. Do you want me to call for a reservation?"

"I'm not really hungry, but maybe a walk in the park will do me good."

"I think it will. I wasn't thinking. New York is cold this time of year. I'm so used to island life. I'll need a coat. Do you have one I can borrow? I can look for one tomorrow."

"No need for that. I have an extra one."

"And you don't have to eat. Maybe some dessert." Jessie dialed the number and made the reservation.

In Gina's bedroom she saw a picture on the dresser of Josh and Gina, of when they were little, playing on the beach. It wasn't taken at the island but at Coney Island. You could see the Ferris wheel in the skyline. Gina was always scared of the Ferris wheel, but Josh loved it. Josh was a real daredevil. He would try anything. She had to always be on guard when it came to him. Once at age five, he had gotten away from her. She caught him attempting to climb up the high dive.

Gina waited while her mom freshened up, and then worked on covering traces of her red, swollen eyes. "Theater tricks," she said.

“Have a nice walk," Dave said as they left the building. "The park?"

“Yes, Dave, the park,” Jessie said with a grin.

Jessie wrapped Gina's coat up around her neck. A hint of snow pervaded the air. Taxi horns blared and became muffled as they got deeper into the park. The island seemed only a faint memory.

She remembered the route to the tavern. Everything was coming back to her. She had had a set routine when she lived in New York. She guessed it was like riding a bicycle. The old habits were returning. Except this time, she was with Gina, her daughter, a young woman now.

CHAPTER 16

LAMPS GAVE off a dim glow, although darkness still captured parts of the park. They passed joggers and couples, walking, talking and holding hands, some glued tightly together in embraces. The island would be completely dead by this time.

The area they were in was safe enough. Parts of the park weren't. Jessie had learned to stay away from the nooks and crannies, the ones that invited danger. They would reach the restaurant before total darkness set in.

Autumn leaves covered the walk way. Jessie missed the fall colors. That was something she didn't get to experience much of on the island. She took Gina's hand as they walked. She was so proud to be walking with her daughter once again.

It had been windy. They stepped into the bathroom to

comb their hair while they waited on their table. Jessie didn't have change to tip the attendant. Gina said, "Here, Mom, let me, and put a quarter in the bowl." Although Jessie had been methodical in planning for the trip, she had forgotten about the constant tipping in New York. Tipping on the island would have been lunacy.

The maître d' escorted them to a small table in a back corner where a waiter filled water glasses and handed them a menu. Little seafood was on it. Seafood was the majority of the menu back home. She considered the island home now. Jessie ordered mushroom soup and salad. Gina wanted only desert, something to cheer her up. Crème brûlée.

They didn't talk about the break up during the meal. Gina asked about the island and how life there was. Jessie told her about Jackson and Amy and about the yoga class she would be taking when she got back.

Gina arched a brow. "You've never exercised in your life."

"I walk. I've always walked."

"Everyone in New York walks. I thought you walked because you hated the subway."

"I do hate the subway, but I also love to walk. Remember all those walks we used to take with Clare. Have you seen Clare lately? I have to visit her while I'm here."

"I got a card from her on my birthday. She sent it to Dad's knowing it would get to me."

"Did you like the gift I sent? You never said."

"Yes, I thought it was sweet. It looked like my old doll, Annabelle."

"Speaking of Annabelle, where is your dog?"

“I ended up giving her to one of my theater friends. I just wasn’t settled enough to take care of her.” Gina frowned and added, “Actually, Chris didn’t like her.”

"Oh, sorry. Maybe we can go see Clare together. We can call tomorrow. Are you free tomorrow? Gina, I don’t even know if you are working anywhere or what you’ve been doing. We haven’t talked in so long. I hope you can let me in on your life.”

“Mom, I'm sorry. What can I say? It’s not that I meant to exclude you. It’s just…Well, you know. Life here is so hectic, and we’ve never communicated that well. Josh always seemed to be the buffer between us. I meant to write or call you. I just kept putting it off.”

“No, I’m sorry, Gina. You know how much I love you, don’t you?”

“Yes, I do. I mean, I suppose I do. It’s just that after Josh died you more or less got lost in your own world. And then you moved. I had to deal with Josh’s death on my own. I guess I resented that fact. Even before Josh's death you were always off into your own world or that world where you were dealing with Dad. I felt like I was caught in the crossfire. Josh knew how to handle it. I didn't. You never saw that."

“I know, Gina. And, I’m so sorry for that. But now I’m doing much better. And, I always was asking you to come down to visit me at the island.”

“I know. I know. I just didn’t want to then. Maybe now I should get away for a while. I don’t want to stay in your old apartment with Dad, and I don’t want to be on my own either just now."

“Gina, you are always welcome to go back with me or just come down anytime you want. It’s your cottage, too.”

Jessie wanted to ask about Chris. She wanted to find out what he was like. He must have been something to shake her up like this, but she didn't dare pursue that topic. It was all too fresh. It had only happened this morning. This morning seemed like a different world, a parallel universe.

Jessie didn't have experience in this matter. She had never been heartbroken over a boy. Her dissolved marriage with Gino didn't count. There wasn't any sudden breakup. Their marriage could be defined as a slow, destructive process, suicide in installments. She was only too glad to get out of it. The only heartbreak she suffered was over Josh. That wasn't the same.

There was Malcolm. There wasn't any heartbreak there. She didn't love Malcolm. He didn't love her. They were using each other for solace. Neither one of them had any expectations. They both were married.

Jessie felt incredible guilt over the whole situation. Clare was the only one who ever knew. Jessie trusted Clare with her secret. One day, she just let it all spill out after Josh's death. Clare made no judgment. She just hugged her and said it was understandable.

It happened while Josh was in Korea. Gina was sixteen. She didn't want to leave her school friends to go to the island that year. Besides, she had her summer theater camp. Jessie knew how important it was to her, so she said it was okay. Gina was at that age she was breaking away from Jessie. Gino also begged off, as usual. She knew Clare wouldn't leave her husband for two solid weeks, but she asked just the same.

Jessie rented a car and took off for the island on her own but never made it. Just a little out of New York, she had a flat tire. Malcolm stopped to help her fix it. He put the spare on but said she needed a new one, and followed her to the nearest garage.

That was how their romance began. He insisted on waiting at the garage with her. Jessie thought him younger, but sensed he was attracted to her. It didn't matter. He had a wedding band on, as did she.

She told him all about the island and how she had been taking the children there since they were small, and how her oldest was serving as a medic in Korea. She told him about Gina, who was in high school, and how she loved theater, that she was attending a summer theater program and that's why she wasn't going to the island with her.

Malcolm asked why her husband wasn't with her. "Business," she said. "He's a workaholic. He quit coming to the island years ago. It's basically always been just me and the kids." She gave a sigh. "And now it's just me."

She asked about his wife and why he was alone. He told her he lived in Chicago but had been to New York on business. He came to New York two or three times a year. "My wife and I lead separate lives."

"Why?" Jessie asked.

If he found her forward, he didn't let on. "She wanted children," he said with a slight sadness. "We couldn't have any. The fault was mine, not hers. She lost her attraction for me after that. As a salesman, I was always on the road. It was just as well. We would have gotten a divorce, but she is a strict Catholic. It was out of the question for her. She is from Chicago, and all her family and friends are there. Even if getting a divorce weren't against her religion, she would have never been able to live down the disgrace."

Malcolm was English. He had been living in America since he turned twenty. That had been five years ago. He married after being in America two years. He still had a thick accent. That was part of Jessie's attraction to him. She had always wondered what her life would have been like if she had remained in England. What if she had stayed and married a proper Englishman? When she told him she was also from England, he had told her he had detected a slight accent. He said another Englishman could always tell.

Jessie didn't want to be on the road after dark so decided she would find a nearby motel and start again in the morning. But she ended up not going at all. She and Malcolm found a small diner, sitting in the back corner where they had apple pie with vanilla ice cream and hot tea. They would have had crumpets if they had been on the menu. They must have looked like star-crossed lovers. They got plenty of stares.

They confided in each other, telling each other their woes. Jessie had never been able to talk to a man in this manner before. She told him things she was too embarrassed to tell Clare. They ended up staying in that roadside motel for a whole week.

Both of them were lonely and needed the attention. She had to admit there was a fair amount of lust involved on both of their parts. Malcolm continuously told her she was beautiful, something Jessie desperately needed to hear. He was the first man to ever tell her that. He was the only man to ever tell her that.

And the sex, it wasn't quick with him. He took his time. Jessie discovered what making love was supposed to be like. For the first time in her life, she felt like a woman. She knew she had been missing something with Gino, but she never knew what up until this point. It was more than just the sex. It was the way he listened to her and understood. They talked non-stop all week, except when they were making love. They talked about life back in England. They talked about almost everything from their earliest childhood memories. They talked and made love until they could do neither anymore. Jessie knew it was time to say good-bye.

After a week, she felt like she had to make a decision, either go on to the beach by herself or just return home. She decided to return home. If she had gone to the island, she might have thought about the situation too much. She might have begged Malcolm to go away with her. That wasn't realistic. There was still Josh and Gina, and there was his wife. She couldn't let this go any further in her mind or in her heart.

Malcolm talked about meeting again when he came back to New York. Jessie considered it. The universe intervened. Josh came home from Korea. A month later, he was dead. Everything in life changed from that point on. Another segment of her life began — a long dark segment. Malcolm was a brief, happy interlude.

Jessie had confided to Clare that it might have been a sin, but that it felt like a Godsend to her. She reasoned the tire blew out at just the right moment, at just the right time in her life. It was all meant to be.

As they were leaving the restaurant, Jessie noticed Gina watching a wedding party that had one of the rooms reserved. Gina was calm but somber.

Outside there were carriages lined up along the green.

"It's been a long time since we've had a carriage ride. Do you want to go for it?" Jessie asked.

In the cool night air Gina looked more relaxed. "Why not."

CHAPTER 17

FOR THE first time all day, Jessie saw a glint of sparkle in Gina's eyes as they snuggled under the coarse blanket. The carriages had certain routes they followed. The horses clopped over the routes like wound up toys. Jessie asked if the driver would drop them off close to the apartment building.

Day in and day out, the horses followed the same path. Jessie used to watch them in the park. A change in course was more trouble for the drivers. The horses would get a little flustered at first with the change in plans and become harder to control. After a bit, they seemed to like the change. She knew the horses would thank her for this, just like she thanked Amy for getting her out of her own doldrums.

Her sole purpose now was to help Gina out of her

melancholy. Jessie leaned in closer to Gina under the blanket. No matter how old Gina got, she would still be the baby that had her days and nights mixed up. She would still be the little girl who carried her doll around until it was in tatters.

Annabelle. Gino had gotten so tired of her clutching onto that ragged little doll. He said a child of his should have a nice doll. The one she had was a disgrace as well as a petri dish for germs.

He asked Jessie why she hadn't bought her a new one. Gina didn't want a new one she told him. He always threatened to take it away from her. How she cried.

One day, Gino took matters into his own hands and brought home a new doll, one with a porcelain head with hand-painted features. Its eyes, with eyelashes, opened and closed. Gina would have nothing to do with it. This wasn't the kind of doll that a little girl played with, but Gino didn't know that. It wasn't one she could take to the beach. The doll had beautiful golden hair that curled on the ends and a red velvet dress. The doll was meant for a display case, not for a child.

Gina pushed the doll aside. She held tightly onto Annabelle covered in remnants of the band-aids from the shark bites. One night while Gina was asleep, Gino put Annabelle out on the curb for the trash man to pick up. Gina was lost for an entire week. Finally, she picked up the new doll and began combing her hair. It wasn't long until she grew tired of dolls altogether.

Jessie felt Gina tense up. Her eyes were fixed on the woman in the park, the one who fed the pigeons. Jessie reached over and held tightly onto Gina like Gina had held onto Annabelle all those years ago. "Don't worry,

Gina. She's perfectly harmless."

They both called it a night, early for New York. Jessie thought about what people were doing back on the island. All the restaurants and businesses would be closed. Everyone would be snug in his or her cottage. Amy and Jackson might be out walking on the beach. Maybe they were back at her cottage. Maybe that's what Amy thought giving her the key meant — free reign. She guessed it didn't matter.

After Gina had finished in the bathroom, Jessie ran herself a bath. Of course there was no bubble bath. Why would Gino have that? Ivory dishwashing liquid from the kitchen sufficed. Jessie loved bubble baths. She needed one tonight more than ever. She offered to run Gina one, but Gina only wanted to go to bed.

She tried to relax her mind while soaking in the tub. Recollections had started coming back to her on the island, but coming to New York had intensified those memories. It was harder to push things away here. There was no sound of the ocean to swallow the emotions up. On the island, she had been thinking of Josh and Gina as small children. Now she was thinking of them as adults.

She had always thought Josh would get some sort of engineering degree in college. He had an inclination for it. He started out with Lincoln Logs when he was just a toddler. For his fourth birthday, his dad bought him a boat he could sail at Central Park. He used it as a model to make his own. It consisted of any scrap parts he could find along with an old kitchen pot as the base.

"Mommy, this will float won't it? Just like the soap bar?" he asked.

"Yes, Josh, just like the Ivory."

His dad got him a bigger boat the next year.

He was always building. It was sand castles at the beach. Later, he would take pieces from various models and make something entirely different from ground up.

Jessie thought it was his intent all along to go into engineering or architecture. But, he started out with general courses, saying he didn't know what he wanted. After two years at Columbia, he came home one day and said he had enlisted in the army. He was going to be trained as a medic. He already had some biology and chemistry courses under his belt. The announcement coincided with a visit from some recruitment officers at the university that day along with Gino having met him for lunch on that same day. What they talked about, she wasn't privy to.

The proclamation threw them both for a loop. Gino immediately wanted to pull strings. Josh was emphatic. "Dad, no!"

Jessie worried about Josh being in the service as any mother would. But it was Josh's decision, and she respected that. Gino had just missed being drafted during World War II. He was over the age that was being selected. Still, Jessie always wondered if some of Gino's connections had helped keep him out of the war. The war had turned out to be a profitable time for Gino. But then, Gino could turn any horrible situation into a profit.

Jessie never felt like they were making the same war effort that was encouraged and that other families were making. Gino had even brought her some silk stockings home one day, which he had acquired from the black market. Jessie felt ashamed and shoved them into the back reaches of her drawer. Fortunately, she could tell people two of Gino's brothers had served their country. She was so glad they both came back unscathed.

Jessie went to the theater just to see the newsreels of the war. Her home country was taking a severe beating. She never knew if the house she had grown up in had escaped the bombs. She had never tried to find out.

After Josh's training, he was shipped off to Korea. She now understood what wartime mothers went through. Gina was getting ready to graduate high school during this time and spent most of her time with her friends. Jessie saw Clare more and more. Jessie had an empty nest, and Clare didn't have a nest to begin with. Clare thought of Josh and Gina as her own.

She looked forward to calling Clare tomorrow. Clare would be surprised that she was back in New York. Clare had given up hope that she would ever come back to the point that she quit asking in her correspondence.

When Josh returned home from Korea, Jessie breathed a heavy sigh of relief. He returned to Columbia, this time majoring in medicine. Jessie always wondered if Gino had influenced him in this direction. He bragged way too much about having a doctor in the family. If anything, Josh would have an exceptional bedside manner. Jessie had never noticed any inclinations in him towards medicine before the medic thing. Little did they know, he had so little time left to live.

Gina graduated from high school and also started Columbia, majoring in theater, a no-brainer. They both lived on campus. Jessie would have rather kept them at home, but Gino said it would give them character.

He always felt Jessie smothered them, especially Josh. Maybe she was afraid Josh might follow in his father's business pursuits. She had done her best over the years to put Gino's business as well as his infidelities out of her mind. But somehow, it pleased her just a little that she didn't lose out to other women. Maybe it wouldn't be for other women, but this was much easier for her to accept. Besides some of the most brilliant people in history went this direction. She didn't have any judgment on the lifestyle, just on herself for not seeing the signs before she married him. She did her best to put all that behind her after her fling with Malcolm. Even if she once had a speck of judgment, she had no right to put a sentence on anyone for perceived misdeeds.

At any rate, Jessie was so glad that both children were still close by, and that they had not decided to go to schools far away. Josh had considered it. For some reason, she could have more easily accepted Gina going off somewhere else, but not Josh. In retrospect, now she wished he would have.

Both she and Gino would meet them for lunch sometimes, just not together. They were already going their separate paths, even more so after the kids left the house. Josh seemed to be available much more than Gina. He dated a little. He was rather shy around girls. Gina was popular on campus, belonging to a sorority. She had lots of dates. Jessie suspected Gina wasn't a virgin and worried. Before she went off to college, Jessie had tried to talk to her about it and asked her please, if she was doing anything, be safe and use condoms. And yet, she was sure Gina knew more about sex than she ever did.

Gina, not denying anything, said, "Mom, don't worry. I know what to do."

Josh kept a watchful eye on his sister, and Gina adored

her brother.

After Josh's death, Gina dropped out. She enrolled again the following year but started to lose interest in school. Jessie didn't realize how much Josh's death had affected her. She had been too wrapped up in her own grief. Jessie regretted not being there for her.

Gino was also dealing with the grief. He had mellowed out. At least he was handling the pain in a more constructive manner than she was. He began making changes. He did a complete turnaround in his business, starting with the pharmaceutical thing. He had business cards printed with the name Gene instead of Gino. She was sure he never showed the cards to his mother or any of the family, lest it get back to Rosa.

Jessie hadn't asked him to do any of it. It was something he had done on his own. Earlier, it might have mattered, but now, none of it was important. She had more or less zoned out, leaving both Gina and Gino to their own devices. She was seeing that now.

Jessie toweled down her pruned body and dug into her luggage to get her gown. She hadn't brought much, and what she had brought wasn't suitable for New York or the New York weather.

She got those clean sheets Gino told her about out of the hall closet. She looked in on Gina just like the old days. She was sound asleep. That gave Jessie a feeling of peace. Jessie fell asleep herself, almost as soon as her head hit the fresh pillowcase.

CHAPTER 18

JESSIE LOOKED at the clock. She had slept almost twelve hours. She had wanted to get up early so she could have breakfast made for Gina, or so she could at least go out and get some croissants for the both of them. Maybe it wasn't too late. Gina usually slept in. Jessie grabbed her robe and peeked in Gina's room to find an empty bed. A note was on the kitchen counter.

Mom, you are tired from the trip. Let you sleep. Got an early call from a girlfriend in the theater group. She said she had heard about the breakup yesterday and wanted to let me know Chris would be out of the apartment all morning. So, I'm taking the opportunity to get my things out now. Took a taxi. Will meet you at Clare's after lunch. Hope that's okay? Your old key to the apartment is in the side drawer.

Love,
Gina

* * *

Jessie started to pick up the phone to call Clare, and then, she thought, no, I'll surprise her. She hoped she wouldn't be the one surprised and that Clare would be home.

Jessie hopped in the shower. The only warm clothes she brought were some slacks and a light jacket. She looked through Gina's closet and found a sweater. She knew she wouldn't mind. She would have to get a few things while she was here or keep borrowing from Gina. She had planned to shop. It just wouldn't be for a mother of the bride dress.

In thirty minutes, Jessie was out the lobby door.

Dave held the door open. "Have a nice walk in the park today."

"Not going to the park today, Dave. Would you hail me a taxi?"

He gave a smile of approval and waved his white-gloved hand at the approaching yellow cab. She didn't look like the sad park lady today.

She took the taxi as far as Brooklyn Bridge. She wanted to walk across it. She and the children had always loved doing that. They would stop along the way getting a treat from one of the vendors that was set up on the bridge and watch the artists paint. She looked forward to walking back across the bridge with Gina later. The rectory wasn't that much farther.

The house still looked the same. Clare always made it so inviting. What caught Jessie's eye were the pink roses out front. Clare had always kept the church adorned with roses. She had a flare for growing them. Clare had a flare for any type of gardening. The church kept a plot off to the side where they raised vegetables, most of which they donated to the soup kitchens. Clare was in charge of all kinds of charitable operations. Clare's many abilities always amazed Jessie.

Jessie knocked on the door.

Graham broke into a broad grin. "Jessie! Is that you? Well, I'll be. You didn't tell us you were coming."

"I wanted it to be a surprise. Please tell me Clare is home."

"This *is* a surprise. And yes, she is at home. Well, she went across the street to the church. She and some women are setting up for a bazaar. I'll go get her."

"No, I'll just go over. I want to see the look on her face when she sees me. Oh, Graham, I'm so happy to see you. It's been so long."

"Me, too, Jessie. Me, too. Clare will be overjoyed."

Jessie walked across the street, going through the back to where she knew they would be setting up. Jessie had been in the church plenty of times with Clare, just not too much in the pews. The times she did attend, she remembered Graham's robust sermons. She called him Graham when it was only she or Clare around but referred to him as Reverend in front of anyone else. When he did Josh's funeral, he couldn't keep back his own tears. It was as if he and Clare were burying their own child.

Jessie walked in. A few women casually glanced up, thinking she was there to help. Clare had her back turned, and Jessie lightly tapped her on the shoulder.

Clare turned and exclaimed, "Oh, my! I can't believe it." Clare grinned from ear to ear and covered her mouth with one hand. She took it down and grabbed Jessie's hand. "Jessie, is that you? Of course, it's you. I just can't believe it."

"Believe it, Clare."

They stood there and stared at each other for a while. Jessie saw some gray streaks running through Clare's hair. Clare touched her hand to the side of her head. "I've meant to cover those up, but Graham doesn't seem to mind, so I've never gotten around to it." She and Clare had a way of knowing what the other was thinking.

"I'm getting a little gray myself. It's just that the sun and the beach wind lighten my hair so much you can't tell it."

Clare and Jessie simultaneously reached out for each other. They rocked back and forth, hugged, and jumped up and down like boarding school girls. They finally let go. All the women in the church had quit what they were doing to look at them. They were quite the spectacle.

"Let's go back to the house so we can talk. Ladies, this is my good friend Jessie. We haven't seen each other in three years. You don't mind finishing this up, do you?" Heads nodded approval as various voices chimed in "No, you go on, we can handle it."

"So, Jessie how long will you be staying? You're not back for good are you? I would love it if you moved back here. It would be like old times."

"Old times! You make us sound ancient. How long I stay, well, it all depends on Gina."

"How is Gina? I sent her a birthday card. I never hear from her anymore."

"Well, Clare, that's why I'm here."

Clare laughed. "I didn't think it was because of Gino."

Clare's sense of humor was coming back to Jessie. She

could always use it to diffuse tense situations as well as telling it like it was.

"Before I tell you, can we go back to the churchyard cemetery?"

"Of course. What was I thinking? You would want to go there first."

Josh's headstone was one of the biggest in the cemetery. Gino had insisted. It had fresh mums on it. Jessie had always sent Clare money to keep flowers on it, although Clare would have done it anyway. Jessie sat on the bench just looking at the few fall leaves strewn about his grave. They were the same ochre color as the mums.

"Clare, I'm so glad Josh's body is resting here because you are here. I know you are watching over him, you and Graham. I know he would like that, too. I sometimes feel guilty not coming back to see his grave, but I know this is just his body. I think about him every day. I sometimes feel his presence. He loved the island so much, too, you know."

"I know you do, honey." Clare sometimes called Jessie honey. After all, she was older than her by five years. She was one year older than Gino. Gino had never called Jessie honey, nor she him.

Jessie got up from the bench, and they made their way back to the house. Graham was just leaving. He kissed Clare on the cheek. "Hon, I'm going over to the church office to get some work done. I know you girls have a lot to talk about."

"I'll see you a little later, I hope, Graham," Jessie said.

"You had better."

Jessie followed Clare into the kitchen.

"Do you want some tea? We can pretend we are back in jolly old England." Clare still had some distant family there. Jessie knew she corresponded on a regular basis. But Clare had never been back. She talked about it but never got around to it, just like Jessie. Except Jessie had nothing to go back to.

"So what's up with Gina? I hope she's okay," Clare asked.

"I think she will be, at least with time. I got a call from her a couple of days ago. It feels like a week ago. Funny how travel will do that to you. She called to say she was getting married."

Clare almost dropped the tea set. "Gina getting married! That's so wonderful. I really didn't see her ever settling down. She stills seems like a little girl to me in some frilly little dress."

"She's not. I mean, she's no longer a little girl, and she's no longer getting married."

"But you just said."

"I know, but as soon as I got here she said it had been called off. Clare, she's devastated. She hides it well. But, she's torn up."

"I take it he called it off and not her."

"That's right."

"Where is she now?"

"She left the apartment early this morning before I got up. She got a call from a girlfriend saying Chris, that was her fiancé, wasn't going to be home. She wanted to get her stuff while he wasn't there. I had planned on going with her. I was so jet lagged I slept through the phone and everything. In her note, she said she wanted to let me sleep."

"Well, she'll be all right. She has you here with her now."

"She plans on coming here after lunch."

"Oh, good, so you're staying for lunch. I was going to invite you. Where are you staying? With Gina?"

"At Gino's apartment."

"Oh dear! What?" Some of the tea spilled.

"He moved out for the time being. Both Gina and I are staying there."

"You scared me for a moment. Just when I thought life couldn't get any stranger, you say something like that."

Clare grabbed Jessie's hands. "It's just so great to see you. And don't worry about Gina. She's young. She'll bounce back. It's better she didn't marry the wrong guy."

"Yes, I can attest to that."

Clare looked down and then looked Jessie directly in the eye. "I sometimes blame myself for that."

"What do you mean?"

"You know, back in England, I pushed you to come over here to see Gino. And then, when he wanted to get married as soon as we hit dry land, I encouraged that too. It was selfish on my part. I blame myself that you were even with him. If I hadn't intervened you would have never met up with him again after that first day you saw him on the dock when we came ashore. If I hadn't told him where you were staying, a flirtatious wink would have been the end of it.

"But I wanted to stay in America. I was only ever going to be a servant in England. At least over here, I would have a chance, and now my life with Graham has turned out great. And, yours with Gino, well….." She trailed off. "I always inwardly thought you might have blamed me. At the time, I thought Gino was right for you. You were facing life by yourself back in England."

"Clare, I never blamed you. True, I have lots about my life that I have regrets about. I should have stood up to Gino more. I turned a blind eye to so much he was doing. Don't get me wrong. I wasn't the best wife, but I had two wonderful children by him. Maybe I should have left him a lot earlier after the children were born. It would have been as good for him as it would have been for me. Maybe if I had of, Josh would still be alive. I blame myself for a lot of things."

"Jessie, you can't think that. Things happen for a reason."

"Clare you've always been so great not to judge me. You know more about me than anyone, including Gino. You've kept my secrets, even the one about Malcolm."

"Jessie, this might surprise you, but I see Gino once a week. He comes to the grave. Sometimes he stops in to say hi. Don't be too hard on him. He has lots of regrets, too. And everyone has his or her secrets. We both know Gino has plenty."

Jessie looked dumbfounded. "Clare, I don't know what to say. I do know things changed with Gino after Josh's death, but I had no idea he visited the grave regularly. A child's death is always harder on the mother. At least that's what I always thought." Jessie caught what she said too late. "Oh, I'm sorry, Clare."

"No, no, don't be. Graham and I accepted long ago that we wouldn't be blessed with children. I'm just fortunate that I was blessed with Graham. Graham forgave me long ago for that before we were married."

"What do you mean?"

"Like I said, we all have our secrets. And, I hope you won't judge me for mine."

"I could never do that. You've been the best friend I've ever had. And like it says in the Bible, let he who is without sin cast the first stone."

"Do you remember the day you wanted me to go to Coney Island with you when Josh was just a baby? I begged off, saying I had some important errands to run. It was the time you came by the boarding house the next day, and I was sick in bed. I told you I had a virus and that you and the baby should stay away."

"Yes, I remember. You were better and up and around in a week's time."

"It wasn't a virus." She hesitated. "How do I say this?" Tears welled up in Clare's eyes. She held her head down and almost in a whisper said, "I had an abortion. You know how wild I was back in those days."

Jessie thought again of the middle child, the one she knew she lost. It was still painful.

"The abortion went bad somehow," Clare continued. "Minor things would flare up because of it from time to time but not enough to keep me bedridden. It got better over time. But the guilt of taking my own child's life got me down. I never wanted you to know. I didn't want you to think less of me. I know you always looked to me for guidance. You were so young when you had Josh. You were a baby yourself.

"I told you I met Graham in church. That wasn't a total lie. I went to his church just to talk to a preacher about it. You know Graham was the new minister at the church at that time. He counseled me. He forgave me. He said God forgave me. We fell in love. He knows all about my past. I didn't know at the time it would keep me from having children later. You know the story from there.

Graham continued to forgive me and accepted it was God's will. We all just have to forgive ourselves. It's all we can do."

"Oh, Clare, I'm so sorry." Jessie hugged her. "I could say I wish you would have told me, but you were right in not doing so. I don't think I would have been there for you the way you have always been for me. I was young, naïve, and having all the problems with Gino. I'm the one who should be asking for your forgiveness."

"Let's just call it square and let this be a new beginning for the both of us," Clare had a way of cutting to the chase.

"If anything, this trip is making me aware of my many shortcomings. I have lived in a vacuum for the longest time, but things have begun to change for me."

In the kitchen Clare rolled out some dough that had been rising and handed Jessie a cutting board, some potatoes and a knife. Jessie chopped in a precise cathartic rhythm, while telling Clare about Amy and Jackson and about her learning about yogis and about how she was going to take up yoga. She talked more about Gina and how she thought things were changing between them.

Graham came in and set three plates at the table, some silverware, and poured them some ice tea. Clare and Graham moved in perfect sync, something that Jessie admired and envied. After Graham said grace, they dug into Clare's shepherd pie, which reminded her of her childhood. They continued to talk about New York, the island, the church, the upcoming presidential election, and this and that. Jessie told Graham the whole story of why she had come back. Graham assured her it would be okay and even offered to talk to Gina. Jessie had hoped that

Gina might talk to Graham and said she would bring it up to her.

Right on cue, there was a knock on the door. Clare set an extra plate. Graham and Clare both gave Gina a hug and told her what a beautiful woman she had grown into before he made his way back to the church. "I'll see you girls later."

Clare gave Gina another hug. "You're just in time. I was just 'getting out the apple pie. I'll put on a pot of coffee."

"Love your rose bushes, Clare. I'm surprised they are still blooming this late in the season. Clare, you have the touch," Gina said.

"Remember when you were little and helped me water and dig in the dirt?"

"Yeah, I remember. I remember when Mom and Dad took us to a Chinese restaurant once. They had roses out front. I picked one for Mom. She didn't know whether to thank me or get mad. She did a little of both."

"Oh, I remember that. I was afraid I would hurt your feelings. You thought you were doing such a good deed," Jessie said.

"Josh explained it to me afterward. Clare, this apple pie is great," Gina said.

"Yes, Clare, it is," Jessie chimed in. "I need your recipe. I didn't tell you, but I've been getting into cooking lately. I made Indian the other night, well with Amy's help."

"Then maybe you should be teaching me," Clare said.

"I'm not that far along, just in training," Jessie said.

They finished their pie and began their goodbyes.

"Mom, I just want to spend a little time at the grave

before we go. I'll walk back over in a bit." Gina grabbed her coat and went out the back door. The house had been a second home to her.

"She's going to be fine," Clare said. "You're here now. She just needs her mother. You know, she'll be a mother one day before you know it."

"Don't make me a grandmother just yet. Well, actually I wouldn't mind at all. In fact, I've been thinking a lot about grandchildren lately."

Jessie got her coat and hugged Clare goodbye. "I'll call you in a couple of days."

She walked over towards the cemetery. Gina was just coming back. Jessie put her arm around her daughter's waist, and they walked towards the bridge.

"Mom, what will you be doing for Thanksgiving?"

"Amy's family invited me to have it with them, but I would rather be with you."

"I thought we could go see the parade," Gina said.

"That sounds great."

CHAPTER 19

FIRST DAY of November. She would mark this day as a new segment in her life, and she wanted to help Gina mark the occasion as a new segment as well.

They left early for a day of shopping. More importantly, it was a day spent with her daughter. What better way to begin a new chapter? If she were going to stay through Thanksgiving, she would have to get some warmer clothes. She would also have to find somewhere else to stay.

Dave opened the door for them with a tip of his hat. "Good to see you both back."

"Good to be back, Dave."

Jessie wanted to go to one of her favorite haunts, a tea shop a couple of blocks away. This place also had the freshest assortment of pastries. Ah, New York. No place on the island served pastries like these.

Jessie loved island life, but she wished she could move the aspects of what she loved about New York onto the island. She wouldn't move any more bookstores in. She wouldn't want to crowd Myrtle out or wreck her little empire. She would just make Myrtle's empire bigger, with more varied themes. There would have to be a whole spiritual section, as well as a rare book section. Rare books would have its own cluttered look and old book smell, just like those little quaint shops here in New York.

Maybe there would be a section that served coffee and tea, and even pastries, with a few scattered chairs and tables, maybe even some plush upholstered chairs Maybe that was already being done somewhere. It sounded like Greenwich Village to her. If not, she should suggest it to someone. Maybe she should do it herself. It would be one of those ground floor things that Gino was always talking about.

Maybe she would invent her own little perfect town while she was at it? A lightbulb went off in her head. That could be her novel. It would be her fantasy world. It would inspire real places like it to spring up all over the world. Everyone would be happily married. Sons and daughters would grow up perfectly in a perfect world. There would be gardens everywhere. Clare would be in charge of them. Children would not die before their parents. No one wrote novels like that. No one would even read a novel like that. Pure fiction. Maybe far off in the future, the year 2000, but not in 1960. For now she lived in a world where people were drawn to war and getting in on the ground floor.

"Ma'am, ma'am? Are you going to tell me what you

want? There is a line forming." It was the lady at the counter.

Gina nudged her. "Mom, snap out of it."

Jessie jumped, startled. "Oh, sorry. I'll take this one with the cream filling." *Typical New York.* The lady didn't have to be so rude. That was one thing about the island. They never served rudeness with the food.

"And what to drink?" the lady asked, before she even finished with the pastry order.

"Hmm, I don't know. Something different for a change."

The lady rolled her eyes like this, was already going to be a long day.

This is why I'm inventing my own town.

Gina intercepted. "Mom, try the tea latte. It's something new. You'll like it."

"What is it?"

"It's tea with milk in it."

"That's not new. I grew up drinking that in England."

"It's different," Gina said. "They foam it on the top."

The lady was growing impatient. A man behind her whipped his rolled newspaper against his leg repeatedly, giving them a nasty stare. Jessie looked down. His black boots were definitely Gestapo issued.

"Ok, I'll take it. Gina, what do you want?"

"Mom, I already have it. Like fifteen minutes ago."

Jessie looked down to see her tray.

"Let's find a table. Over here in the back away from the people in here who hate us," Gina said.

"That table is dirty."

"We'll clean it off ourselves. You don't want to ask the lady to do it, do you?"

"No, I guess not."

"What's wrong with you? You were so spaced out. You're not going senile on me are you? Please say you're not. I don't mean to be selfish, but I don't need any more going on in my life right now."

"No, Gina, don't worry. I'm not. I was just missing island life. I had forgotten how hurried New York is. And I was writing a novel in my head."

"What?"

"Oh, never mind."

"Let's just get this table cleaned off." Gina waved over to the bus boy and gave him a wink. He rushed over, wet rag in hand, saying to Gina he hadn't seen her in here before.

"Maybe I'll come more often since you're working in here," Gina replied with a smile.

He winked and walked over to gather up a load of dishes.

"Gina, is that how you get things done in this town? Openly flirt with waiters and busboys?"

"Oh, relax, Mom. I know him, or have seen him around at the theater. He's an actor."

"Is every waiter and busboy in this town an actor?"

"Pretty much. But back to you. So you're a novel writer now?"

Gina's sarcastic humor hadn't diminished.

"Gina, we need to talk about what we are going to do with the rest of our lives, more specifically what you are going to do. We already know that I'm going to be a novel writer." Or just writer she thought to herself. Who says novel writer?

"Okay, let's get serious." Gina wiped all expression

from her face, looking Jessie straight in the eye.

"I'm worried about you."

"Don't be. Didn't Clare tell you I'm going to be fine?"

"How did you know Clare said that?"

"That's what Clare does. She comforts. Remember how Josh called her Care?"

Jessie smiled. "Yes, I remember."

"No, in all seriousness, Mom, I really am going to be fine. I have it all figured out."

"You do?"

"Yes, I do."

"Okay, are you going to let me in on these plans?"

"Brace yourself."

Jessie held onto the table with both hands, pulling away just as quickly. "Yuck, chewing gum! I think you need to get your friend back over here."

"Okay, Mom, who needs to be serious now?"

"I'm sorry, Gina. For some strange reason, I feel delirious this morning. I'm happy to be with you again. I'm happy to be with my little girl."

"Mom, look at me. I'm not a little girl."

"No, you're not. Tell me what your plans are. Are you going back to school?"

"No. I'm going to California."

"California! That's so far away."

"Not really. We have planes, trains and automobiles, now."

"Why California?"

"Movies."

"Of course, what was I thinking?" Jessie smiled. "I think it's a great idea."

"You do?"

"Yes. I think you were made for the movies. You could be the next Audrey Hepburn. I always thought you resembled her. Maybe even television. I hardly ever turn mine on, but I would if you were on it. I don't think that many people on the island even have them."

Jessie had no idea what the movie crowd was like, but she knew Chris was in the theater group and thought a clean break would be great.

"I can't believe you are encouraging me in this."

"Why wouldn't I? I know you could never be a secretary, a department store clerk, or even a typical housewife. There has never been anything typical about you. I only want you to be happy. You would never be happy at any of those things. In fact, I'm proud of you for wanting to pursue a dream. Have you told your father about this?"

"I had talked about it with him before Chris. After Chris, I let the idea go by the wayside. Chris is all about the theater. Movie acting is not real acting to him. Dad actually thought it was a good idea. He said he might have some connections in Hollywood and offered to pull some strings for me. You know Dad, always pulling strings. I told him, no. I wanted to make it on my own."

"Well, if you have a hard time out there, maybe your dad could just get an introduction to some studio executive for you."

"Mom, I can't believe you said that!"

"Gina, I have every faith in your acting ability. But you know from theater that acting is a dog-eat-dog world, and I have a feeling that the movie business is even more so. This would just be something a father should do for a daughter, like paying her tuition for college if he can. So, no, I'm not against it."

Jessie was thinking to herself it was also safer. She didn't want Gina sleeping with someone to get ahead. She sometimes read the movie magazines. A father stepping in would prevent this, she hoped.

"Well, I didn't want to make the move until after Christmas."

"Okay, we'll talk more. Let's get to that shopping."

CHAPTER 20

THEY RETURNED back to the apartment later that day, exhausted. Jessie tried to be conservative, buying things that would both serve her in New York and on the island. With Gina, she wasn't so frugal. She attempted to put her dwindling trust out of her mind. She wanted Gina to have presentable audition clothes. They unpacked their shopping bags.

Gina reached into her bag, and pulled out a book. "Here Mom."

"What's this?"

"It's a blank journal. For that novel you're going to write."

"Thanks, Gina. This is great! I guess I have to go forward with it now."

As Gina went back to her bedroom, Jessie heard the

key in the lock. It was Gino.

"Hi, Gino. I guess you want your apartment back."

"No, where's Gina?"

"She's in her bedroom. I think she was going to lie down for a while."

"I just wanted to get some clothes and a suitcase. You are welcome to stay here for a while longer."

"Where are you going, not that it's any of my business? But Gina might want to reach you."

"I tell you what. Let's get out of the apartment for a bit. Do you think you could have a late lunch with me?

"Gina and I already had lunch."

"Ok, how about some tea. I'll have coffee. You have tea. As I remember, you could drink tea all day long. I wanted to talk to you about some things."

She remembered Gino's things. This couldn't be good. She gave a long sigh.

"I remember those long sighs of yours, too. Come on. I promise I won't bite or anything."

Jessie knew he wouldn't bite, at least not with her. His bark had always been bigger than his bite. The thought of him even touching her these days repulsed her. It had apparently always repulsed him.

With reluctance Jessie said, "Let me leave Gina a note, in case she wakes up."

Dave opened the door. "Good to see you two again."

Gino ignored it. Jessie looked back over her shoulder at him and shook her head. Dave's jaw muscles tightened as he realized his mistake and mumbled, "Sorry," loud enough for only her to hear.

They went down the street to a corner diner.

He got them coffee and tea. "Also, if I remember

correctly, you don't take anything in it. Is that still the case?"

Jessie nodded. "So, where are you off to?"

"Cuba," he said in a low voice.

"Cuba!" She burst out. He reached over placing his hand over her mouth. She pulled it away with her hand.

"Why?"

"Just some business."

"And I remember that one. Always business."

"I won't be back until Thanksgiving, and I'll be going straight to Mama's house. I would invite you, but well, you and Mama never quite got along, and the sight of you might give her heart palpitations."

She grimaced. He had always pleaded with Jessie to try to get along with his mother like it was all her fault.

"That was an attempt at humor," he said. "Her heart is as strong as ever. So how long will you be staying?"

"Until Thanksgiving. I promised Gina we would go to the parade together."

"That's good." He reached for his cigarettes. "Really, I mean that. I'm glad you are here for her. I'm not heartless. I know you think I am. Anyway, better you are here for her than me right now."

"I never thought you were heartless."

There was some silence as they both sipped on their drinks. So much of their later lives together had been spent in silence. They even parted in silence. The only thing Gino discussed with her was the practical end of the split up. They had both been drained of emotions by that point. She couldn't believe they were talking like this now, actually being civil towards each other.

"Do you know what happened with Chris? Did you

even meet him?" Jessie asked.

"Yes, I met him a few times." Gino added rather bluntly as he took a puff. "He wasn't right for her."

"What do you mean he wasn't right for her?"

"Jessie, I'm the reason he broke it off."

Jessie knew how he maneuvered things around in people's lives. She suspected him of maneuvering Josh's around towards going into medicine. But even Jessie didn't think Gino would do something to break his child's heart, especially Gina's. She was the apple of his eye.

Anger was welling up in Jessie, an emotion she hadn't felt in a long time. She was mad for Josh. She was mad for Gina. Maybe she needed to quit holding it in and let it all out. Maybe they needed to take a quick trip to the therapist they had gone to before. She was now ready to talk; she was ready to emote. She had started the first stages of talking with Amy, and now the floodgate had been opened.

Gino reeled back in his chair seeing her hostility. "Now, Jessie before you lose control, there was a good reason for doing what I did. For once, I used my heart."

Jessie was doing her best at trying to control a possible outburst, not that anyone in the loud, busy diner would even pay any attention. Outbursts and shouting were a way of life in New York.

"I'm waiting for an explanation."

"How do I say this?" There was a pause. "Jessie, he was like me." He repeated, "He was like me. Do you understand that?"

She gave him a puzzled look. "No, I don't know what you mean."

"I looked at him, the way he talked, the way he

conducted himself, the way he treated her. She was marrying her father. I didn't want her making the same mistake you did. I married you for the wrong reasons. Let's face it. You married me for the wrong reasons."

Jessie had once read where a psychologist had said that children often married one of their parents. It was a way of taking care of unfinished business. *Wasn't that what reincarnation was for — unfinished business?* A queasiness overtook her. Would she have to spend the next life with Gino?

Once again the world felt surreal. Why did this only happen around Gino? She didn't know Gino had thoughts like this. She had never tried to delve deeply into his inner mind. Maybe if she had, their life might have been different. The room buzzed around her. A myriad of emotions lit up on Gino's face. He didn't yell; he was having some sort of awakening. Or was it some kind of mid-life crises? He was fifty now. She had even thought for one brief infinitesimal moment of sending him a card to mark the momentous occasion. She put the thought out of her mind as swiftly as it had happened.

Jessie thought he might start crying. The only time she had ever seen Gino cry was on the night he had told her that Josh was dead. That was the only time. He was somber at the funeral but didn't shed a tear all through it. She thought he cried a lot after that but where no one would see him. She could never be sure, though.

She had hoped maybe she could avoid Gino altogether on this trip. But here she was, staying in his apartment, once hers as well, one with lots of memories attached. And now she was sitting in a diner with him, having tea and a conversation, an emotional, maybe cleansing one at that.

Jessie drank her tea to calm herself. If she knew the conversation was going to go in this direction, she would have ordered herbal. On second thought, maybe she would have suggested a bar.

She took a few deep breaths. She commended herself for not being the one who was emotional. She was taking it in like a yogi. She was becoming more curious than mad. "So what was this Chris like? How was he like you?"

"He was ambitious. He was a talker, a lot of bull. I'm sure you can relate to that."

She rolled her eyes.

"He was dirt poor, well is, unless he has hooked up with some other rich girl. He knew Gina had money. She lives on Park Avenue."

"Gino, Gina's not wealthy."

"Maybe not on her own, but she has enough, getting an allowance from me, and you have always bought her things. She hasn't had to work. She hasn't had to take acting all that seriously. I mean she hasn't had to really go after it. Neither she nor Josh had to struggle. We gave them everything."

"Don't bring up Josh. I can't go there." The yogic part she had conjured up was beginning to slip by the wayside.

"Okay, Okay, don't cry."

She let out a deep breath and bit her lip. "Go on. What exactly made him break up with her or dare I ask?"

"I went to see him after she called you. I spelled the facts out for him. I said when she married there would be no more money from the parents, and that he might even have to fork over some for the wedding. He didn't protest. He didn't even show up to get Gina to pick you up at the airport. It was getting late. Gina called him. He wasn't at his apartment. She got a taxi to the theater. She must have found him there because she came back in tears. I tried to comfort her. I had to bring her to the airport. She was a mess. I was glad you were coming back. I knew you could help her."

"I see."

"Jessie, I hope you see this for what it is."

"You're right."

"What?" This took him off guard. He froze, waiting for her to speak.

"You were right. Maybe you weren't right doing this the way that you did it. You maybe could have sat Gina down and talked to her, but I guess that's not your way. But then she wouldn't have listened. She was in love."

Jessie looked down at her tea, and wondered what the leaves at the bottom of the cup signified. "In fact, I can't believe we are even having this conversation now. I see a side of you that I don't think I've ever seen. If he had loved her, he wouldn't have backed down. Just assure me that you didn't threaten his life." Jessie said.

"God's honest truth, Jessie. I didn't do anything like that. He was good looking and a slick operator, that's all. What Gina even saw in him, I don't know."

"You don't?" Her mind went back to that first day she saw Gino on the dock.

Gino put out the remainder of his cigarette. "And Jessie, there's something more."

"What more could there be?"

He looked at her for the longest time. "Jessie…."

"Yes?"

He hesitated once again, and then just shook his head.

"It's nothing. It's good to see you are doing well. Let's get back. I need to get my packing done and catch a plane." He stood and threw some coins on the table.

As they walked out he turned. "You would never tell her would you?"

"No, Gino. She doesn't need to hear that right now. Maybe years down the road you might tell her, one day when she's happy with children. Maybe then she might thank you. For now, this will have to be our shared secret." She remembered what Clare had said about secrets.

He fumbled nervously around in his pocket and pulled out a pack of Juicy Fruit. Jessie had the distinct feeling there was something more Gino wanted to say, but she let it go. This was already too much Gino for one day. They walked back to the apartment without speaking.

Gina was up, reading a magazine when they got back. Gino told her he would be gone until Thanksgiving on business. Gina shrugged it off as normal. She didn't question him. She didn't ask where he was going, and he didn't volunteer the information. Jessie was glad. He grabbed his suitcase and kissed Gina goodbye.

He looked over her way. "Thanks, Jessie, maybe I'll see you at Thanksgiving," he said.

Gina closed the door behind him.

Gina looked at her mom. "What was that all about?"

"We were just healing old wounds."

This time it was Gina who let out a heavy sigh. "That's good."

During the next couple of weeks, Jessie gave Gina her space. On some days, she walked in the park by herself. On other days, Gina joined her. On a couple of days, Clare walked in the park with Jessie.

One day, when Jessie was in the park by herself, she saw a man sitting on a bench. She remembered him from before. She had always imagined him to be a professor or curator at the art museum. He looked the part. He was mature looking, with glasses and a beard. It was the colorful bow tie against the gray suit that spoke of intelligence to her. He always brought a bagged lunch. She remembered how he sometimes looked her way. On some days, he watched the lady who fed the pigeons.

Today, he didn't seem to recognize her. As usual he was reading something. Jessie watched him get up and throw his bag into the waste can. She noticed too late that he had left the book he had been reading on the bench. She would save it for him. He would more than likely be back on the same bench for lunch tomorrow. Jessie picked up the book. It was the same book she had been reading, the one with the yogi's picture on the front. What kind of coincidence was this? She sat down and began reading where she had left off.

Jessie heard a ruckus and looked up from her book, the professor's book, to see ducks rushing to get some tidbits of crumbs a man had thrown into the pond. It was a good ruckus.

She remembered back to one that wasn't so good. The pigeons had scattered as a man in a pinstriped suit made his way over to the woman people called Pigeon Lady. He resembled a gangster that one might see in the movies. He looked like one of Gino's friends. In fact, he looked like Gino. He had discarded a half-eaten pizza in the garbage can. The pigeon lady was retrieving it for her pigeons.

Jessie noticed Pigeon Lady looking in the opposite direction. Jessie saw what she saw, a half-naked man behind a bush. It was the direction that the man had come from. He was mad that she had spied them in some forbidden act. The undeserved angst he displayed towards her was bitter and demeaning. The woman was obviously mentally ill. Why would someone treat her that way? Why was his anger directed at the pigeon lady and not her? She had seen it, too.

Jessie watched and did nothing to defend her. It was something she had always regretted. The man looked over at Jessie, gave her a smug smile, and walked away, justified in his reprimand. Jessie had always wondered why his temper had erupted without any provocation. She wondered what had happened to the pigeon lady, and then she and Gina saw her in the park that night they rode the carriage back to the apartment. Gina felt frightened upon seeing her.

Jessie looked back down at the picture of the man on the book. Pictures were worth a thousand words. Only two came to mind: love and peace. Her thoughts centered on the upcoming Christmas season and the Macy's Thanksgiving Day parade.

When Clare invited her and Gina to have Thanksgiving at her house, Jessie felt relieved. She didn't want to do the whole Thanksgiving thing for just the two of them in the apartment, even though it might have been fun. They had already been having some cooking adventures together. Jessie had tried to cook Indian for Gina one night. They ended up going to an Indian restaurant after it flopped. It was something they both laughed about, and maybe something Gina might tell her own little girl about. Jessie had begun to think about the possibility of grandchildren, but she knew that would be several years down the road. She was just happy they had this time together now and were healing old wounds. Jessie concluded this trip was all about healing wounds.

It snowed during the parade but melted quickly. She had a flight back to the island the next day. She took her luggage to Clare's and stayed Thanksgiving night there to avoid seeing Gino again. Gina stayed too. Since Clare and Graham only had one guest room, they slept in the same bed that night. It reminded her of when Gina slept with her those many nights Gino was working late or never came in at all.

The next morning she and Gina took a taxi to the airport so Gina could see her off.

On the plane, Jessie opened her carry-on bag. She took out her journal and pen and began to write. At first, she drew a blank. Then, she started writing about all that happened to her from as early as she could remember. Dr. Linn had handed her a notebook once and suggested she write. She wasn't ready then. Now, she was more than ready. She was going to need more journals. Part of it was that she wanted to savor every moment she could remember of her mother, real or imagined. She opened her purse and put the locket on. She felt it would guide her on her writing journey. When the time was right, she would give the locket to Gina.

CHAPTER 21

ON THE flight back Jessie stayed wide-awake. There was just too much to think about, too much to fill her journal with. She wrote about her past, but then, her pen was guided like a planchette on a ouija board to the present. She went back and forth, writing about feelings, nothing in chronological order. Every word was self-discovery.

Everything that had happened to her was still fresh in her mind. She remembered what Gino said, about Gina sort of wandering aimlessly, not really giving it all she had. That wasn't exactly what he had said. That was her perception of it. What did he say? She didn't take acting seriously? She didn't have to go after it? Wandering aimlessly?

Jessie realized that she was accessing her own psyche. Wandering aimlessly, that is what she had been doing since she had come to the island. She had started her purposeless trek a good time before Josh's death. Of course, she raised the children, but what did she have that she could call her own? Maybe being a mother was enough.

Clare had something to call her own. She ran a good deal of the church activities, especially those that involved fundraising such as the bazaars. She headed groups of women. She had her garden. Maybe she did all that to take the place of children. No, she would have done it anyway. That was Clare. Clare took charge of life.

Jessie wrote all of that in her journal and more. The only break she took was for the lunch they served on the plane. Only the sound of her stomach growling and the stewardess pushing the cart through the aisle had stopped her from forging her pen furiously on. The conversations, the crying baby, the passengers' movements, and the stewardesses going up and down the aisle had blurred to a hum in the background, like the ocean waves. No, she didn't need a Coke. No, she didn't need peanuts. No, she didn't want a pillow. She just needed to write.

Before she knew it, the stewardess was nudging her. "Ma'am, Ma'am, please put that away and fasten your seat belt. We are going to land."

Jessie stuffed her pen and journal into her purse, as it was too late to get out of her seat and reach into the overhead.

She looked out the window and saw the teal of the ocean and the accompanying blue sky, no clouds to be seen. The island was like that. It was good to be home. As they began the descent, she saw the mainland and the ferry heading across to the island. It would be another hour before the next one. She should make it just in time. She hadn't called Amy or Jackson to ask them to pick her up. She would just get a taxi at the airport and ride it as far as the ferry. From there, she would call Amy. The wait would give her time to write more. That's all she wanted to do now — just write.

On the ferry, she found a seat and did a double-take to make sure she had everything, in particular the gifts. She had found a book for Amy in one of those quaint little bookstores that were so typical of New York. It was about a different yogi, one who had recently moved to America. Maybe she would take a peek before actually giving it to Amy. She would be careful not to wrinkle or smudge the pages.

For Jackson, she got a small wooden boat, reminiscent of the one Josh used to sail at Central Park. She thought he would enjoy the intricacy of the parts and the adjustable sails. Scrolled across the backside of the boat was the name AMY.

Behind her she heard a familiar voice. "Haven't seen you around. Looks like you've been traveling."

She smiled. "Oh, Mr. Roberts. I've been to New York to see my daughter. I've been gone for almost a month."

"From your radiant glow, it looks like it must have been a good visit."

She laughed. "It was."

Her journal was bulging out of her purse. She slipped it down into the bag alongside Amy's book lest it fall out.

"It's good to see you so happy," he said.

"So who's minding the store?" she asked.

"Cork is here for Thanksgiving holiday. I left him in charge."

Cork was Mr. Robert's son. She didn't even know what his real name was. Cork was some kind of childhood nickname he had acquired. It just stuck. She wondered if he used that name in college as well. She remembered Gina and Cork playing on the beach together. Cork was the only kid who would participate in Gina's little made up plays. They used to do silent movies for the other children. But it was the adults who took the greatest pleasure in their plays. Gina and Cork went all out, holding up cards they had made with an explanation of the acts.

"What about Roger and his family? Did he also come for Thanksgiving?"

Roger was the oldest son, the one who had served in Korea.

"No, they decided to have Thanksgiving with his wife's family. So, it was just Myra, Cork, and myself this year."

"Will he be picking you up on the other side?"

"No, I have my car on the ferry. I just saw you sitting over here and thought I would come over to say hi. Do you have someone waiting for you?"

"I thought I might call Jackson or Amy and see if they might come for me. They were kind enough to see me off."

"They've become quite an item on the island. You never see them apart anymore. But you don't have to call them. It would be stupid to call them when I can give you a lift. I'll take you back to your cottage."

"Thanks, Mr. Roberts. I would greatly appreciate that."

"Jessie, there is a condition."

Jessie looked at him with a curious expression. "What's that?"

"You have to start calling me Carl."

"Okay, Carl."

When they arrived at her cottage, he carried her luggage inside for her. "Thanks, Mr. Roberts, I mean Carl. Calling you Carl will take a while to get used to."

He waved good-bye. "I'll see you soon I hope."

"Sure thing."

The cottage smelled a little musty. She opened the back door and gazed out the screen to take in the sound and view of the ocean. She took off the jacket she had worn on the plane, feeling something hard in her pocket. She reached in and pulled out her wedding band. She decided it was time to leave it off. She wondered if Mr. Roberts, Carl, had noticed she wasn't wearing it.

She picked up the phone to call Gina. She had promised she would call her to say she had arrived safely. She told her about seeing Mr. Roberts on the ferry and that he had given her a lift back to the cottage. Gina had fond memories of Mr. Roberts and Cork.

"I'll be there for Christmas. I mean it this time," Gina said.

"I can't wait. I love you. Bye."

"I love you, too."

Not even bothering to unpack, Jessie lit the stove and put on the teakettle. The smell of the loose tea and the recent flight made her think of England. Why not board a transcontinental flight and go see the old estate, that is if it were still standing.

The land had been parceled off into smaller pieces after Aunt Agatha's death. She knew she would have to go back one day to settle up some things, to see what Aunt Agatha had left her. Even with the inheritance from her father and with the sale of the estate and its land, the money wasn't going to hold out forever. She had a year left in her trust at best. If she were frugal, she could possibly stretch it out a bit more. It would have lasted longer if she hadn't used what she had saved up to buy the cottage outright.

She hadn't planned for her future at all. She could have taken alimony from Gino after the divorce, but she didn't want it. With Josh's death, she wasn't thinking financially. Practical matters always had a way of eluding her. During her marriage, Gino always took care of the finances. Before Gino, she had Father and Aunt Agatha. And she knew she always had Aunt Agatha's money to fall back on should the event arise. Good old Aunt Aggie, as Father used to say. She would always come through in a pinch. The pinch was here.

Having had no children Aunt had no one to leave her money to but Jessie, and she didn't have a clue how much it would amount to. She knew it wasn't as much as Father's, but still it had to be enough for her if she was saving. Her father's lawyer had handled everything and advised her to let that sum rest for a rainy day. Now her lawyer's son handled it for her. She got a yearly statement of the assets but couldn't make head or tail of it. She had meant to put it in the children's name but never did. Now, sadly, she guessed she would take the part she had intended for Josh.

In the meantime, maybe she could get a job helping Myrtle out in the bookstore. Amy would be going back to college sooner or later. Amy had mentioned that Myrtle had wanted to expand the bookstore. Maybe she would suggest a business venture with Myrtle, adding a little tea and coffee nook. She could delve right in and take a leap of faith investing what she had left of her own money and be part owner. Would Myrtle go for that idea? Myrtle had charged ahead, and now she was doing okay. So much to think about. The teakettle whistled. Like Scarlett, she would think about it another day. After all, tomorrow is another day. Tomorrow was her future, and she was starting to give a damn. She was beginning to face forward. Dr. Linn would be pleased.

CHAPTER 22

HER GUT whispered more change in the air. The ocean was not at all like she had left it. A weird calm had settled over it. She grasped the hot mug of tea as she sat on her new porch swing. She sat in reflection until darkness fell and then retired to her bedroom.

From the open window of her bedroom, not even a breeze stirred. Shrugging off the eerie feeling, she dove into the book she had bought for Amy, turning each page with a cautious reverence. Sleep came easy. It wasn't until almost ten o'clock the next day that a rap on the door stirred her.

"Hi, I heard you were back. Mr. Roberts told me. How was your trip? How was the wedding?" Amy asked.

"The wedding?" She had almost forgotten. "It got called off, but it's okay. Gina is okay or will be. It still turned out to be a great trip. Something I really needed. "

"Oh no! I'm sorry about the wedding. Still I want to hear about everything. Can you come to dinner tonight? At my grandma's house? There is someone I'd like you to meet."

"Okay, that would be great."

"Well I have to run. A lot to do. See you at 6:00 tonight. Don't be late," Amy said.

"I won't. Do you want me to bring anything?"

"No, just yourself. You know Grandma. She loves to cook, so it won't be Thanksgiving leftovers."

Jessie went back to bed and continued to read.

By noon, she started to stir about the cottage and scrounged around in the cupboard for something to eat. She found a can of tuna and some questionable bread. She pulled off the mold spots.

She still hadn't unpacked. She would put it off another day. Most of the clothes in the suitcase were something she would wear in New York, not on the island. She thought she was buying clothes suitable for both places. Somehow, they didn't seem so appropriate now that she was back.

Her pedal pushers and sandals felt like old friends. She got her bag and headed for the grocery. She eyed the wine in the store, thinking she really should take something to dinner. It occurred to her that Mr. Roberts, Carl, had a small wine selection. After dropping her groceries off at her cottage, she found herself headed to Carl's store at a New York pace. She cautioned herself to slow down. No hurry. She had plenty of time. She was back on the island.

The bell on the door rang, and the old floor squeaked. She looked to see, not Carl, but Cork behind the counter.

"Hi, Cork. Haven't seen you in quite a while. How's college going?"

"It's going well, my last year."

"Got plans after that?"

"I'm going to help out my dad until I can find work on the mainland."

"I hope it goes well for you."

"Thanks."

Jessie perused the scant wine selection. She guessed a red. After all those years with Gino, she still knew relatively little about wine.

When in doubt, opt for the wine with the prettiest label. That was her motto for most things, books included. It was the cover that drew her in. Maybe that is why she never got into romance novels. It was always some beautiful woman in the arms of a shirtless, muscled man. Who actually looked like that? Well, Gina might be able to pull the female part off. But somehow she knew Gina wouldn't go for that type of guy. On the other hand, maybe she would. That guy was typical of Hollywood.

The cover was crucial. It suggested what lie within. The cover with the saintly appearing yogi compelled her to read it. She hadn't even thought of the cover for this imaginary book she was going to write. Something colorful.

Jessie caught a glimpse of Carl back in his office and waved. He came over. Jessie noticed a sparkle in his eyes, when she said, "Hi, Carl."

"Sauvignon Blanc? You can't go wrong with that one. Important occasion?"

"Amy invited me to dinner tonight. I thought I should take something."

"Oh, then you'll meet her father."

So that was the surprise. Amy's dad was here. She remembered he had come to see her for Thanksgiving to meet Jackson. It all seemed so long ago now. It was as if she had been back in New York for forever. Would Jackson be there as well? Of course he would. Carl had said they were inseparable. For all Jessie knew, they could be announcing their engagement tonight.

She wondered what Amy's father had thought of Jackson? He liked him. Jessie was sure of it. She was a parent. She liked him for Amy, and he would too.

She would have even liked him for Gina, although he wasn't Gina's type at all. He was nothing like any of Gina's boyfriends, the ones Jessie had met. But then, Gina had never met her type. Jessie hoped, from what she had heard of Chris, if Gino's appraisal was accurate, and she was sure for once it was, that Chris wouldn't be her type down the road.

"She told me she had a surprise for me. I guess that's it," Jessie said.

"Oh, I didn't mean to let the cat out of the bag. You won't say anything, will you?"

"No, cross my heart."

"And Jessie, I'm glad you finally took off that wedding band."

Jessie looked down at her finger. There was a faint trace of white skin where it had been.

He spoke cautiously. "I hope I didn't say anything I shouldn't have."

"No, I consider you a friend. After all, we're on a first-name basis, right?"

"Right." He winked.

She hesitated, but the timing seemed appropriate. "Carl, I hope you don't mind me asking, but for some reason I got the impression you didn't think much of my ex."

"I didn't know him, but what little I saw of him made me think you two didn't fit. I always thought you deserved better. Myra thought so, too. Well, Jessie, have a great time tonight."

"Thanks for everything, Carl." She gave him a quick hug.

Back at the cottage, she laid out an assortment of clothes on the bed. What would she wear? Long pants. Yes, it would have to be long pants. Her legs were starting to show stubble.

She and Amy had talked about having a contest to see whose legs were the hairiest. This had been after their visit to the pottery shop or yoga shop. She didn't know what to call it. It was a little bit of everything. The sign out front had said, 'Follow Your Dream,' a catchy name that fit.

Jessie had told her the contest would have to wait until after she got back from New York. She was sure she would win. Amy was blonde. She probably only shaved once a week. Or would she lose? She wasn't sure who would be considered the winner, the one with the hairiest legs or the other one. They made no mention of underarms. If she wasn't going to shave her legs, then she wasn't going to bother with her underarms.

The weather was getting chillier. She was beginning to wear light sweaters now. She wouldn't be wearing sleeveless tops until spring again. How long was this contest supposed to last? Had Amy changed her mind? She had someone to shave for now. Jessie doubted Jackson cared one way or the other. Jessie couldn't imagine him ever criticizing Amy for anything. She was a sure winner or loser, but which was it?

Jessie looked in the full length mirror. She was presentable, not too dressy, not too casual. She grabbed the bag with the gifts, and the bottle of wine, its outline apparent beneath one of those discreet brown paper bags. She had seen winos on the streets of New York drinking from such bags. There was nothing discreet about them. They were as obvious as neon signs. If anyone saw her on the way to Myrtle's, they would know, but then, who on the island cared? The laundromat ladies? Jessie didn't.

She walked past the cottages encased in their white picket fences. No one, other than herself, was on the street. Where was everyone? She tried hard to envision the locals, out working in their gardens, painting their pictures, or walking their dogs. Often, the locals came across as nothing more than shadows.

It was during times like these that she could hear Dr. Linn's voice in her head, "Jessica, Jessica!"

She ignored him. He was back in New York. She was on the island. She now had her life on course. Electric shock therapy? She would have no part of it. She didn't need his clinical mumbo jumbo or his treatments. She didn't need his interference. She concentrated. Oh, there was Mrs. Gibbons. Jessie waved. And now, she could see Myrtle's cottage, it's white picket fence encasing her perfect garden.

Amy opened the door, and Jessie handed her the wine. Jessie was glad she had gotten red, since it didn't need chilling. She did know that much about wine. Amy took it and said, "Thanks, but you didn't have to."

She took her into the living area. Jessie had remembered the house from a book club meeting. The furniture was Victorian. It reminded her of the furniture they had on the estate. That was all gone now. Jessie had kept nothing but the locket.

A tall man with salt and pepper hair was stirring up the logs in the fireplace. He turned around and smiled at her. "You must be Jessie. Amy talks about nothing but you and Jackson." He looked over at Jackson and smiled. His approval was apparent.

"Jessie, meet my dad, Michael," Amy said.

Jessie had never heard Amy say her dad's name. It was always just *my dad* when she spoke of him.

Jessie did her best to hold back her surprise at how handsome he was. She couldn't see too much of Amy in him. Jessie conjectured Amy took after her mom in looks.

He had a strong cheekbone and a straight nose, not too long, not too short. Gino had a long nose. Michael wore glasses, wire rims. Gino had always had perfect eyesight. Michael's eyes were somewhere between gray and green. Gino had dark brown eyes. Didn't all Italians? Michael had a slight dimple. He wasn't skinny, but maybe just a little close to lean. Gino had a small potbelly when she saw him last in New York. Between the speckled gray throughout Michael's hair, she could tell it had once been dark brown. Gino had black hair in his younger days. Now it was graying and receding. He looked to be around six foot tall, definitely taller than Gino. Why was she comparing him to Gino?

His hand reached out to her, and she took it. It was his right. She looked down at his left — no wedding band. She thought he might still wear it. A lot of men did. It had only been a year since his wife had died. Amy mentioned he was in construction. Rings could be dangerous in construction.

"I'm so glad to finally meet you. Amy has also talked a lot about you."

"And, she has talked about you as well."

Jessie asked if she could help Myrtle in the kitchen, but Myrtle assured her everything was almost done. It was going to be simple. It was eggplant lasagna. Amy had insisted the meal be vegetarian.

Jackson had brought some breadsticks he had picked up at one of the pizza places. Leave it to a man to bring something simple.

Sometimes the islanders had potlucks. They were to raise money for upkeep of the boardwalk or wooden steps leading to the beach. The single men always brought either the beer or the chips.

Jessie's contributions weren't too far removed. She had once taken tortilla chips with her homemade guacamole. Everyone raved about it and wanted the recipe. Did they really like it, or were they being kind? She told everyone it was a family secret. She didn't want anyone to know she had mashed up avocados adding a jar of prepared salsa. The salsa was some of the best. Gino once brought home a case of it, one of his perks. It had come from Mexico.

Amy and Jackson snuggled on the couch while she, Myrtle, and Michael sat in the Victorian chairs. There just happened to be three. Jessie remembered the additional folding chairs at the book club meeting.

Amy spoke up, "What's in the bag?"

Jessie had forgotten about the gifts. "Oh, I brought you and Jackson something back from New York. It was only right since you were kind enough to take me to the airport and see me off."

Jessie pulled out the book. She felt her journal in there. She had forgotten to take it out. "I wasn't sure if you had this. I came across it, and well, since we have been talking about yoga recently, I thought you would like it. Okay, I didn't exactly just come across it. I purposefully went to one of those great little bookstores that New York is so famous for and found this for you."

Jessie looked over at Myrtle. She hoped she hadn't made a faux pas. "Myrtle, I love your bookstore."

"No, I didn't take any offense. I always go into any bookstore I come across when I'm off the island. It's partly for competitive reasons, but mostly just because I love bookstores. I keep thinking about expanding but don't have the resources just now. It's just a dream of mine."

Jessie lit up at the mention of expanding the bookstore, but she thought it wise to be quiet on the subject for now. She would talk to Myrtle when the time was right, when she had her alone. Maybe she would do some serious meditating on it first.

Michael reached over taking the book from Amy. "I've heard about him. He has an ashram in the states. I've thought about visiting it."

So Michael was into these yogis, as well. It wasn't just Amy's mom who was into them. "Well, I hope you like it. Hope you don't mind, I started reading it myself, and may have to borrow it from you when you are finished."

Michael interjected, "So, Jessie, are you interested in Eastern religion or philosophy?"

"I am reading up on it and find it all fascinating."

She reached into the bag and carefully pulled out the

boat. It was wrapped in tissue. She handed it to Jackson. "Be careful with it. It's somewhat fragile."

"Now, what could this be? Feels like Christmas." He took his time unwinding the tissue paper. "Wow! I love it."

Amy let out a gasp. Michael laughed. Myrtle didn't know what was going on.

Jackson had the boat's stern turned away from him. He didn't see the name of the boat. They told him to turn the boat around. As he did, Myrtle saw it, too and let out a loud laugh. Everyone got a blast out of it.

"Okay I know it's like Christmas now. Jessie, this is so incredible. Thank you!"

The timer on the oven went off, and Myrtle said, "I guess that's our cue to sit down to dinner." Michael found a corkscrew and opened the wine. Amy sat out the wine glasses while Jackson put out plates and silverware. He seemed to know his way around Myrtle's.

Michael poured the wine. "What should we toast to?" he asked.

"How about to Amy and Jackson?" Jessie said.

"To young romance, and not so young romance," Michael said.

As their glasses clinked, Jessie blushed, not knowing if she had reason to or not, and just hoped no one noticed. Maybe Michael found her attractive. He had looked her way quite a lot. Maybe he was just being polite. Maybe he had met someone back home and was referring to her. Why was she even thinking these things?

"And while we're at it, let's also toast that Myrtle's dream of making the bookstore even bigger and better comes true," Jessie added.

They ate and polished off the wine and talked about

island life. Michael and Jackson talked construction a great deal. Michael told his mother if she did want to expand the bookstore he and Jackson could maybe work together on it. Jessie found out that Michael did some architectural work as well when he offered to draw up some plans for his mother.

About that time, the outside lit up with lightning. There was thunder and heavy wind. The lights flickered.

"Mom, do you have any candles? We may be needing them," Michael said.

The rain came down in sheets. Jessie worried, thinking about her open bedroom window.

"This storm isn't going to let up anytime soon, and it sounds serious," Jackson said.

Just then, the island's warning siren went off. Amy grasped Jackson's hand. Putting his arm around her, he said, "Don't worry. The storm is bad, but we are past hurricane season."

"Mom, this island hasn't had any hurricanes since you've lived here, right? What about you Jessie?" Michael asked.

"No, I haven't known about any since I've been coming here, and that's been since the thirties," Jessie said.

Just as she thought she gave away her age, Michael said, "Since you were a babe in diapers?"

The lights took their final curtain call, preventing him from seeing her face redden.

"So what do we do when a siren goes off? This all happened so suddenly. Just yesterday I thought the ocean was the calmest I had seen it in a long time," Jessie said.

"You know what they say, the calm before the storm," Jackson said.

"We're supposed to either go to the mainland or seek higher ground on the island," Myrtle said. "Since the storm came without warning, it's too late for the mainland. The ferry wouldn't run in this storm. The church is on the highest ground on the island, and since we are almost next door to the church, we are as safe as we are going to get. So, we all better sit tight till it passes."

Michael suggested they all go to the living room, which still had the glow of the fireplace. He took a candle and lit it in the fire. He lit a couple more, placing them in holders around the room.

Myrtle suggested they have dessert in there. It was ice cream, and since the electric was off, it wasn't going to keep. Amy and Jackson took a candle in the kitchen to get bowls and spoons.

Michael looked over at Jessie. "Should we be chaperoning them?"

"I think it might be a little late for that."

Michael put another log on the fire as Amy and Jackson passed out the bowls of ice cream.

"It's mango," she said. "I made it from scratch. Dad brought the mangos."

Jessie had expected vanilla, but she should have known Amy would come up with something original.

As much as they were all trying to remain calm and enjoy the ice cream, the sound of the ocean and wind took precedence. Lightning once again lit everything up, disclosing the worried looks that had settled on their faces.

Jessie had always been scared of storms since she was a little girl. She worried about their safety and wondered if she had seen Gina for the last time. If she had, at least it was a time when they had truly bonded. She felt confident

Gina would be okay if anything happened to her. Gino knew about Aunt Agatha's money. She knew she could trust him to see Gina got it if anything happened to her. She was making too much of this. It was merely a storm. It would pass.

She worried about the rest of the island inhabitants. She wondered if her cottage would make it through the storm. Her mind went to the metal box on the top shelf of the closet. If she survived, she hoped the letters would survive. She couldn't stand the thought of losing the letters. She was wearing her locket. If the cottage got flooded, the letters would be safe since they were up high. Maybe it was nothing more than a bad storm. But she sensed everyone else was as nervous as she was.

Jessie tensed. She was immobile as if she was strapped down to her chair. A sudden warmth on her hand loosened her constraint. It was Michael. He had placed her hand inside his. What would Amy think? It was just natural. If anything she felt sorry for Myrtle. But then Michael put his other arm around his mother. Just when he couldn't get any more attractive to her, he did. She could tell he and his mother had a much different relationship than the relationship Gino and his mother had had. It was a much healthier one.

As if the sound of the ocean and rain weren't already loud enough, a tremendous crashing sound came from nearby. Michael loosened his hand from hers and wrapped his whole arm around her. Jessie instinctively pulled as close to him as was physically possible. It felt good.

Jessie looked over at Amy, wrapped up in Jackson's arms. Amy attempted a smile. Jessie took this to mean that her father's arms around her was acceptable.

They sat that way for what seemed like hours into the night just waiting for the house to lift off and fly to Oz. The noise finally subsided as daylight emerged. They were still intact, but what of their surroundings?

Michael said to Jackson, "We need to find flashlights and see what's going on outside."

"Agreed," Jackson said.

With one small flashlight between them, they opened the front door. Amy, Jessie, and Myrtle hovered behind them. They all let out their own gasps of horror as they looked out over the debris.

The street looked like one giant garbage dump, lots of wood, shingles, broken glass, and tree limbs. Sand was everywhere. Myrtle's house was relatively unscathed compared to most. It was one of the oldest structures on the island, well-built. It was one of the few brick ones. The fact that it set further inland didn't hurt either. She had lost shingles and a couple of shutters. Her beautiful garden and picket fence were entirely demolished. Jessie doubted if a picket fence would be left standing anywhere on the island.

Michael and Jackson ventured out onto the street. Others were beginning to stir. Dogs barked. Jessie's mind rushed to the horses. Were they okay? She didn't even want to think of human victims. She, Amy and Myrtle stayed cowered inside for a couple of hours. Michael and Jackson still weren't back.

There was still no electric. To keep spirits lifted, Myrtle dug into the utility closet and found a camping burner. Jessie offered to make tea using the burner. It still had some propane in it. She lit it with a match and filled the teakettle that Myrtle always kept on the stovetop with water. She rummaged through Myrtle's cabinets looking for tea bags. She was making herself at home. She may no longer have a home for herself.

They sat in silence, drinking their tea. Myrtle brought out some cookies to go with the tea. She said they would need to keep up their strength.

About three hours later, Michael and Jackson returned.

"It's bad, but it could have been a lot worse," Michael said.

"The pier is no more, not a trace. There are a few houses along the beach that were washed away, those closest to the pier," Jackson said.

Jessie breathed a little easier. Her cottage was a good mile away from the pier.

"Boats are all along the beach," Michael said. "From what we've put together through various reports, the mainland took minor damage, only what a strong wind might do. The houses down by the pier, the ones that did survive, are severely flooded. We could only get on the street side of them. The water is starting to recede. The island has no electric or telephone at this point."

"What about lives?" Myrtle asked.

"Mom, at this point, we just don't know. No one is reporting anyone missing. There is a crowd at the church, now only the women and children. The men are all out doing what they can. Jackson and I will take a couple of those cookies and head back out."

Myrtle got out her battery-powered radio. The local station came from the mainland. So, they were in luck as far as keeping abreast of the news. They were getting reports of a heavy storm all up and down the East coast as far as their island. They had taken the brunt of it. At this time, no casualties were reported. Various response teams from the mainland were being dispatched. The news just kept repeating the same information over and over. New developments were being added as they made new discoveries. People were being interviewed. Jessie recognized most of the voices. Since it was a holiday weekend, some were stuck on the mainland, not being able to get back to their homes. The ferry had shut down.

Jessie thought how much worse it could have been if this had happened during the tourist season. Two-thirds of the cottages were now vacant, especially the ones close to the pier.

The news reported that the mainland airport had been damaged by the wind. Planes would not be taking off until they could get the runway cleared. There was the emergency landing strip on the island. It was more than likely covered with debris as well.

Michael was scheduled to leave tomorrow. Now he would be staying a few days longer. She wondered if this news had reached Gina. Was the storm big enough to report nationally? The phone lines were also down. There was no way to reach her. If she had heard, then she would have also heard no casualties reported at this time. She could breathe easier at least.

The rest of the day was just waiting to see what happened next. They found more batteries just in case the radio started to give out. It was their lifeline to what was going on. Michael and Jackson would return periodically to dry off and get some sustenance. They reported that Red Cross had set up inside the church. They asked Myrtle to gather all the blankets she could muster so they could take them over.

The women wanted to do something, but Michael told them they would let them know when they could. Right now, it wasn't safe to walk through the streets. Plans were being made to ferry over bulldozers and heavy equipment. Michael was going to take the next ferry as soon as it was up and running for regular passengers back to the mainland after the equipment came over. He wanted to call his partner about getting his own crew down.

It took a full day to make a head count of the island. There were injuries, nothing gravely serious. All dogs and cats were miraculously accounted for as well as the horses. For some reason, Jessie was greatly relieved about the horses. Maybe it was because there had been horses on their English estate. Maybe it was the horses she was so used to in New York.

The broadcasters announced one death. No! Not Mr. Roberts! Jessica broke down, covering her face with her hands. He went to his store to gather supplies, flashlights, batteries, water and whatever he could find. He was taking them back to the church.

He had made it to the store and filled his car with supplies. A falling telephone pole crushed him in his car on his way to the church. That was the loud crash they heard. She thought of Myra, Roger, and Cork. They surely knew about this long before it was reported. The authorities were making sure his family knew first. Roger and his family had to be reached back on the mainland.

For the next two nights they slept at Myrtle's. The water had receded from the flooded areas, but the electricity and phone lines were still out. Crews were working around the clock. Propane powered burners had been set up inside the church, and the Red Cross was doing everything possible.

Jessie, Myrtle, and Amy were doing what they could to assist. Myrtle instructed Jackson to go to the bookstore and gather as many children's books as he could. That would help keep the children occupied to some extent. Amy and Jessie played games with them.

One of the first places Michael checked was the bookstore. There was no flooding, but a new roof was in order. The only books ruined were those in the storage area where the roof had leaked. Jessie thought of the professor's books. Michael had covered the worst parts with tarps. On the second day, the runway on the mainland had been cleared enough for planes to come and go. Michael requested a supply of tarps be flown in, along with other supplies including various sizes of rubber boots.

'Follow Your Dream' shop on the mainland sent over every candle they had in stock. People were planning to gather after Red Cross's last meal of the day to honor Mr. Roberts, Carl. Everyone would light a candle for him. A proper funeral would be held after the island had gotten back to some sense of normalcy.

On day three, Jessie saw her own cottage. She donned rubber boots and walked through the debris hand-in-hand with Michael. What a way to start a relationship — if they were indeed starting a relationship.

Jessie felt needy, but not like when she had come across the ocean for the second time and married Gino. She was now older, and hopefully, wiser. She had found a new lease on life during her visit with Gina.

While they maneuvered through the street making their way towards her cottage, she solemnly looked out over all the devastation. As bad as it seemed now, she knew that it must have been worse two days ago. Right now, besides the letters, the thing she wished had survived the storm the most at her cottage was her toothbrush.

They came up to the cottage, entering through the front. Things didn't look too bad at first glance, that is on the front end of the cottage. The picket fence was gone. That was to be expected. The shutters were God knows where? That was also to be expected. The yard hadn't been much to begin with, so there was virtually no difference there.

Maybe spring would be the time to plant that new garden. Michael and Jessie made their way to the back of the house. Light was coming from the bedroom. A whirlwind had struck in there. They looked up. There was no roof on that whole section of the cottage. It could have been worse. The closet door was still shut. At least the closet was on the driest side of the room. The letters were safe. Her unpacked luggage, along with the bedside table, lamp and whatever else had adorned her bedroom were all in one pile either on top of the bed or surrounding the bed. The rug on the floor was drenched from the rain, but there was no flooding.

Michael tried to make light of the situation. What else could he do? "If you ever wanted a skylight now is the time." She laughed. It was better than crying. Then she thought of Carl.

They went through the kitchen. The cupboard had turned over. Not much on the floor. Luckily, she hadn't bought much in the way of groceries. She was glad now.

She opened the refrigerator door. She gagged at the smell. She closed it again with a loud bang. She looked at Michael, while holding her nose. "I won't be inviting you to dinner anytime soon."

They made their way out to the back. The beach was a mess. The boardwalk was gone. The wooden steps down to the beach were no longer there, and her beach chairs were probably long out to sea. The rocking chair had vanished. The bicycle that had turned to rust had also disappeared. No great loss there. The swing was intact. Was that some kind of sign? If it were, it was a good one.

Michael checked the swing to see if it was structurally sound. When he concluded it was, they both sat down. They gently swung back and forth. He put his arm around her and said, "Don't worry. I'm not leaving the island at least until things start to get back to normal."

Amid all the disaster, she felt safe. It was one of the few times in her life that she had felt that way.

CHAPTER 23

THEY SAT in the swing a while longer. She didn't want to get up. Jessie found herself reveling in the present moment. Everything seemed perfect despite all the disaster surrounding them.

Michael asked if she was ready to make the trip back to Myrtle's. She said, no, that she preferred to stay at the cottage.

"But you can't stay here. You have a big gaping hole in your roof."

"I can sleep in the other side of the house, and the bathroom section still has a roof, and we have cold water. I'll be okay. More than anything right now, I want to shower even if the water is freezing, and I want to change clothes if I can find some dry ones. I'm beginning to feel crusty. And more than that I want to brush my teeth. I must look awful."

"No, not awful at all. In fact, quite pretty."

"You're lying I think, but I like it. I'll feel prettier when I can get that shower, even a freezing one. I must stink."

"I know what you mean," Michael said.

Jessie looked at him a bit perplexed.

"No, no, no, I didn't mean you. I meant me. You smell like, hmm, well, like scented candles."

They both laughed. She had seen enough candles for a while. She had once thought them romantic, but not so much now.

He said he would return with tarps, and then he kissed her forehead. "I hope that was okay."

She didn't know what to think. She wasn't sure what was happening, but she knew something was. Or then again, it was only a kiss on the forehead, maybe nothing was going on. She smiled and said, "Perfectly fine. Be safe out there."

She walked with him towards the front of the house. He helped her lift the cupboard back upright before leaving. It was a start.

She went back into the bedroom. She wanted to jump into bed, but she couldn't. It was covered with rubble and soaked. The letters! She opened the closet door. There was still a roof attached over that section of the bedroom. She rummaged through clothes on the top shelf until she felt the metal box. Everything appeared dry. The box was where it had always been. She was relieved.

She opened her luggage to find the contents damp. She spread clothes throughout the house so they could dry, trying to smooth them out as much as possible so they wouldn't wrinkle. She didn't know why. She didn't see herself wearing any of the New York clothes anytime soon.

She found some sweat pants and a sweatshirt up in the closet where the box was stored. That was what she needed now. Underwear, that was a different story. Everything in her dresser was wet. In fact, the dresser would have to be loaded into a dumpster. She would have to go commando.

She took a brief shower in the ice-cold water, not washing her hair even though it needed it. She combed baby powder through it to remove some of the oil and grit. She put on her sweats and rubber boots, the ones that Michael gave her, and began to put things in order as much as possible. She put on a jacket over her sweatshirt, not so much because it was cold, but because of what the cold was doing to her being braless. She did what she could and then made her way over to the church to find out if she could be of help to anyone else.

She did her best to help most of the day. Everyone who was old enough placed garbage in dumpsters.

She needed to call Gina. She was sure almost everyone on the island needed to call someone. She walked by Carl's store. A wave of sadness rushed through her. Funny how long it had taken her to finally call him Carl, and now he was gone. What would happen to his store now? She guessed Cork would take over for the time being, maybe for good. The store was a landmark. It had to go on. The workmen had already removed the telephone pole that had fallen in front of it as well as the crushed car. No one wanted to be reminded of the tragedy.

She saw Amy and Myrtle in the distance. They were carrying hot coffee to the workers.

She slept on the couch that night in her sweats. As the sun was rising, she heard a vehicle pull up. There was now a one-way lane where emergency vehicles could get through. Running to the front window, she saw it was Jackson. Michael was on the passenger side. The bed of the truck was filled with wood and shingles and a large ladder.

She answered the door. "We're here to patch your roof," Michael said.

"I'm grateful, but shouldn't you be helping some of the more less fortunate victims first?" Jessie asked.

"We are prioritizing. The bad ones have to be rebuilt from the ground up," he said. "Construction on them won't start until spring. A new pier will go up at the same time. The boardwalk won't start until spring either. The coast guard is working on the stranded boat situation. Considering all this, you are one of the top ones on the priority list. So, grab a hammer and give us a hand," Michael said.

"Me?" She had never held a hammer in her life. She never even knew Gino to have one in the house. He wasn't much of a handyman. Putting together the children's bicycles had been a struggle for him. That's why he always got everything preassembled.

"I believe Amy told me you had divided your life into segments. I think this is going to be a new segment for you." He continued to hold out the hammer in her direction. Jessie took it with some hesitation. The next thing she knew, she was up on what was left of the roof. She remembered all the times she had watched men up on the skyscrapers guiding beams across those narrow walkways, and even eating their lunch up there like it was nothing. They balanced as if they were walking a tightrope. They looked like ants scurrying about up there. She couldn't be more than fifteen feet off the ground, and it made her dizzy.

So, he knew about her life segments. "How much did Amy tell you about me?"

"She said you were going to take a yoga class together. She said you were divorced. I'm sure she told me as much about you as she told you about me. I know Amy likes to talk. I have to confess that since I met you, I've been asking her for the lowdown. I have to warn you. Don't ever trust her with a secret. She's well intentioned, but she just can't do it."

"And you still want to talk to me?"

"More than ever." He smiled. "More nails please."

By the end of the day, they had the tarpaper on, and she was ready to change careers from a novel writer to a carpenter.

"Okay, let's call it a day." Michael was clearly the boss.

Jackson left to go back and see Amy, leaving her and Michael alone.

Michael looked at Jessie. "I thought he would never leave."

"I would offer you something to eat, but there is not much to offer. I can light the stove and make you some tea, that is if I can find a dry match to light the stove."

"I have a better idea. Why don't we get out of our work clothes?" Michael said.

Her eyes widened. She hadn't dated anyone since the divorce, but wasn't this a little fast?

He could tell what she was thinking. "Let me finish." His face turned red. "I mean get dressed up a bit. We could go to the mainland and grab a bite to eat. That is, if the ferry isn't too crowded. I think most of the island is headed that way."

"That would be great. Also, I could find a phone and call Gina."

"I'll pick you up in an hour if that's okay. I'm sure Jackson will let us use his truck."

She checked her underwear, almost dry. She did find a dry match and lit one of the gas burners holding it over the heat for about five more minutes. That did the trick. She hopped once again into the freezing shower.

She still couldn't bring herself to wash her hair, even for this first date. She would just have to tie it back. She looked at herself in the mirror, wrapped herself in a dry towel, and began putting on makeup, making sure her lipstick covered her entire lips. Poor Mrs. Gibbons. She was probably oblivious to the storm going on around her.

Jessie finished up with some mascara. She couldn't believe he was actually asking her out on a date. He had undoubtedly seen her at her worst. Everyone on the island was pretty much at his or her worst right now. At least she was bypassed by the camera crews that had been filming and interviewing people earlier.

What would she wear? She had no idea whether this was casual or not. It had to be casual. He said *grab a bite to eat.* With all that had happened, it had to be casual. She put on her black pants, a pair she had purchased in New York. The stubble on her legs had softened down and turned downy by this point. She had a white top and black jacket to go with that. It was pure New York, not overstated but not under either. She finished it off with low black pumps, the ones she did all that walking in while she was in the big city.

Right on time. Michael pulled up in Jackson's truck. He wore jeans and a denim blue shirt with loafers. She might have been a little overdressed, after all.

"You look beautiful! For a moment, I thought I might be back in New York."

She laughed.

He opened the door for her. She never remembered Gino ever doing that. Okay, for a few hours, no for the rest of her life, could she just erase Gino from her mind? Why was she even thinking about him? It was just that Gino, with the exception of that week with Malcolm, had been the only man she had ever known. If only there had been childhood boyfriends while she was growing up. But then if that had been the case, there would probably have never been a Gino. Okay, she thought, tonight there is only going to be Michael and Gina. She had to call Gina.

Michael got behind the wheel. "Okay, are we all set?"

"Yes." This whole thing felt strange to her, but a good kind of strange.

They stayed in the truck during the ferry ride, talking about Amy, Jackson and Gina.

"I hope you like Chinese. It's one of the few restaurants that is easy to order vegetarian," Michael said.

She had forgotten that he was vegetarian. She knew Amy was. She would be too, tonight, she decided. "Yes, I love it," she said.

The first thing she did was use the pay phone that was down the street from the restaurant.

"Gina?"

“Mom, are you okay? I’ve called and called. I knew the lines must be down. Are you okay? It’s been all over the news.”

“Yes, I’m fine.” She told him about Mr. Roberts.

“That is so sad. I started thinking about Cork after our last conversation. He was about my age. I haven't thought about him in forever.”

“Well, I’m on the mainland now. I will call you as soon as the phone lines are up and fill you in.”

“Okay, and Mom, I still plan on coming for Christmas.”

“I’m still looking forward to it, and love you.”

“I love you, too.”

After she got back into the truck, Michael asked, “Is everything okay?”

“In spite of everything it couldn’t be better.”

He smiled and drove to the restaurant.

“Do you like bean curd,” he asked.

“I don’t know. But I’m willing to give it a try.” She was so glad he hadn’t picked an Italian restaurant.

They talked until one of the waiters gave a boisterous "ahem." They looked around to see they were the only patrons left. The restaurant was closing, and the staff wanted to go home.

She had never felt so comfortable with anyone in her whole life. She told him about her ideas for Myrtle’s expansion. He talked about having Jackson as a son-in-law. They both agreed it was the real thing, what he and Amy had. With all the needed construction on the island, he was going to expand his business to the island and put Jackson in charge. She thought that was a good idea. Jessie also took that as a sign he would be coming to the island a lot, an idea she liked. She told him about her trip to New York and about the called off wedding but how she thought it was for the best.

They made the last ferry back in the nick of time. They had lost track of time. He walked her to her door and kissed her on the lips this time. That was all. He didn't try anything else. She didn't know whether to feel disappointed or relieved. She thought relieved. She wanted it all to be so special if that time should come. Plus she remembered her hairy legs and underarms. She didn't know if he was into French or not. And, there was her bed, still damp.

"I'll see you early in the morning. You have coffee and tea ready. I'll bring the donuts. Then we'll get started on that roof," Michael said.

"Okay, boss," she said with a grin.

CHAPTER 24

DURING THE middle of the night, she heard the buzz of the refrigerator. It happened several times. Things were looking up. She fell back asleep on the couch. The next thing she knew, her alarm was going off. She had set a wind-up clock on the table near the sofa so she would be sure to wake up before Michael arrived.

Even if she was going to only be a carpenter's assistant, she wanted to be the best looking one she could be. That would mean rising up early enough to hop once again into that cold shower. She had read that the Himalayan monks took excruciatingly cold baths in the mountains. Then, she would put on just a dab of make-up. They didn't do that. They were content with their inner beauty. She was not.

Once again she heard the refrigerator. She flipped on

the light switch."Yes!"

She got in the shower, this time shampoo in hand. The water was just beginning to warm up. Clean hair at last. She plugged in her blow dryer. She again pulled back her hair. Long hair and being upon a roof just wasn't an option. She put on that dab of makeup and put her sweats back on which were stiff and crusty against her clean skin.

Michael was right on time, alone, and he was carrying a bag. He said there were no fresh donuts to be found anywhere on the island, so he had brought some prepackaged store ones.

Jackson was helping elsewhere on the island. He had every faith in her newly acquired carpentry skills to finish the job without him. Today they would lay the shingles. Jessie was glad it would be just the two of them.

She got out her new teapot and the loose-leaf tea.

While they ate their donuts and drank their tea, he told her half the island currently had power. He added the phones should be back up by the end of the day.

After breakfast, they climbed up onto the roof. He began placing the shingles and showed her how to get started. He carried them up the ladder one at a time, handing them to her. He stopped her at a certain point and measured out a section of the roof area. "We are going to go around this spot with the shingles," he said.

"Okay, I don't mean to question your construction genius, but why? I thought we were covering up the hole in the roof."

"I thought you wanted a skylight."

"I thought you were joking."

"No, don't you think it will be great? We, I mean you, can look up at the stars and the moon at night."

She smiled at his slip.

"Yes, I think it will be fantastic. Now hand me some more shingles."

They finished the roof before nightfall, except for the skylight area. Michael said it would be coming on tomorrow's ferry.

They sat out on the beach that night. He held her and kissed her several times. He walked her back to the cottage, holding her hand, and kissed her one more time. He said he would be back tomorrow when the skylight came in. He would be helping out with other construction up until then. Jessie, beaming with pride with her new skills, offered to lend a hand. He said he would definitely take her up on that later, but for right now she needed some more apprenticeship. She gave in. Michael was the boss as far as the construction business went.

That night she checked her phone. Good news, a dial tone. She dialed Gina's number. It was late for the island but not for New York, but then, Island time had gotten so off kilter since the storm.

She told Gina about the roof and about how it was already being taken care of. Gina said, "That was fast. Do you have special connections there or something?"

Jessie replied that she sort of did. She said she knew one of the contractors pretty well.

Jessie assured her that with all the work crews and volunteer labor, the island would be up and running in no time. Jessie added with optimism, "Maybe near normal by Christmas!"

CHAPTER 25

JESSIE SPENT the next day trying to bring the inside of the cottage back to some order now that the hole in the roof had been temporarily patched. She wanted to make room for a Christmas tree this year, not that she had much furniture to move around. She hadn't put one up in the three years she had been here.

Finally, she was feeling festive. She knew that the reason for her holiday spirit was that Gina was coming down. Michael didn't hurt the mood either.

She would have to break Michael to Gina slowly. Jessie had to consider Gina's feelings, having just called off her wedding. Might a wedding be in Jessie's future? She was taking everything too fast. She told herself to just slow down. Is this what falling in love felt like? Did he feel the same?

She piled up everything that needed to be washed.

There was no need in even trying to get into the laundromat. A couple of kids had been going door-to-door volunteering for that job. Since the island children had been excused from school for a couple of weeks, they took your laundry and returned it to you only charging for the detergent and the cost of the machines. They were making a pretty good haul since people were tipping them. It was one less worry for people to have to attend to. The kids considered it an adventure. Plus they were making their Christmas money.

She waited for Michael, but he never showed up. The window was due to arrive today. It wasn't until nightfall that he finally came by. She figured he had just got caught up in other construction. She didn't want to monopolize his time when so much work needed to be done on the island.

When she did see him, he greeted her with a kiss and then said, "There was a bit of trouble with the window. We had to order a new one."

"Oh? How come? But more importantly, I was a little worried when you didn't show up. But I thought you and Jackson were out saving the day on the island with your trusty hammers and nails, which was fine. I shouldn't be taking precedence. People might start to talk."

"Trust me, they already are."

"Really, I would think they would have bigger fish to fry right now than a little gossip."

He laughed. "It provides a little something for them to take their mind off of things."

"So, what was the problem with the window?"

"Jackson and I took his pickup truck down to the ferry at noon to wait for it. Sure enough, it arrived. I was kind of surprised, since it's not a common item. I thought it might be put on back order but was keeping my fingers crossed."

"But you said there was trouble with it? Wrong size or something?"

"No, even if it were, we could adjust at this point," he continued, "I don't know if Amy told you about her previous boyfriend?"

"She mentioned a little. Myrtle told me he was trouble."

"He had come across on the same ferry that the window was on. He saw me as he was getting off. Jackson and I had just got the window off and were loading it onto the back of his pickup truck. David came up to me and asked about Amy. Someone they had class with, who didn't know they had broke it off, had asked him if Amy was okay. She had heard about the storm on the island. That's how he knew where she was."

"Oh dear! Where is he now?"

"I told him Amy didn't want to see him, but he was getting insistent. Jackson was a little confused at first, but soon figured out he must be an ex-boyfriend. Amy apparently hadn't told Jackson about him, which I find a little hard to believe.

"He was getting loud and yelling and demanding to see Amy. He was throwing in some foul language. We had stopped mid-process in loading the window. Before I knew it, he and Jackson were in a fight.

"It wasn't much of a fight. David lunged at Jackson. Jackson had the upper hand, and punched him hard. David was on the ground with a bloody nose. That was after his body hit hard against the skylight we had just started to load onto the back of the pickup truck. It fell to the pavement along with him. As good as it was packaged, we could still hear the glass shatter. David got up and walked away, heading back towards the ferry. We waited to make sure he got on. We took the next ferry over to the mainland with the damaged skylight. That one's supposed to be picked up and a new one shipped. It may take a couple of weeks now."

"I'm sorry about David showing up. Do you think he will try it again?"

"No, he's a lot of talk. If he had known about Jackson, he would never have come in the first place."

"I'm glad. About the skylight. Maybe we just should forget it?"

"No, you want it don't you?"

"Well, I had never thought about having one before, but the thought of having one sounds good. But it seems to be too much trouble. And there are more important things."

"In the construction business, there are always setbacks. It goes with the territory. And you will be able to look at stars at night before you fall asleep, one of life's great pleasures. Isn't that worth a little complication? Plus, you will be the only one on the island to have one. You would be doing the island a favor by adding value to the property."

There was that word — complication. It was a new beginning in her life. Maybe it took a little complication to get there. The skylight represented a new beginning after the storm.

"After an argument like that how can I refuse. I just hope everyone else won't be jealous."

Michael smiled and held his hand to his stomach. "I'm starved. I heard the pizza place across from where the pier used to be has reopened."

"Only if we don't get tomato sauce on it."

"And only if we don't get pepperoni or sausage as well."

She laughed. "Deal."

They walked hand in hand together down the beach. The debris had been cleared. There was no boardwalk, no walkways to the cottages, no beach chairs or umbrellas sitting out. The actual beach area was almost back to the pristine condition it had been in before the island ever had tourists or maybe locals, for that matter.

The waiter took their order. He remembered Jessie ordering it without sauce before so didn't even blink an eye as he wrote it down on the pad. They ate their pizza and drank their Cokes. They talked. They laughed. They didn't even notice anyone else in the room.

They walked in silence back along the beach towards her cottage. They sat down on the sand. Michael spoke first, "Can we talk seriously?"

"I guess."

"So why don't you like tomato sauce on your pizza?"

"That's what you consider serious?"

"No, that question was playing on my mind. I just wanted to get it out of the way."

She explained about being so nervous when she married her first husband and how they had eaten pizza that first night. She told him about how the marinara had upset her stomach. From that day, she tried to avoid it. One thing led to another. Before she knew it, she was spilling her guts about her life. She told him about Josh's death. She began to cry. It was as if the flood wall had finally broken down. He just listened and held her.

He continued to hold her for the longest time. He offered his shirtsleeve for her to dry her tears.

"I'm sorry. I didn't mean to let all that out. You said you had wanted to talk about something serious," Jessie said.

He smiled and kissed her. "I think that was serious, and it's okay. Sounds like you needed a good cry. I'm glad you told me everything."

She had feared he might just walk away after that outburst. No, he wouldn't do that. She didn't know him that well, but at the same time she did know him well, even though she had met him less than two weeks ago. Maybe they had known each other in a past life.

"Remember, I know what it is to lose someone, not a child, but you know I lost Carol. A spouse is hard enough to lose, but I couldn't imagine losing Amy."

That was the first time she had heard him say his wife's name.

"I'm so sorry. I know she was an exceptional person. Amy really misses her."

"I know. So do I."

Jessie looked up at him feeling kind of strange. Here he had this great marriage, and she didn't. Their circumstances were so entirely different. She wondered if she could measure up to Carol.

"Of course you miss your wife." She gripped his hand tighter.

Maybe this relationship wasn't as serious for him as it was for her. Jessie hadn't even intended on this. It just happened. Maybe that's what he meant about being serious before she just emotionally exploded in front of him.

Maybe he was going to say what never actually started was over. No, she told herself. He just took her to eat, and they had a great time, and now he was holding her on the beach. Jessie tried to push the insecurity from her mind.

Silence ensued. Only the sound of the ocean could be heard, as they sat on the sand and Michael held her. She thought that could be a good sign or a bad sign. She told herself, *Jessie, just live in the moment. It is what it is. Whatever it is, let it take its course.*

What was he thinking? Why do women always want to know what a man is thinking? No, that's not true. She usually didn't want to know what Gino was thinking. She reminded herself. *Don't let Gino ruin the moment.*

After a while, he spoke. He started talking about Carol. At one point, he had tears in his eyes. They came quickly and went quickly. Men held feelings in much more than women, but he was talking to her about it and how scared he was at the time about losing his wife and about Amy losing her mother.

Then, he talked about how he felt. He was lost for the longest time. Jessie could definitely relate to that. He was afraid he wasn't there for Amy when she needed him. She could also relate to that. She assured him that he was, thinking unlike the way she wasn't there for Gina. It was his turn to talk now, and she wanted to be there for him. He said he was ready to start a new segment of his life.

He turned to her and said, "Now for the serious part."

"This wasn't the serious part?" she said with a bewildered expression.

"I was interjecting humor in a tense situation, Jessie."

He looked into her eyes. "Can we start seeing each other?"

"I thought we were. We are sitting here. I see you and you see me."

He grinned. "Funny, I see you are interjecting some humor, too."

"If you are asking me to go steady, the answer is yes."

"I just wanted to make sure. I'm a little rusty at this. Is that what they call it for folks our age, going steady?"

"I don't know what they call it. I'm sure the ladies at the laundromat will know. Believe me, you couldn't be as rusty as I am. Maybe we should ask Amy's advice?" She paused and asked, "Maybe we should ask Amy's approval."

Michael smiled. "I think we already have it."

They sat for a bit more, both in contemplation over what had just taken place. Michael finally got up and pulled her up. They wiped the sand off and walked back to the cottage. He kissed her at the door. She didn't know if sex was next or what. She inwardly started to panic, thinking about the deal she and Amy had.

"Well, we have an early day tomorrow. Do you want to apprentice with me?" Michael asked.

"I'll be ready."

"I'll bring the donuts."

She threw off her clothes, ran a bath, and shaved her legs.

CHAPTER 26

AS SOON as she got out of the tub, she heard the phone ringing. It was after midnight. Who could it be? Something wrong with Gina immediately popped into her head. Or maybe it was Michael. Maybe he missed her already. Maybe shaving her legs would pay off. She stumbled over the pile of laundry and reached the phone before the caller decided to give up.

"Hello."

"Mom."

"Gina, are you okay?"

"Yes, why do you keep asking me that?"

"You'll understand when you are a mother."

"I'm the one who should ask you if everything is all right. It's after midnight. I thought I would give it one more try before calling the police. Where have you been?"

"I was out on the beach."

"You must have been out there for a good while. I've been calling since eight o'clock."

"So what's wrong?"

"Dad wanted me to call you."

This was already sounding ominous. "What about?"

"It's Grandma."

"Is she okay?" Jessie immediately felt remorse thinking she was ill or maybe she had even died. Maybe her heart wasn't as strong as Gino had suggested it was.

"She's okay. She just wants to see you, this week. And, I think Dad wants to see you, too. They are going to Italy. Grandma said The Old Country."

Jessie was taken aback. They had never been back since they had come to America. Gino had never even once talked about going back. But Rosa was always talking about it. After so many years had passed, Jessie had thought it was nothing more than talk. Gino did favor her in that regard.

"Why?"

"That's all Grandma has talked about lately. She says she's getting old, and she wants to go back, maybe to die. She insists that Dad be the one to take her. She wants to say her goodbyes to everyone, specifically you."

"Me? Are you sure about this? And, is your dad going to stay there?"

"Not forever, but he does plan on staying until after the New Year. Mom, I'm just as puzzled over it as you are.

Don't shoot the messenger. Anyway, they have plane tickets for the end of the week, so as soon as you could get here would be great, that is if you will even see her. I know you just came up here and all. Dad even offered to pay for the plane ticket, both ways if that helps."

This must be important. This whole night had been full of serious. Now, the complication side of serious was beginning to manifest itself.

Jessie let out one of her heavy sighs. "I need to sleep on this. I'll call you back in the morning. This won't change your Christmas plans will it, me coming back up there?"

"No, I still want to come to the island. Maybe after you talk to her, I can just come back with you."

"Okay, well, let me call you tomorrow."

"Okay, Love you, Mom."

"I love you, too, Gina."

Jessie sat on the bed. This was all so strange — stranger than strange. Why would Rosa want to talk to her before she left for Italy? Maybe she wanted to put some Italian curse on her. No, not even Rosa would resort to something like that. She had never heard her curse anyone. Her revenge was subtler than that.

And why did Gino want to talk to her? Hadn't they aired out their grievances towards each other while she was up there? She couldn't sleep now. She looked up at the closet. She got down the box with the letters. She placed it on the bed, just staring at it. She hadn't read them since coming to the island. So many times she had started to but never even got the box as much as opened.

CHAPTER 27

WITH REVERENCE and trepidation, she opened the first letter with the return address of San Antonio.

July 1, 1951

Mom and Dad,

This is to mostly let you know that I arrived safely at Fort Sam Houston in San Antonio. On the train ride, I saw some beautiful country. Every state was different. I especially liked Kentucky.

We went across the Mississippi River. I kept imagining Mark Twain on a riverboat. I remembered all those Mark Twain books you used to read to Gina and me. I did see a riverboat, but mostly I saw barges.

Entering Texas was a different world. I can't say I like it much.

There isn't much green, even this time of year, mostly tumbleweed and oil wells. Jim said we were lucky the windows on the train were closed. It stunk to high heaven. Jim got on the train at Tennessee. He's a fellow medic. We hit it off right away. I think it's his hillbilly accent and his peculiar way of phrasing things. He has an opinion on almost everything. I thought if I stuck with him it would be a learning experience.

Texas just went on and on, and San Antonio is just a small part in. I can't imagine riding a train all the way across the state. I slept a good deal on the train. That is, when Jim shut up and finally went to sleep himself.

So many different accents. Guys are here from I think every state. I know there are a lot of accents in New York, but I hadn't heard hillbilly before. Don't think I'm downgrading hillbillies. Jim has such a wide range of knowledge on about every subject there is, like a self-taught Abraham Lincoln. Only Lincoln was from Kentucky. I'm hoping we turn out to be good friends. I can already tell he's someone you could depend on. We've agreed to watch each other's backs when we get to Korea.

Sorry, this is so short. We're not given much free time, and barrack lights will be off soon, so must close. Training starts early tomorrow. Will write again as soon as I can and have more news to report.

Love,
Josh

July 15, 1951

Mom and Dad,

* * *

Sorry I didn't write any sooner. It's taking me a while to get settled in. Training is tough. As luck would have it, Jim and I got assigned to the same barracks. It's one long big metal building. I'm in the upper bunk, and he is in the lower.

Our instructor is a Dr. Hoffman who got his degree at Berkley, California. I can't say much for his bedside manner, but the nurse who works under him sure is cute. Maybe I'll like being a medic, after all. Right now, it isn't too glamorous. Yesterday I had bedpan duty. They put us through the rigors of all aspects of what we might encounter, one by one. Tomorrow I learn the proper way to administer tourniquets.

On the 4th, there was a big display of fireworks at the base. You can count on the military to have real fireworks, even better than New York City. There was also lots of beer to go around. Hope you, Dad and Gina had a great Fourth of July. I thought you might change your mind and go to the island. If you are there, I hope this letter gets forwarded to you.

Love,
Josh

August 1, 1951

Dear Mom and Dad,

Only two more weeks of training! I haven't gotten my orders yet, but rumor has it that I'll be shipped to California before heading to Korea.

I probably won't write again until then. They keep us pretty busy here. So far, I've managed not to be disciplined. Jim hasn't been so lucky. One day I want you to meet him. He can be outspoken, something they frown upon in the military. He considers it his duty to give his opinion on almost every subject. The sergeant doesn't like that at all. Some of the guys find him annoying. I must be odd. I really like his company. I do tell him he should learn to keep his mouth shut, but that's like telling a dog not to bark. He has one of the kindest hearts.

Tomorrow I start weapons training. That's something I totally don't understand. They are training me as a medic to save lives and also teaching me how to kill. I can handle the bedpans and blood, well mostly. I'm not so sure how I will fare on the guns, having never touched one. Jim, an avid hunter, found that hard to believe. He's good to have around. He may just save my butt one day.

Don't worry. Hopefully I'll never have to use the gun, and Jim will never have to save my butt.

Love,
Josh

P.S. I didn't mean to brag about saving lives. That's the doctors and nurses' job. I'm merely a glorified first aid bedpan man who gets to wear a fancy uniform.

One by one, she continued to read, savoring every bit of her son's essence that she could, lingering over each letter as if in meditation.

August 15, 1951

Dear Mom and Dad,

* * *

We made it to California. The base we are at is dull and boring. All I see is sand. Tomorrow will consist of parachute training. I'm glad I'm not scared of heights. Maybe it was growing up in New York with all the skyscrapers. Unless I flunk skydiving, I will have a week here with plenty of free time before being shipped out to Korea. Jim and I plan on taking advantage of it.

We've made a list of places we want to see: Oakland and San Francisco, the Golden Gate Bridge, Fisherman's Wharf, and any other tourist sites that the locals might recommend. I look forward to the San Francisco Bridge the most. It's a work of engineering genius.

I'll do my best to write again before getting shipped out.

Love,
Josh

August 29, 1951

Dear Mom and Dad,

I apologize for not writing sooner like I said I would. I can only imagine your worry. Everything has been so hectic I couldn't write until now. I got shipped out sooner than I expected. Jim and I boarded a private plane. It was one of those contract things that the army does.

We did get to see all the tourist sites and more as you can see from the enclosed pictures. Mom, maybe you can start me a scrapbook.

The pictures fell out. After his death, she just didn't have the heart to start that scrapbook. Maybe now it was time.

* * *

The plane we came on was a huge cargo plane. There were no seats, only benches along the sidewalls of the aircraft. It was noisy and a rough ride. We were also carrying oil. The government agreed to buy the oil if there was any kind of leak. Luckily that didn't happen.

We stopped on Wake Island to refuel, but the fuel sheds had been wiped out by a storm. We made do with 55 gallon drums of fuel, all that was left. The runway started in the sea and ended in the sea. I have to hand it to our military, especially the pilots. They are well trained.

We stopped again in Hawaii for fuel. They let us get off for a cup of coffee. Nothing beats Hawaiian coffee. I know, Mom, you wouldn't touch the stuff, but Dad, you'd love it.

One of the most beautiful parts of Korea was seeing the mountains as we flew over before landing. We ate at the mess hall. I can't say much about the food. I sure do miss New York in that respect. Then we were put on a truck headed for a small village near Seoul. The two doctors and a nurse assigned to the mash unit we were headed for rode in a jeep in front of us.

When I say unit, don't expect anything like buildings. Everything is set up in tents, the hospital, the barracks, the mess hall, etc. The only actual building which is just a shed houses the generator. The generator broke down once. I ended up fixing it even though I wasn't assigned to and became the hero for the day. Everything around here is state of the art makeshift if that makes any sense.

Jim and I, being the low men on the totem pole, stay in a separate tent from the real medical staff. What tent you are in depends on your rank. Of course, the few women that are here share a combined tent.

There is only one tent with showers. Men and Women are

allotted different times. It's scorching right now and never stops raining (monsoon season). Some of the guys just stand outside naked (don't mean to offend you, Mom) for their showers. The women here are tough as nails and just ignore them. Being nurses, they've seen it all anyway. Other than the injuries, all the mud is the bad part.

Don't be discouraged. I look at it all as a learning experience. I couldn't get anything like this back at school.

Love,
Josh

September 15, 1951

Anyong Haseyo

That's hello in Korean. There is a young boy who is a patient in the mash unit. He's been trying to teach me a little Korean. His name is Young-Ho. He's only 15 and lost his leg in a land mine. Those are a real danger around here. Spence, that's the doc's name, put me in charge of teaching Young-Ho how to use his crutches. You're probably wondering why I call a commanding officer by a nickname. Everything is real casual around here. They keep us so busy. It's all about saving lives and keeping everything in working order. The doctors and nurses are great, well everyone is. They perform miracles in the most primitive conditions. Everyone I work with is top notch.

We only have sand for floors, even in the hospital. And the privies, well we are talking really primitive. For the guys, it's not so bad, but I really feel sorry for the women, but they seem to be able to handle anything the men can, and sometimes more.

Young-Ho is doing quite well. He follows me around, and I let him help. He wants to come to America one day. You would think he would be depressed or bitter, but not at all. I admire his courage.

Haven't seen much of Jim lately. He had night duty. Even as casual as it is around here, his opinions can still get him into trouble. He definitely has a unique perspective on life, one of the things I love about him. When we get out, I want him to visit New York so I can show him the sites.

I wanted to make this a long letter to make up for the short ones, but duty calls. Stretchers are coming in with wounded.

Love,
Josh

September 30, 1951

Dear Mom and Dad,

So much has been happening, more wounded than we can handle. That's why I haven't written. By the time I get back to my tent, I'm exhausted.

I'm glad to hear everyone there is doing well, and tell Gina I hope she gets the part. Mail here is erratic. I got your last four letters in one bundle. I so much appreciate your letters from home.

Now, for my sad news. Jim was shipped up near the front line to the single tent battalion aid station. It's where they bandage the wounded up before sending them back here for surgery or whatever else they need. That's the most dangerous place for a medic to be other than out fighting which we shouldn't be doing. He was shot and died instantly.

The sad part is that I was the one who was supposed to be on the front line. Orders were changed last minute. No one speaks of it, but everyone knows why. It was because Jim was different, not because he was outspoken, but because he liked men. I liked Jim. It didn't bother me, but you know how prejudiced people can be. I'll really miss Jim. I feel so bad that I wasn't there to watch his back. I feel like I owe my life to him. One of the first things I want to do when I get back is to go to Tennessee and visit Jim's parents. I want them to know how brave he was.

She gently rubbed her fingertips across the letter where his tear stains were.

I don't want you to worry about me. Spence insists I stay here. They think I'm handy to have around, not just for bedpans, but to fix the equipment when needed. There is always something that needs fixing. I've kept the generator going more than once.

Young-Ho went back home. I'll miss him. I'm sure as heck going to miss Jim.

Love,
Josh

October 8, 1951

Dear Mom and Dad,

I think the rain has finally stopped. Everyone had a big beer bash to celebrate.

A couple of the doctors got their papers to go home. That was cause for another celebration. We use any excuse to have a party around here. We are a bit shorthanded at the moment. A new doc is supposed to be here by tomorrow. We're so short-handed that I've been training in x-rays. They even pulled one of the truck drivers in, teaching him how to operate the x-ray machine. His name is Alvin, and he's from California. The captain said we were best suited for the job since we both knew machines and how they worked.

We have rations for everything. I gave my beer rations to Alvin since I don't much like beer. What I've really been craving since I've been here is a Nehi Grape soda. Remember how you, me and Gina used to get those in Mr. Robert's store? Since I've been here, I've learned to appreciate those little things in life.

Last week, a vaudeville act came by the mash unit and performed for us. Back in New York, I would have thought they were appalling, but here, we are grateful for any diversion. We've heard that Bob Hope is coming. Everyone is looking forward to that, but I don't think it's Bob Hope everyone is excited about, though. There's been rumors that Marilyn Monroe is coming with him. I hope that's true.

Until next time, and please keep your cards and letters coming.

Love,
Josh

November 29, 1951

Dear Mom and Dad,

The cooks in the mess hall went all out for Thanksgiving. There was plenty of turkeys to go around, probably one too many. I'll explain.

One of the new nurses is a Brit, a male nurse. Talk about an odd duck. That's how the Brits would label him. You probably already know that, Mom. Sometimes I forget I'm part Brit myself. Well, anyway, he kept a pet turkey. Some of the guys keep pets around here. Sometimes it can be an actual zoo. There was a Turkish guy here who even had a deer. It had a broken leg. He had put a splint on it, which only did more damage. Doc operated on the leg but ended up amputating. The deer didn't last too much longer after that.

Back to the Brit's turkey. Come Thanksgiving he couldn't find him anywhere. The turkey had completely vanished. He refused to eat Thanksgiving dinner in the mess hall. Later he caved in on his hunger strike and had pumpkin pie. Not to worry, the turkey turned up the next day. We later found out some of the guys had hidden him in a cage as a gag.

I don't think I've ever been so stuffed. It was the one time we got seconds. Tomorrow back to the same old mess hall food.

Love,
Josh

She continued reading all the letters and then came to the last one.

July 1, 1953

Dear Mom,

Is everyone okay? Dad wrote and said he had something important to talk to me about when I got home. My first thought was Grandma or Granddad.

I hope this is one of the last letters I write. There is talk of the war ending soon.

I don't know what my plans are when I get back. I would love to travel some. I think I would like to visit Europe, specifically

England and Italy. I've had a hankering to trace my roots. Hankering is a term I got from Jim. Definitely somewhere without rice paddies. I know there must be scads of relatives still living in Italy.

After seeing so much blood and watching the surgeons work, I want to rethink this doctor thing. I know it would dash Dad's hopes, but I don't know if I'm cut out for it. Maybe I'm just tired of the war. Maybe I'll have a new outlook when I get back home. I do love helping people. That made all this worth it.

Will go for now.

Give my love to everyone,
Josh

There was a knock at the back door. She looked over at the clock. Seven AM. She had been up all night reading the letters.

She opened the door, and Michael greeted her with the usual kiss and a funny expression.

"Good Morning! Why are you still in your robe? Why do you look so sad? Your eyes are puffy. You've been crying! You're not breaking up with me already are you?" His face lost its cheer and turned grim.

"No, of course not. I took a long bath and didn't go to bed. I've been up reading all night."

"Must have been a good book or a very sad book."

"I read all the letters that Josh had written while he was in Korea."

"Oh, I can see why you are sad. Do you want to talk about it over tea and donuts?"

"I do have something I want to discuss with you." She put on the teakettle and got out the coffee pot.

"You'll have to help me make the coffee." She got out the can of Maxwell House. "I always forget the scoops. You'll have to walk me through it."

He put his hand over hers with the scoop and guided her in dipping out the coffee. She smiled up at him. "If this is the way you make it, maybe I could learn to like it."

"Now what's the big discussion about?" He laid the donuts out on the table and pulled the journal out of the other bag he was carrying and put it on the table as well. "You left this at Mom's the night of the storm."

"My journal! I had totally forgotten about it."

Jessie stopped in her tracks. "Did you read it?"

His face looked guilty. "Well, maybe a peek. No, no, honest, I didn't. I was just kidding you."

She hesitated again. "What about Amy?"

"No, I'm sure she didn't. Mom, on the other hand, well I don't know."

She pretended to throw a donut at him.

"So, what is it you want to talk about?" he asked.

"Gina called last night or rather this morning after we got back. Gino had asked her to call. He wants me to come back to New York. Even offered to pay for the plane tickets."

"Whoa, this is serious. Does he want to get back together? Should I be worried?"

"No, and no. Rosa, his mother, wants to see me. And, he wants to see me, too. They are going to Italy."

"Forever?"

"Maybe Rosa. Gino will be back after the New Year."

"Oh shucks. Do you want me to go with you?"

"You would do that?"

"Of course."

"That is so sweet, but you need to stay here and help with the rebuilding. Besides, it would be better if I went on my own. That is if I go. I haven't decided yet. I'm supposed to call Gina back today. It would have to be almost right away. They are leaving this weekend."

"I think you should go."

"You do? Are you trying to get rid of me? Maybe it's you who wants to break up."

He reached over and kissed her with powdery lips. "Remember, I just said I would go with you. We are both so paranoid since we said we are going steady. Maybe we should call it something else."

"Okay, when you think of what to call it let me know."

"Jessie, in all seriousness, you should go for closure. You need some type of closure. Why else would you be up all night reading your son's letters? And if there is anything left between you and Gino, I want to know before I get in too deep and get my heart broken."

"Trust me, there is nothing left. I'm not sure why we were ever together in the first place, maybe some past life karma."

"I had better get to work. Looks like I won't have my apprentice by my side. You need some sleep and need to make some arrangements. I'm going to be the one who takes you to the airport this time."

"Okay, I look forward to that."

After their kiss, as she was closing the door, he said, "By the way, you have beautiful handwriting."

CHAPTER 28

OKAY, MAYBE he did read her journal. She had spilled most of it to him last night anyway. That was the least of her worries for now. It was still early, but she dialed Gina's number.

A groggy Gina answered, "Hello." Oh, good. Gino didn't answer.

"Tell your dad to make the flight arrangements and call me back. I have to get packed and get to the airport. So, tell him either the last flight out tonight or make it tomorrow morning."

"Okay, Mom."

"Gina, did you get that? You still sound asleep."

"I did, but if you want to talk to Dad?"

"No, I trust you got it. Call me back as soon as he has it worked out. I'll start packing. Love you."

"Okay, love you."

Jessie hauled out her suitcase once again and began to pack. She threw in her journal. She anticipated filling it up.

A different type of nervousness enveloped her as she went through the procedure of laying out her travel clothes. It was dread. This time if something went wrong like missing her flight she would call it fate and maybe dodging a bullet. Now she just had to take a nap and wait for Gina's call to wake her up. She lay there for half an hour. Sleep didn't come. She opened her suitcase back up and took out her journal and began to write. She wrote about Michael.

She had gotten ten pages in before the phone rang.

"Hello, Gina?"

It was Gino. "Sorry, I know you were maybe expecting Gina to call you back. She had to go out. Your flight leaves the mainland at four. Hope that's okay. Tickets will be at the check-in counter. Gina and I will be there to pick you up at the airport."

He paused. "And thanks, Jessie, for agreeing to see Mama and me."

She had just enough time to grab some lunch and find Michael to let him know.

Michael waited with her until they called for boarding. He kissed her long and hard. She looked back to see him watching her board the plane. She was supposed to call him when she got there. He told her he would be waiting by the phone.

Maybe it was all his reassurances at the airport. Or maybe it was because she couldn't hold her eyes open any longer. Maybe it was the turkey sandwich and Nehi Grape she had at the deli. That combination called out to her after reading Josh's letters. She felt his presence on this trip. She closed her eyes and didn't open them until the stewardess came by to tell her to bring her seat forward and fasten her seatbelt. They were getting ready to land. The captain announced they would be circling until they received clearance. Jessie peered out the cabin window. She saw the Statue of Liberty and the big green gap amongst all the skyscrapers, Central Park. She thought she could even see the Park Avenue apartment building.

Her feet felt like lead as she disembarked from the plane. The first time, she thought she was going to a wedding. This time, she felt like she was going to a funeral. She came through her gate, and there was Gina, standing in front of Gino. She was glad to see her daughter's face first. They hugged like they hadn't seen each other in a long time. It was the hug she had expected from a happy bride-to-be the first time.

Gino had the same awkward stance, but their roles were reversed. Gino looked like he had been crying, while Gina looked fine.

"Are you both okay?" Jessie asked while kissing her daughter.

"Yes, Mom. Doing much better now."

"I'll get you back to the apartment to freshen up, and then maybe we can talk if that's okay," Gino said. He pulled a handkerchief from his pocket and wiped his nose. "A bit of congestion," he said.

It was dark out, and she was tired from the flight and the stress, but Jessie knew she wouldn't get any sleep until she found out what this was about. It wasn't exactly established where she would be sleeping, but she trusted it would work out. "Okay, that will be fine," she said.

"And, then we'll go see Mama tomorrow," he said.

Again, she agreed. She was too tired to do anything else but agree.

Gino picked up her luggage and hailed a taxi. They arrived at the front of the apartment. Dave had the usual big smile plastered across his face. "Dave, do you ever take a break from the door? Jessie asked. "You deserve one."

"So glad to have you back, ma'am," he said, like a programmed robot.

When they were in the apartment, Gino asked, "Do you want something to eat? Something to drink?"

"Maybe just water," Jessie said, although a stiff drink crossed her mind.

He took a glass and filled it up at the tap and handed it to her. He sat down on the sofa and reached for a cigarette, and then put it back down. "I'm sorry, habit. I know you don't like these. I won't smoke."

That was a first. Whatever was going on, it must be out of the ordinary. Everything lately had been out of the ordinary.

Gina yawned. "Well, I think I'll call it an early night and get to bed. Have to get that beauty sleep so I can put on my happy face tomorrow for Grandma."

"Good night, Gina. See you in the morning," Jessie said.

"Night, Mom. Night, Dad."

Gino just nodded. He then looked at Jessie. "So, do you want to get freshened up or anything? I thought we might take a walk."

"A walk?"

"Yeah, maybe you should get a hat. It's kind of chilly."

This was indeed strange. Gino being thoughtful? That was the least of it. Maybe he was going to propose again or something? Preposterous thought. *Just think of Michael. Whatever it is, thinking of him will get you through it.* Michael! Oh my, she had forgotten to call him.

"Gino, I have to make a call. Then we'll go for the walk. Can I have some privacy?"

Gino looked surprised. "Sure, I'll just step out on the balcony for a bit and have that smoke."

"Hello."

"Michael, I'm sorry. Maybe I should have called from the airport. But I'm back at the apartment now. The flight was uneventful, or so I guess. I slept through it."

"I'm so glad it went okay. I'm glad you were able to sleep. What apartment?"

"Gino's."

"Gino's? Should I be jealous?"

"No, Gina is living here, too. Gino wants to go for a walk. There is something he wants to talk about."

"Do you know what?"

"No, I don't have a clue."

"You'll be safe with him, won't you?"

"Yes, he would never do anything to physically hurt me. I'm pretty sure of that. He's never hit me."

"Okay, well, will you promise to call me after the walk? I don't care what time it is. I'll sleep by the phone."

"Okay, I promise."

"I'll let you go. The sooner you find out what this is all about, the better. I…, Well, good night, Jessie."

"Good night, Michael."

She hung up. Was he about to say those three words? She was pretty sure he was. She almost said them herself.

But the time needed to be right, and it needed to be in person. Maybe that's what he was thinking.

Well, better get this over with. "Gino." She tapped on the balcony door. "I'm ready."

They walked out of the building together. Dave wasn't at his post. Maybe he did take a break after all.

In Dave's absence, Gino waved for a taxi.

"I thought you wanted to walk," Jessie said.

They got in the back seat.

"I thought we would ride as far as Brooklyn, you know our old stomping ground. Is that okay?"

"Sure, I guess. So, what's all this mystery?"

"I just need to get some stuff off my chest," he said rather grimly. He did his best to summon up a smile. "So, what was the phone call all about? Are you seeing someone?"

"Actually, yes, I am."

"That's good. I'm happy for you."

"And you? Are you seeing someone?"

He looked at her surprised, "No."

"I meant a therapist."

"No, no therapist. You've always did have that dry sense of humor."

"It wasn't humor. I think maybe you should talk with a therapist. You keep wanting to talk to me. Maybe you should speak to a professional."

He let out a sigh that she, herself, had been famous for. "Driver, you can pull over here." They had stopped on the Manhattan side of Brooklyn Bridge. Gino paid the cab driver.

He and Jessie began to walk. He looked up. "No stars out tonight. Do you remember our first walk here?"

"How could I forget? Our wedding night. We walked all over Brooklyn that night."

"It wasn't all bad, was it, Jessie?"

"No, Gino, I can't say it was all entirely bad."

There were others out walking on the bridge, mostly young lovers. They remained silent for a good deal of the way. She thought Gino might stop in the middle where they could be off to themselves a little before he came out with whatever it was he was going to tell her. But he didn't. They just kept walking. She could tell he was trying to get his courage up.

They were nearing the end ramp. "Are you cold?"

"No," She lied. She feared he might try to put his arm around her or something. She remembered how he held her that night so long ago. That girl that he held back then just wasn't her anymore. Gino, of course, had changed too. At this point, she couldn't tell how he had changed. She just knew that things were somehow different with him.

They had walked until they were down by the river.

"Do you remember being here?" Gino asked.

"This is where we walked on our first night of marriage." She looked at Gino's expression for any signs of malevolence. Maybe he was going to throw her in the river, after all. Maybe he regretted not doing it that night. She told herself she was being melodramatic.

There was a couple in the distance. He wouldn't be so foolhardy around witnesses. No, she told herself, don't be absurd. His mother wanted to see her tomorrow. Gino wouldn't do anything to upset his mama. She suddenly felt so ridiculous. She was letting her imagination run wild.

She came to a dead stop. "Okay, Gino, whatever it is

you want to tell me, quit putting it off. Tell me now."

"Jessie." He paused, and looked down, and then looked back up at her, "Jessie?"

She had never felt so sorry for him in her entire life. He looked at her like a wounded puppy.

Tears started flowing down his cheeks. "I didn't mean for anything like that to happen. It should have been me."

"Gino, you're not clear. What do you mean it should have been you?"

"It should have been me, not Josh, that night."

She started to tremble. "I don't understand."

He started to touch her. She jerked away.

"Here, you're cold. Just take my coat," he said.

She complied, even though she knew her trembling wasn't from the chill.

"Explain what you mean, Gino."

"That night Josh got killed. There was no hit and run."

She started to feel faint.

Gino took her arm and led her over to a bench and sat her down. She didn't protest.

He continued, "Jessie, this is so hard, but I have to get it off my chest. Mama insisted. She said you had to know."

"Whatever this is, your mama knows?"

"She wanted me to see a priest. I refused. She even said to talk to Graham. I could never tell him anything like this."

Jessie tried to regain some composure, "Gino, please just tell me."

"I was with Josh that night. I had asked him to meet me at Grimaldi's. We were walking back home, and there was a gunshot. It came from a car."

Gino broke down. He got on his knees and cried like a baby. "Jessie, please forgive me. Oh, God, what have I done?"

If the couple was looking at them, she didn't know. If anyone else were around, she didn't know. This was some kind of nightmare. She felt isolated and alone. This couldn't be happening.

Gino tried to sober himself. "Jessie, it was a hit. It was meant for me. They didn't know that they had shot Josh instead."

Jessie felt as if the whole city was spinning around her. She felt as if she were going to pass out any moment. She so wished Michael were here now. She needed him so badly. Right now, Michael was a whole different world. Did he even exist? Did happiness even exist? Josh was so innocent. He didn't deserve this.

She could hear words coming from her mouth, but it was like someone else was speaking them. "Gino?" She could hear herself say Gino. It was like she was reaching out to him for comfort like on their wedding night. She felt like that young girl again. He was the only one here, the only one to reach out to. Yet, he was the reason for everything that was wrong, and she was clinging to him, to somehow make it all right. She didn't know why she was doing this.

She didn't feel hate. She didn't feel love. She didn't feel anything. She only questioned. Why. She wanted God to tell her why this was all happening.

Her voice was barely audible. "Gino, did he suffer?"

"No, he died instantly." It was a lie, but he had to say it. In her gut, she knew that.

The only person Jessie could think of was Clare. "I

need to see Clare." She knew they would be in bed, but it didn't matter.

"I'll get you there," Gino said.

He got a taxi and helped her into the car.

The driver asked, "Man, is she sick? Does she need to get to a hospital?"

Jessie felt her body go limp. She heard Gino give the taxi driver Clare's address, and could feel his arms around her as he held her up and then his touch as he laid her across the back seat of the cab. Her body lurched forward when the taxi came to a stop. The door opened, and she heard the lone echo of footsteps and a bang on a door. Then a porch light came on. In the distance she could make out part of the conversation.

"Gino, what is it?" It was Graham.

"Jessie's in the car. She needs Clare."

Then she could make out Clare's voice but couldn't hear what was said.

"I don't know. Something about Jessie. Gino's at the door. Get dressed." It was Graham again.

The next thing she knew, Graham was at the door of the taxi helping her out. Gino said, "Take care of her, please." The taxi door slammed shut and drove away.

Clare gasped, "Oh, my, Graham, what's wrong? She's so pale."

She held Jessie's hand and said, "Get some water. Get a cold washcloth."

Graham hurried. He handed the cloth to her. "Clare, maybe we should call an ambulance?"

"No, no," Jessie protested. Her voice sounded like a little child. "He murdered Josh."

"Jessie, slow down." Clare turned to Graham. "Help

me sit her head up a bit." Clare gave her the water. "Now, honey, tell us what you mean."

"Josh's death is Gino's fault. I always knew it was something like that. I didn't want to think about it. Now I know for sure."

Clare and Graham looked at each other. It wasn't a look of shock, just one of puzzlement.

Jessie tried to get up. She didn't know why. She didn't know what she wanted to do.

Clare put her arms around her. She rocked Jessie back and forth like she was a baby. Then Clare laid her head back down on the couch. She looked up at Graham. "You go back to bed. I'll sit up with her. Maybe she will fall asleep. Maybe she'll make more sense in the morning."

"Maybe we should call Gino to get to the bottom of this," Graham said.

Jessie tried to lift up again, but Clare gently pushed her back down. "Call? No, not him. I need to call Michael."

Once again, Clare and Graham looked at each other with the same puzzled expression. "Who's Michael?" Clare asked.

Jessie tried to speak, but couldn't muster the strength

"We'll both sit up with her. I'll put on some coffee," he said.

Jessie closed her eyes and drifted off to sleep.

CHAPTER 29

THE SUN peeking through the window and a heavy banging of a garbage truck outside caused Jessie to stir. She opened her eyes to see both Clare and Graham sitting by her side. She was trying to remember why she was there. The nightmare was coming back to her. She couldn't remember what was real and what wasn't. Tears started to flow down her cheeks.

"Jessie, are you able to sit up?" Clare asked.

Jessie nodded.

Graham went into the kitchen and brought out some chamomile tea. He handed her the cup and said, "Here, Jessie, try to drink this."

Jessie took a sip. Then she looked at Clare and Graham and said, "Josh is dead because of Gino's mafia connections. It wasn't a hit and run. It was all a lie. I just feel so numb, Clare. I don't know what to do."

Tears began to flow down Clare's cheeks as well, and she just held onto Jessie.

"What time is it? What day is it?" Jessie asked.

"It's 7:30 in the morning. It's Friday," Graham said.

"Oh, I have to call Michael. He'll be so worried."

"Okay, okay," Clare said, and Graham pulled the telephone and the cord over. Jessie dialed the number with shaking fingers.

Michael answered on the first ring. "Jessie, are you okay? I was just getting ready to book a flight. You didn't give me a number to reach you. I didn't know what to do."

"Michael." Then her voice just sort of trailed off.

Clare took the phone. "Michael, this is Clare." There was some silence. Then Clare said, "She has had a shock. She's just going to need some time."

Jessie heard Michael's muffled voice on the other end. Then Clare said, "Who are you? Obviously someone close to Jessie. She only just mentioned you last night. She kept saying she had to call you."

Again, she couldn't make out what Michael was saying.

Clare looked up at Graham and responded to Michael, "Oh, I see. Well, she is really going to need you now."

Michael was saying something else.

"No, not just yet," Clare said. "Give me your number and we'll call you back after Jessie is more coherent." She motioned for Graham to hand her a pencil and paper. She took down the number. "We'll call you back a little later, okay?"

She hung up the phone.

"Honey, I'm going to run you a nice hot bath. Then

we're going to have some breakfast. Don't worry I won't leave you," Clare said.

Graham left to run Jessie a bath.

Jessie finally got up, and with Clare's help, made her way to the bathroom. Clare helped her undress and get in the tub. Clare put the commode seat down and sat there while Jessie soaked. Jessie laid her head back on the rim of the cast iron tub and let out a heavy sigh.

"That's good, honey. Just let it out. Cry if you need to. Talk if you need to. I won't leave you. I spoke with Michael. He loves you. He is ready to come up at a moment's notice."

"No, no, I don't want him to come up. I want to get this over with and go back to the island. You heard what I said, didn't you, Clare?"

"Heard what, honey?"

"That Gino killed Josh."

"Jessie, you must be confused. Gino couldn't have killed his own son."

"He might as well have."

"Jessie, tell me what you mean."

"It was a mafia hit, Clare. The bullet was meant for Gino, but they killed Josh instead."

"Oh, honey! I don't know what to say."

"What could you say?"

"He wants your forgiveness Jessie, or he wouldn't have told you."

"How can I forgive him? If it were your son, could you forgive him?"

"I know, Jessie, but Josh was his son, too. There's nothing you can do about it now. The only thing you can think of was what would Josh want."

"Josh was so good, wasn't he?"

"Yes he was."

"I just read all of his letters from Korea last night, no the night before. I'm losing track of time. This is like him dying all over again. No, it's like me dying all over again."

"Let's get you out of the tub. You're turning into a prune." Clare handed her a towel, then a robe.

They came out of the bathroom. Graham pulled out a chair in the dining room and placed some toast and juice in front of her. "You need to eat something, Jessie."

She drank the juice and took a bite from the toast. She wanted to be on the beach in what warmth of the sun was left during this time of year. She wanted to forget this day had ever happened. She wished she hadn't come. But Michael said she needed closure. Closure was too painful.

"What do I do now, Clare?"

"You have to think about Gina. You have to forgive Gino and go on with your life. There is nothing you can do to bring Josh back. Gina is what matters now. She doesn't need to know this about her father now. You know that. Maybe she never needs to know. Take her out of New York, away from him, at least for now. Let time heal."

"She's going back to the island with me to spend Christmas."

"You have to pull yourself together. You have to be strong for her, Jessie. Maybe I don't have the right to say, but this is what being a mother is all about. By being strong for her, you're being strong for Josh."

Jessie knew she was right.

"Rosa, wants to see me."

"You don't have to see her if you don't want."

"She's leaving for Italy on Sunday. Maybe for good. I can't see Gino again. I can't ever face him again."

"Don't worry. You're staying here. I'll call Gina. We'll figure something out. Something that won't be a lie."

Jessie sat in silence.

"Do you still not want Michael to come?" Clare asked.

"Yes, Gina doesn't know about Michael."

"You two are getting married?"

"No, we just started going steady."

"Going steady? He said over the phone that he loved you and wanted to marry you. Going steady? Isn't that for young people?"

"I'm young, Clare." A smile broke across Jessie's lips. "Really? He said he loved me and wanted to marry me?"

"You didn't know? And how well do you know him?"

"I know I love him. We haven't said it yet."

"Well, don't let me spoil the surprise when he does tell you. I'm going to call Gina, and I'm going to ask her to come down with your clothes," Clare said.

"Okay."

"You're going to be all right, honey," Clare said with authority.

"Yes, it's just all been a bad dream."

CHAPTER 30

GINA ARRIVED a couple of hours later, bringing in her luggage. "Dad said you were feeling sick last night, so he brought you to Clare's. Are you feeling better?"

Jessie looked over at Clare and Graham. "Yes, sweetheart, I'm doing better."

"Mom, I don't think you've called me sweetheart since I was little."

"You'll always be a sweetheart."

"I'm going to start lunch," Clare said.

"I'm going to take my luggage into your spare bedroom and change out of your robe," Jessie said.

"I'll help you with lunch, Clare. So, is mom doing okay?" That was the last of the conversation Jessie heard as she shut the door behind her.

"Mom, are you feeling better now? Gina asked, when she reappeared. "Clare said you had an upset stomach." She rolled her eyes. "I told her that and Grandma."

"Gina, do you want to set the table for me?" Clare asked. "Jessie, I think you should be able to handle these mashed potatoes. Gina helped me make them. I'm putting on the teakettle for some peppermint tea."

"Clare, did I ever tell you that you are the greatest?" Jessie said.

"No, not in those exact words."

"Ditto, Clare. That goes for me, too," said Gina.

"I do remember that one time when you called me the wicked stepmother," Clare said.

"I did? I don't remember that."

"I asked you to dust for me, and you told me you were Cinderella and I was the wicked stepmother."

"I don't remember that."

"Do you remember me telling you about that, Jessie?"

"Oh, yes, I remember how we laughed over it."

"You were always play-acting," Clare said.

"You know I'm going to California."

"Yes, your mom told me. Maybe I'll see you in the movies one day."

"Maybe you will. Maybe I'll play Cinderella."

"Well, have a seat everyone," Graham said. After grace, he said, "So when are you going to the island, Gina?"

Gina looked at her mom. "I guess not too long after we see Grandma off. I've got to start packing."

"Do you want to leave Sunday?" Jessie asked.

"That soon?" Gina said.

"I really want to get back." Nervously, Jessie kept talking, trying to get her mind off the night before. "We've got to get a tree and decorate for Christmas. And, I've been helping with some of the carpentry work."

"You? Carpentry work?" Gina asked, baffled.

"Helped put on a roof. I didn't tell you I'm putting a skylight in?"

"Are YOU putting it in?" Gina asked.

"I'll probably help. You know, it keeps the labor costs down."

Graham and Clare looked at each other. Jessie noticed their concern. "You two, I'm really feeling better."

"Is the island getting back to normal?" Graham asked.

"It's getting there. There will still be plenty of stuff to do come spring. The pier has to be entirely rebuilt, and the boardwalk, as well." Jessie said, "I have this incredible idea." She paused. "Graham, why don't you and Clare come to the island for Christmas? I have one spare room. Gina and I can double up in my room." She winked at her. "Under the new skylight."

"The one you're putting in? I hope we don't get rained on." Gina teased.

That brought a laugh to everyone, including Jessie. Clare reached under the table and squeezed Jessie's hand.

"Clare, Graham, you haven't answered. I'll buy the plane tickets." She thought about Gino paying for this trip and almost lost the enthusiasm she was trying to muster for Gina's sake. She didn't want to ever think about Gino again.

"Yes, Clare, Graham," Gina pleaded. "You've always said you were going to come to the island but never have.

Now is as good a time as any. Graham, Mom could use your help with that skylight. I know you've done your fair share of church renovations. You'll help us out, right? Please, I don't want to sleep under a leaking skylight."

Graham protested, "We have all the Christmas activities at the church. How could we just leave those?"

"You have an assistant pastor now," Clare said. "Let him spread his wings a little. I think we should do it. We haven't had a vacation in, well, I can't remember when we've had one, and we're not getting any younger." Jessie noticed the stern look that Clare gave Graham. She knew she had won the argument.

Graham hesitated before starting to protest more, but Clare headed him off. "Jessie needs us."

"Mom needs you?" Gina said in surprise.

"For all that carpentry work," Clare added.

Graham looked down at his mashed potatoes in defeat and then raised his head and smiled. "Okay, by gosh, we'll do it."

"That's great," Gina exclaimed. "I'm so excited. Let me clear and wash the dishes. Then I've got to be off so I can start packing before seeing Grandma tonight."

"Gina, you don't mind if I don't go to see your Grandma?"

"It's fine, Mom. Clare already said when you were in the bedroom that you would see her in the morning."

Jessie gave Clare a look of appreciation.

When Gina went to the kitchen and wasn't in earshot, Clare leaned over to Jessie."We'll sleep on it and work it out in the morning."

A little while later, Gina came into the living room where they were sitting and kissed everyone, saying her goodbyes.

After Gina was out the door, Clare said, "You need to call Michael. The poor man is frantic. Graham, we've got packing to do. Let's give her some privacy."

Jessie dialed the number. Her hands were less shaky.

"Michael?"

"Jessie, are you all right?"

"I'm better now."

"Do you want to talk about it?"

"Not on the phone. So much has happened. I'll tell you when we get back."

"You and Gina?"

"Me, Gina, Clare and Graham. You don't mind do you?"

"Why should I mind? I would love to meet Clare and Graham, and especially Gina."

"Gina doesn't know about you yet. I think maybe I need to break it to her slowly. After all, she just got jilted."

"Jessie, however you want to do it. I'll wait forever if need be."

"I didn't know that going steady was a wait forever thing."

Michael laughed. "Maybe it's more than going steady." Jessie felt a funny feeling in her stomach. It was a new sensation. Maybe it was those butterflies that she had read about.

"Michael, thank you for being there for me."

"I wish I would have come with you now."

"This is something I needed to do myself, well, myself, Clare, Graham, and Gina. I've kept you from saving the island for too long, with all that waiting by the phone you've been doing. You need to get back to it."

"I'll see you soon, Jessie."
"I hope in no time."

CHAPTER 31

JESSIE RESTED and tried to get her mind on more pleasant things. Graham was spending time at the church, and Jessie could tell that Clare wasn't going to go too far away from her. She didn't know what she would have done without her, to be honest. She might have just jumped into the river if she had been left on her own.

She was doing her best to stay strong for Gina. There was a part of her that wanted to cry, but if she started, she would never stop. There was a part of her that was dead, just when she was starting life anew. She had to make a decision. She had to face forward for Gina, for Michael.

She would come up with some reason tomorrow for not seeing Rosa before she left. There was no way she could ever face Gino again.

On Sunday, after Gino and Rosa's departure, she would feel safer. They could all sit down and make plans for Christmas. Christmas was two weeks away. Normally, the island would be full of decorations. Not one light had been lit when she had left. There would be no garland-covered picket fences this year. Jessie would take on the project of making the island festive. It would be her mission. If not this year, next year. It would be in remembrance of Josh. He loved Christmas.

She would single-handedly make sure the island was decorated. No, what was she thinking, not single-handedly, but with the help of Gina, Clare, Graham, Amy, Jackson and Michael, and maybe even Myrtle. Maybe even the kids doing the laundry could help. She was beginning to feel a part of something. She was beginning to think of herself as one of the locals.

Maybe she could buy the decorations herself. Blow the rest of her money. She still had Aunt Agatha's money to fall back on. These were all positive thoughts. She had to keep thinking positive thoughts. Never again would she have Gino thoughts. Maybe she would resume therapy.

There was a knock at the door. She heard Clare say, "Rosa!" There was a pause. Jessie's heart pounded. She cracked the door. "I don't think Jessie is in any shape to see you," Clare said.

Why is Rosa here? What in the world? Jessie felt herself crumbling again.

"Clare, I'm not leaving until I see her. I'm not budging. She has to come out sometime. I won't go back to the old country until I talk to her," Rosa said.

Jessie held her ear tightly to the narrow slit of the bedroom door. What could she do? All her positive thoughts had been replaced with panic and dread. Where was Gina? More importantly, where was Gino? Clare would never let Gino in. She would call the police first. Jessie was sure of it. A lot of good that would do. He and his friends owned the police. They did the night Josh was shot.

Clare was pushing against the door. "Jessie, let me in."

Jessie cracked the door.

"You heard?" Clare asked.

"Yes, I heard."

"I'm going to call Graham at the church and have him come back over. We are going to be here for you. We won't leave your side. Just let her say what she has to say. I don't think she means you harm. She has tears in her eyes."

Jessie looked at Clare in desperation. "You won't leave me? And Graham won't either?"

"I promise for both of us."

She went back in to call Graham. When Graham arrived, Jessie came into the living room.

"Jessica, I want your forgiveness before I go to Italy," Rosa said with woeful eyes. "I know I haven't made life easy for you. And, I know how hard it was with Gino. Please remember Joshua was my grandson. I loved him."

Jessie broke down and began crying. The world was spinning around again. Would this nightmare ever end? Clare held onto her.

"Where is Gino?" Jessie asked. "He's not here, is he?"

"No, no, I know you don't ever need to see him again. I don't think you should ever see him again, at all. Bella brought me. She's outside in the car. I wanted to talk to you alone."

Jessie summoned courage and said, "Clare and Graham are staying. You will have to say whatever you have to say in front of them."

"Okay, I guess it's all right. I insisted that Gino tell you about that night. I've always said he should tell you."

"How long have you known?"

"The day after it happened."

"Maybe you should have told me."

"Maybe I should have, but I'm a mother first. You see, Jessica, I love my son, maybe too much if a mother can love a child too much. I turned a blind eye when it came to him.

"Gino is the reason we came to this country. We had a good life back home. There was no reason to leave. We uprooted the entire family at my insistence because of him. His father argued that we had other children, and they shouldn't be made to suffer for Gino. His father said 'no, absolutely not,' but I wouldn't let it rest night or day until he finally gave in.

"I'm afraid he kind of became a broken man after that. But he has made a life here now and doesn't choose to go back with me. He said he left the old country behind long ago. I knew he wouldn't go. That is why Gino is taking me. But, really, I had an ulterior motive in asking Gino. Maybe I can talk Gino into staying in Italy, at least until I die. He doesn't need to be around Gina either. I know about the wedding, too. Maybe he did a good thing there.

"Jessica, Jessie, I'm asking you to forgive him. The night Joshua got killed, Gino was trying to do something good. He wanted him to be a doctor so badly, but he knew it wasn't what Joshua wanted. He was meeting with him that night to tell him to give it up and do what he wanted. He only wanted Joshua to be happy. It all went so terribly wrong.

"You have to understand and forgive Gino. I'm asking you as one mother to another. Gino had it so hard before. There are reasons he is the way he is. I know your marriage wasn't the way it was supposed to be. I was so happy when you became pregnant. It gave me hope. I thought maybe Gino had turned around, at least in that respect. His father and I knew he was odd from when he was a child. His father would have shunned him, but a mother can't stop loving her son, no matter what.

"The way he was may have been the reason, or it may not have, but Gino kept getting into trouble. The police came to our door more than once. He was always in hiding and always up to no good. He would be with older men who would take him in. They were racketeers and who knows what else. Well, God only knows what they were doing to him.

"Then one night he got beaten up to the point that he was near death. He was found in a ditch. He couldn't even say his name. A passerby was kind enough to load him in his wagon and take him to a doctor in another village. He stayed there with the doctor.

"We didn't know where he was. I was frantic. His father said maybe it was for the best.

"The doctor saved his life. He was kind to Gino and let him stay there with him. Gino wanted to be like the doctor after that. He tried to learn but working with the sick just wasn't in him. He never forgot what that doctor did for him. You see why he wanted Joshua to become a doctor? He wanted his son to make up for what he thought were his own failures. Joshua was good, like the doctor man. Gino saw that in him.

"Gino came back home. I was so happy to see him. His father wasn't. It wasn't long until Gino began getting into trouble again. The same men were always after him, always using him. When it wasn't them, it was the police. There was nowhere left to hide.

"That is when we came to America. I thought Gino could have a fresh start. But working at the docks wasn't good enough for him. He always had to prove himself. He ended up repeating the same mistakes over here. I guess he was drawn to what he knew best. I knew he was mainly marrying you to cover up things, to make himself more legitimate.

"I thought maybe if he married an Italian girl we could have kept it in the family. I didn't think an English girl coming from wealth could adapt to Gino. Believe it or not, I felt sorry for you. I knew Gino could never change, even though you had children. I saw that after a while.

"Jessie, please forgive me. I feel I am to blame for Gino. I don't know what I could have done differently with him." Rosa broke down, her head was down and turned away from Jessie's face.

Jessie walked over to Rosa. She extended her hand towards Rosa's shoulder but pulled away. A physical touch was just too much for her. "I don't know what to say. I just feel numb at this point. Maybe if I had known all this from the beginning, things could have been different. Just too many lies. How can a relationship be based on lies?"

She looked over at Clare and thought of her abortion. She could easily forgive Clare. Maybe she could forgive Rosa. Maybe she could forgive herself for turning a blind eye herself to Gino and not speaking up. At least Rosa spoke up out of love for her son.

Jessie saw how fragile Rosa really was, not unlike herself. "I don't know what to think at this point. Maybe in time I will understand it all. Maybe in time we will all understand."

"That's all I have a right to ask, Jessie. I hope you can find happiness. Now, I'm going to sit by Joshua's grave and ask for his forgiveness as well," Rosa said.

With that, she said goodbye.

The next day was rather sober for Jessie and Clare. They merely sat drinking herbal tea and rested. When Jessie spoke, it was about Michael. When she wasn't talking about Michael, she was writing in her journal. Somehow, putting everything on paper helped.

While Gina was at the airport seeing her father and Rosa off, Jessie spent the time at the cemetery sitting by Joshua's grave. She wasn't even trying to make sense of it. Only God could make sense of it all. She didn't want to blame anyone, including herself. She just wanted to sit silently at his grave. She placed roses from Clare's rose bushes on his grave and kissed the ground.

"Josh, it's time I tried to move on. I hope you are now free from this world and happy. I know in my heart that you are. You took everyone and saw the good in them. You didn't judge. You were just too good for this world. It's the rest of us that are such a mess."

She went back to Clare and Graham's. She was now ready to make plans for their trip to the island.

CHAPTER 32

AFTER GINA had returned back to Clare's, they decided that they would leave the next day for the island. Clare and Graham would finish things up at the Church and come down the day before Christmas Eve.

Jessie thought it just as well, as it would give Gina and her time to make the cottage festive and get everything ready for them.

While they were on the plane, Jessie brought up Michael. She talked about him to Gina as if he were just a friend, someone her own age.

After a while, Gina said, "Mom if he is more than just a friend, I don't mind. In fact, I'm happy for you. You need someone in your life right now."

"Thank you, Gina. Well, he has become more than a friend. But we haven't…."

"Mom, just keep that to yourself."

"We're just going steady at this point."

Gina gave her a motherly look, "Okay, Mom. When is that stewardess going to serve beverages? I need something more than Coke."

"So, Gina, what kind of decorations for the cottage do you have in mind?" she asked, changing the subject.

When they disembarked from the plane, Michael and Amy were waiting at the airport. Michael reached for Jessie's hand, clasping it tightly. Otherwise, he restrained himself. "We are so glad to see you back safe and sound."

Jessie laughed. "She knows. It's okay."

Michael kissed her passionately.

"Hi, Gina, I'm Amy. I've heard so much about you."

"Likewise."

Amy whispered to Gina, but not in such a low voice that everyone couldn't hear. "I think we might be sisters soon."

Gina looked back at her mom and Michael. "Looks like it."

They worked the entire week getting the island as cleaned up and decorated as possible. Jessie wanted to contribute decorations to go along the white picket fences, but that would have to wait until next year. There were no picket fences left to decorate. There was no boardwalk to decorate either. Getting the island back into shape wasn't going to be quick. Michael and Jackson kept busy on the construction end. Myrtle was busy keeping the bookstore going. Gina and Amy were combining forces in keeping up spirits. Both Jessie and Michael were pleased to see Amy and Gina hitting it off so well.

She and Michael hadn't talked about any future plans. She didn't even know how much longer Michael could stay away from his business in Long Island. If they did have a future together, she didn't want to live in New York anymore. There were just too many memories there. She was content to spend the rest of her days on the island, even if she had to spend them alone or in a long distance relationship. She would become a yoga spinster, reading spiritual books, and meditating on the beach. Besides, Michael hadn't even said those three words to her yet.

Clare and Graham would be arriving the day after tomorrow. Clare told her that Michael loved her and wanted to marry her. She hoped Clare hadn't told her that because of the condition she was in at the time. No, she knew Clare wouldn't lie to her.

She hadn't seen Michael all that much since they had returned. Maybe he was rethinking things. Maybe she just had too much baggage. She couldn't blame him. He would have to be getting back to his construction business soon. The only thing she knew to do was to keep busy and enjoy being with Gina while she had her here with her. Michael could be keeping a little distance to give her time with Gina.

Jessie hadn't even bought Michael a Christmas gift. She hadn't done any Christmas shopping at all. She wanted to keep gifts simple, though. She had been spending a lot lately, with both trips to New York. After the New Year, she needed to check on what Aunt Agatha had left her and get it all straightened out. Whether she went to England or not, she had to tend to the matter, one way or another.

That afternoon, she did see Michael. Amy came by, also. Michael suggested that Gina, Amy, and she go out shopping on the mainland. He said they needed a break from all the work they had been doing on the island. Jessie was surprised that he didn't suggest just Amy and Gina go so he might spend time with her. She tried not to be too hurt. Both Gina and Amy thought it was a great idea. Reluctantly, Jessie joined the majority and said okay. After all, she did need to buy Christmas presents, and she was running out of time. She didn't have a clue what to get for Michael.

Their first stop was 'Follow Your Dream'. Angela asked when she and Amy would start the yoga class. Jessie assured her after the New Year they would. She thought Michael would have to go back to Long Island by then and what else would she have to do?

Jessie picked out a tea set for Clare and Graham, and she got Amy a new yoga mat. For Gina, there was her mother's locket. She still didn't have a clue about what to get Michael, and then she thought about Jackson's work in the garage. She asked Amy if Michael knew about Jackson's hobby. Amy said no. Jessie thought that would be perfect, and Amy agreed. There was the shop on the mainland that sold his work.

Jessie picked out a wooden clock with the workings exposed. How could Michael not like it? It was a little expensive but not too exorbitant. It was a gift that said 'we're serious, more than just going steady'. She knew Michael wasn't charging her for all the labor on her cottage. In fact, he was giving all the labor on the island away at this point. If she were overstepping their relationship boundary, then she would just scratch it up to saying it was more than Christmas. It was a thank-you.

They grabbed some dinner, and then, it was time to catch the last ferry back. When they got back to the island,

Amy insisted that Gina spend the night with her. She said they wanted to have a good old-fashioned girl's pajama party and wrap their presents in secret. Jessie remembered back to her days at boarding school and about her coming out party, which was her last pajama party. How could she protest?

Jessie noticed a glow coming from her cottage. It was the Christmas tree. She had forgotten to unplug it. She was so glad the cottage was still standing. She didn't need it burning down after having fixed the roof. The roof was only fixed in part, though. A tarp was still placed where the skylight was to go.

As usual, Jessie entered through the back door. She heard a pop and crack as she laid her bags on the kitchen table. She walked into the living room to see a fire in the fireplace in addition to the Christmas tree being all lit up. Michael was sitting on the couch, a glass of wine in his hand. "I hope you don't mind that I let myself in." He handed her a glass. "Have some wine? I know you're not a drinker, and neither am I. But tonight is a special occasion."

"It is?"

"It's a surprise."

Lately she had nothing but bad surprises, but this one looked to be different, which was a good thing. "Maybe I will have some wine."

"What shall we drink to?"

She thought of that perfect fantasy world she had envisioned. That was unrealistic.

"We'll drink to a new beginning," she said.

They brought their glasses together. "A new beginning for the island and especially a new beginning for us,"

Michael concurred. "Now, I want to show you your surprise."

A diamond ring was her first thought. No, he wouldn't propose this fast. But Clare said he wanted to marry her.

He led her into the bedroom, pointing to the ceiling.

"The stars! They're beautiful. This is my surprise?"

"This is the surprise."

"I thought the skylight wasn't going to come in for another week."

"I totally harassed them. I wanted it so badly for you. Today's shopping was a setup."

She tensed.

"Oh, oh, sorry, bad word. It was something that Amy, Gina, Jackson and I were in on. We wanted to get you away long enough so we could get it in."

"And what about Amy and Gina spending the night together?"

"Also planned. I hope you don't mind."

"No, I don't. Neither do the laundromat ladies."

"The laundromat ladies? That's the second time I've heard you mention them."

"I'll explain later."

There they stood, in the bedroom, beneath the stars. Before she knew it, she was making the first move. Maybe it was the wine. It was the only move she knew. She simply kissed him. He kissed back long and hard and started undressing her. He stopped abruptly and asked, "This is okay?"

"Yes, this is okay."

"I want to warn you. I'm really rusty."

"You couldn't be any rustier than me."

The next morning, she awoke to a man holding her

and to sunlight above her, hearing the roar of the ocean outside. He said, "Good Morning. I wanted to wake up before you and serve you breakfast in bed, but after last night, well, I slept well. How did you sleep?" he asked.

"Better than well."

"Don't move a muscle, and I'll be right back."

She heard cabinet doors opening and closing and smelled coffee brewing. Then, the teakettle whistled. A little while later, he brought in coffee, tea, and some toast with jelly. He apologized. "I'm sorry it isn't more elaborate. This was all I could find. I would have planned ahead if I had known I was spending the night."

"Really? You hadn't planned on spending the night?"

"Really, no. I planned, well…"

She picked up a piece of toast and let out a slight squeal.

"That is what I planned." He smiled. "But I didn't mean for it to scare you. I hope that isn't a no."

"No, I mean, yes!"

"I didn't know your size. We can get it resized."

"It's beautiful." She hugged him and began to cry.

"I also didn't mean to make you cry."

"It's just this is all so beautiful, the way you proposed. And this is a good cry. I've needed a good cry for so long."

"And now we can say we are engaged and drop the going steady thing."

"Yes, I think both Gina and Amy thought it was kind of ridiculous. Did they know, about this, the ring?"

"No, and I hope they don't scream, too."

"Amy might scream. Gina will take it all in stride."

CHAPTER 33

GINA AND Amy were elated at the news. Jessie and Michael were acting like teenagers and admitted it. Gina and Amy, a bit embarrassed, agreed.

Gina and Amy stayed behind to fix dinner for everyone while Michael and Jessie went to the airport to pick up Clare and Graham. They were using Myrtle's car. "I will have to drive my car down, and I will have to sell my house in Long Island," he said.

"You don't plan for us to live in New York?" she said, both surprised and relieved.

"We have a lot to discuss," he said.

And discuss, they did. They used the trip, the ride on the ferry, and the time waiting at the airport to do nothing but discuss their future plans.

Michael had another surprise for her. He announced

that he was selling out his part of the construction business. Over the last few days when she hadn't seen him, he had been on the phone working out a deal with his construction partner. He wanted to start fresh on the mainland if she didn't mind. Of course, she didn't.

Michael said maybe soon Jackson would be his new partner, but he would wait until he and Amy finalized their plans. Amy still had to finish college. He didn't usually interfere since she was technically an adult, but he was going to insist on it or at least strongly suggest it.

Jessie agreed that Amy should finish college. "But maybe she could transfer from Columbia. Maybe she could go out to California with Gina and find a college out there if that is what she wants."

"Maybe she would go for that. Either way, she is going to be away from Jackson. I have a feeling that Jackson is the deciding factor in this whole scenario."

"Yes, you're right. But you will be keeping Jackson plenty busy starting up a new business here."

"That's true."

"Michael, you're giving up so much for me. I mean, you're totally uprooting and moving, selling your business and starting over."

"I'm doing it for me as well. I'm doing it for us. There is no you and me anymore."

That sounded good to Jessie.

"I love the island, too," Michael continued. "And, my mother is here. She is getting up in years. It will be good if I am close to her."

Michael told her the city fathers and mothers had already assured him he would have the job of rebuilding the pier and the boardwalk. He had already talked with the real estate agency that owned the demolished cottages by the pier. That reconstruction deal looked like it was going through, as well.

He told her it might be a little rocky at first, restarting a business, but Jessie said she didn't mind. She told him about her trust and how it was running out. She also told him about Aunt Agatha and that she still had money to fall back on, but whatever it was, Gina was to get half. She wanted Gina to have a good start in California. She would take the half she had planned on giving Josh. She told Michael that whatever she had was his, too. "As you said, it is us now. So it is ours, not mine."

He assured her he wasn't destitute. Construction on Long Island was extremely profitable. He just wanted to let her know unless big hotels started building on the island, this wasn't going to be anything like his Long Island business. He and his partner had been building mansions up there. He was ready for something more laid back and relaxed. There was something he admired about Jackson's outlook on life. He added, even if hotels might be good for his business, he didn't want that. He didn't wish to see the island change the way Long Island had. Michael said, "I know it will eventually happen. Everything is building up so."

They were on the cusp of 1960. Everything was changing. They talked about how people might be scared because of the storm. The tourists might not come back for the summer, but they concluded that people loved the ocean too much and would take the risk. After all, it wasn't a full-blown hurricane, and nothing like that had happened for as long as they could remember. Jessie told him what her Aunt Agatha had said after crossing the ocean the year after the Titanic sunk. *Lightning doesn't strike twice in the same place.*

"We have to set a date. And, where do you want to go on for our honeymoon? The mountains, maybe?" he asked.

"I'll let you set the date." Before even giving it any thought, she blurted out. "I want to go to England."

"England! I'll have to get a passport."

"Me too. So, it's okay if we go to England?"

"I would love to see where you grew up."

"That's what I want to see. I don't even know if it's still there."

"New Year's Day," Michael said.

"What?"

"That's the date I want to get married."

"That soon?"

"Why should we wait?"

She thought for a moment and said, "It's a good idea because everyone would be here, Gina, Amy, Myrtle, Jackson, Clare, and Graham. Graham could marry us. That would be good. We shouldn't wait."

Michael hugged her. "That's what I was thinking. See, we've already started finishing each other's thoughts, like an old married couple."

"We are going to have to rush those passports," she exclaimed. After a pause, she said, "Michael, you can say no, but what if we take everyone on the honeymoon, well, the girls and Clare and Graham. I would love for Gina to see my original country. Clare has always talked about going back but never did. I don't know if they would go for it, but we could ask.

"Gina was planning on going to California, but she

can wait a little while. We can settle up my inheritance from Aunt Agatha. Surely, my part would be enough to pay for the trip."

"Jessie, how rich was your Aunt Agatha? I hope you don't think I'm marrying you for your money."

"Well, you're selling your business and moving to the island to be with me. No, I don't think you are marrying me for money. You're giving up a lot."

"No, I'm not giving up anything. I'm gaining."

"Aunt Agatha wasn't as rich as my father was but maybe half I'm guessing."

"And you've lived off of your father's estate for thirty years? And, your Aunt Agatha's money, half of your father's, has set in a bank for thirty years accruing interest? I think you might be surprised. But even if it's not a great fortune, we'll make it just fine. I'm not worried."

"I'm not either. We could start a shop like yoga couple."

"Who?"

"I'll tell you later. Look! Clare, Graham!" Jessie grabbed them both as if she hadn't seen them in ages, instead of just a few days ago. "Clare, Graham, meet Michael."

Clare took hold of Jessie's hand as they walked to the baggage claim. "What is this?" She held Jessie's hand, admiring the stone.

"What does it look like? We have a lot to tell you."

"I'm sure you do. I'm so glad to see you smiling."

"The island can do that for you, Clare."

"It's more than the island, Jessie."

"You're right. I have the most important people with me now, Gina, Michael, Amy, you and Graham. It's going to be a Merry Christmas."

On Christmas morning, they opened their presents. Clare and Graham loved their teapot and cup set. They in turn had brought Jessie and Michael a collection of gourmet teas and coffees from New York.

Michael marveled at the clock. "Jackson, you made this? And I was having you nail down shingles. I'm going to have you draw up plans for those new cottages. You could come up with a better boardwalk with gas lamps, something to give the island lots of charm."

Amy opened hers. "Can always use a yoga mat." She handed Jessie her present, "A yoga mat! I guess I can't get out of those yoga classes now."

Gina opened hers from Amy, "I think I'll be joining you." She laughed.

Jessie had gotten Jackson a beautiful set of chisels. "Jessie, I love them."

Michael handed Jessie her present. "Whoa." She almost dropped it. "It's heavy. What is it?"

"Open it!"

"Yes, Mom, open it."

"A typewriter? What do I do with a typewriter? Manage your accounts?"

"No, silly. It's for that novel you're writing."

"Who said I was writing a novel? What do I have to write about?"

Michael held up her bulging journal.

"Wow, Mom, you filled that up quick. I'm glad." Gina handed her a package.

Jessie opened it. "A stack of journals. Thank you, sweetheart. Looks like I'm going to be doing a lot of writing."

At this point, Jessie handed Gina her gift.

"Mom, this was your mom? My grandmother?"

"Yes."

"I'll treasure it," Gina said.

"It will bring you good luck in California."

"Last but not least, Myrtle, this gift is from both Jackson and myself." Jessie got something a little large from her bedroom and set it down.

"What could I use that is so big?" Myrtle asked.

"Just unwrap it, Mom," Michael said.

The sign said, "Myrtle's Tea and Book Nook."

"Jackson contributed the woodworking skills, of course," Jessie said.

"I guess I'm going to have to expand now, and I'm depending on my new daughter-in-law for guidance," Myrtle said smiling.

"I don't think she'll settle for anything less than partner." Michael laughed.

"I thought maybe you might want to add a little café corner with a few tables and comfortable chairs. You could serve tea, coffee, maybe some pastries, good ones, like the ones back in New York. You have the construction guys right here to make it work. I know what makes for a good café. I frequented them enough in New York. So, yes, it could be a joint venture if you want. I'm ready to sink some money into it. What do you think?" Jessie asked.

Myrtle paused, and then said, "I think I like the idea. The only spot for expansion would be on the back wall where Walter's urn is, but if I took it down for a while, I'm sure he wouldn't mind. We could drape heavy plastic over the work area so the bookstore wouldn't be too disturbed during business hours."

Jessie hugged her.

"Now, Jessie and I have an announcement to make," Michael said. "Actually, we have several announcements and some important questions for you. We've set a date, New Year's Day. We wanted to start the New Year out right, and what better way than to promise our love than in front of all of you."

"And, Graham, we want you to marry us," Jessie said.

"Mom, let Amy and I take care of the arrangements." Gina looked over at Amy, who showed total agreement. "Don't worry. We will keep it simple. I think the ceremony should be on the beach where Josh and I used to play. What do you think?"

Jessie looked over at Michael. They both agreed in unison.

"Now for the other news," Jessie said. "We haven't made the arrangements yet, but we want to spend our honeymoon in England. We want to take you, Amy and Clare and Graham with us. Gina, you can put off going to California for just a bit can't you?"

"Mom, it sounds like a great idea, the England trip, and yes, I would love to go, but wouldn't your honeymoon be a little bit crowded?"

"No, Michael and I both agree we want you to go," Jessie said.

Clare and Graham had been quiet the whole time.

Jessie looked at them, "Clare, Graham?"

Clare looked at Graham, "Graham, we never had a honeymoon of our own, and how often have I talked about going back?" She looked at Jessie. "How long would we be gone?"

"A couple of weeks."

Clare stared at Graham intently, ready to plead, but it wasn't necessary. "

Graham kissed her and looked at everyone. "We'll do it. It's never too late for a honeymoon. I must be getting soft in my old age."

"Now that that's all settled, shall we start dinner?" Myrtle asked.

After Christmas, it was rush, rush, rush. They all carried out different tasks. Gina and Amy dove right in as wedding planners.

They found the most beautiful dress for Jessie on the mainland. It was simple but elegant and perfect for the beach. Jessie loved it, and it was a perfect fit.

While there, they took care of the airline tickets and reservations. They made sure everyone had everything that was needed for passports. It was a bit stressful as much more maneuvering was needed in order to get them processed during the holidays. Luckily, it worked out. Everything would be picked up on the day of the flight, the morning after the wedding. Everyone would be staying at Myrtle's on the night of the wedding to give Michael and Jessie a proper honeymoon night in the cottage. The calendar indicated a full moon on the wedding night.

"If we are lucky, it will be visible through the skylight," Michael said.

"That would be auspicious," Jessie added.

The day of the wedding came, and almost the whole island turned out. Jessie wished Carl could have been there. There had been plenty of weddings on the island. This one being on the first day of 1960 after the storm would be one that would go down in history. Gina was maid of honor, and Amy was the bridesmaid. Jackson stood in as best man for Michael. There was a thunderous applause as Graham said, "I now pronounce you man and wife. You may kiss the bride."

They retreated to the cottage, and when they finally came out late the next morning, everyone was quietly waiting outside with their luggage. Jackson was in his pickup truck. He would take Gina and Amy. Myrtle was there with her car to take Michael, Jessie, Clare and Graham. They all squeezed in the vehicles and were off to the airport for Merry Old England.

After a night at their hotel, they rented two cars in England. Michael and Jessie drove up ahead, and the rest followed. They went slowly up a paved road taking in the countryside. Some of the old cobblestone showed through the pavement.

Jessie peered out the window, which she had rolled down to get a better view. "I know this must be it. It looks so familiar."

"Well, these are the directions we were given at the pub," Michael said.

"I remember now. I remember that barn and riding my bicycle past it," Jessie said.

They continued on. Traces of snow dotted the ground, giving the land a pristine look, like something one would see on a postcard. They passed sheep in one field, cows in another.

Jessie pointed. "There's the caretaker's cottage."

They came around a sharp curve and over a slight hill. There stood the house.

"That's it. That's my house, or the house I grew up in."

"Wow, it's huge. I would call that a mansion, not a house," Michael said.

"It's smaller than I remember," Jessie commented.

Michael raised an eyebrow looking at her. "Surely, you're joking."

"You know how everything looks bigger when you're small."

Both cars bounced on the circular drive which had remained cobblestone. As they got out of the cars, a man walked around from the back, a beagle hound shadowing him. He called out, "And who might you all be?"

Jessie walked ahead, rather sure of herself. "I used to live here, long ago. I've been in America. I just wanted to come back and see the home of my youth."

The man gave her a once over and then exclaimed, "Jessica, is that you."

"Yes, do we know each other?"

"I'm Jimmy. My father was the caretaker before me. I was a bit older but remember you. You rode your bicycle all over these roads."

"Jimmy!" She hugged him. "Jimmy, I want you to meet my husband, and these are our daughters. And, this is Clare and her husband, Graham. Clare was here too, during the last year I was here."

"You wouldn't remember me," Clare said. "I worked in the house. My goodness, this place sure brings back memories."

"Jimmy, can we look around?" Jessie asked.

"Sure, you obviously came a long way. The owners are away. They went to a warmer climate for the winter. I know they wouldn't mind. You can go inside and even look around and get warm."

Jessie showed them where her father's study was. The bookcases were still there, but everything else had changed. "And, this was my bedroom," she told Michael. "I remember looking out the window on gray days. We had plenty of those here. You see that tree. It was much smaller."

Clare showed Graham the spots she remembered.

Gina was in awe, and considering it was hard to impress Gina, Jessie was pleased. The whole estate floored Michael, Amy, and Graham. Jessie reminded them that it had once been a much bigger operation. Jimmy explained how most of the land had been sold off. Various farmers now owned all the farms they had seen on the drive up.

They walked out to where the garden had been. Her swing was still there, covered in a thin layer of snow. Jimmy said he had kept it in good repair. Both owners had children, and they liked to play here. The house had gone through two different families since Jessie and Clare had left.

They walked past a shed in back of the house. Jessie looked in and stopped dead in her tracks upon seeing something rusty propped up against the inside wall. Jessie had been holding Michael's hand on the whole tour, dragging him along to wherever she chose to go next. He relived her memories with her. She let go of Michael's hand and ran towards the object she spied in the shed. Michael followed. Jessie placed both her hands on the handlebars of the old bicycle.

"This is vintage and still in decent shape," Michael

said as he enthusiastically explored the components of the bicycle while Jessie held it up. "Can't be ridden now, but it could be fixed easily enough."

Jessie, after some time, laid it back against the wall. "She was an old friend."

She thanked Jimmy and hugged him again.

A week after they returned, Gina left for California. Clare and Graham had said their goodbyes in New York at the airport, the first stop on the way back from England. Michael and Jackson were busy on the mainland starting the new construction firm. Jessie, Amy, and Myrtle were busy drawing up plans for how they wanted the new section of the bookstore to be. They hoped to be open for business before the tourist season.

Amy was going to begin the school year in the fall at Berkley, in California. She and Jackson would become engaged before she left. Michael was right in his predictions of Aunt Agatha's estate. She had left a tidy little sum, nothing to be laughed at.

A month after they had returned from England, Michael returned home after work in the company pickup truck. "Jessie, come out to the front of the cottage. There is something I want you to see." He lifted her old bicycle out of the back. Only, it didn't look old anymore. It had had a complete overhaul. Jessie couldn't believe her eyes.

"You had this shipped from England?"

"With Jimmy's help. Well, what are you waiting for? Take it for a spin."

"I can't ride."

"No pun intended, but it's just like riding a bike." Michael laughed.

Michael held it for her as she put one leg over the middle and sat on the seat. He let go. She began to pedal down the street, moving from side to side at first. She started to straighten up as she went faster.

She yelled back, "I'm not wobbling anymore!"

EPILOGUE ONE

"HAPPY SIXTIETH Birthday, Michael." Jessie leaned over and kissed him, placing her left hand over his on the arm of the chair. She reached her other arm down to pet the dog.

Michael had a twinkle in his eye and responded, "This couldn't be a better birthday."

The sun was starting to go down. On the beach, Michael and Jessie were sitting back in Adirondack chairs under the umbrella. They watched as their grandchildren played in the sand. The twins, Joshua and Carl, were building a sandcastle. They were seven now. Jacquelyn Carol, who was five, was playfully trying to kick it in. The twins protested. "No girls allowed."

Amy went over and picked up Jackie Carol. "Come on, darling. You shouldn't kick in the castle that your cousins worked so hard to build."

Amy yelled for Jackson to follow them. She pulled back Jackie Carol's blonde curls, "We have to go get you back home and cleaned up. We have to get you into your new dress for Grandpa's big birthday party tonight."

Gina got Carl, and Cork got Josh. "Time to get ready ourselves," Gina said.

Gina kissed Michael on the cheek. "Come on you two. You better be getting ready, also. Remember our theater company is dedicating this play to you tonight, Michael. You can't be late for your own birthday."

Michael took Jessie's hand and patted it. "And tomorrow we'll celebrate your mom's second book coming out."

EPILOGUE TWO

HE WALKED up the concrete steps, seven of them. He had a habit of counting. He paused to take a last puff from his cigarette, discarding the butt in the receptacle before reaching for the white porcelain knob of the door.

He stopped in the corridor to read the name of the doctor etched on the glass. He mentally confirmed he had the right office before entering. He took a pack of Juicy Fruit from his pocket, offering a stick to the receptionist. She politely refused and took his name. "The doctor will see you shortly."

The slim average built man of average height with graying hair was immaculately dressed in a slate gray business suit. The suit matched his eyes. The colorful bow tie matched his personality. He entered the office at Bellevue Hospital where a doctor was waiting for him. "Please, have a seat. Thank you so much for coming in."

The doctor proceeded to tell him about a case he had been working on — a case with another doctor. He apologized that the other doctor wasn't there at the moment. "He had an emergency to attend to. He should be here shortly. I promise we won't keep you any longer than is necessary."

The man was a bit confused, as he didn't know why his presence had been requested, other than it had something to do with Jessica. The doctor had introduced himself as Dr. Hoffman.

Dr. Hoffman began by confirming that the man's name was indeed Malcolm Harrison. Then the doctor asked him if he lived in Brooklyn, NY, formerly from Britain. The man with the slate blue eyes said yes to all questions. Dr. Hoffman then asked if he was the husband of Jessica Harrison, also of Brooklyn. Mr. Harrison corrected the doctor by asserting that Jessica and he had been divorced for many years.

"Mr. Harrison, would you like to see her?"

"Oh, no, Doctor. Why would I want to see her?"

"Mr. Harrison, we called you here today to hopefully shed some light on her case. It might help if you just observe her. She won't see you. We can watch through a one-way glass. She's in the common area now with other patients."

Mr. Harrison hesitated, but said, "Okay, in that case, if you think it might help."

They walked out the door, turning the opposite direction from where he came in. They went down a long hallway until coming into another waiting area. From there someone in a white coat pushed a lever that opened a set of doors.

They entered a different world, one that was foreboding, to say the least. Thick plastic blocked off part of the ward. Workmen were scurrying back and forth. They stepped around some scaffolding where men were installing what appeared to be a skylight. Dr. Hoffman apologized for the construction mess. As they walked, Malcolm felt the squeak of the old hardwood floor.

Rooms lined the hallway on both sides. It was clear that this was the female ward. The half-clad patients with disheveled hair peeked out of their rooms and stared up at him with glazed eyes. One woman sat on the floor rocking back and forth on crumpled white sheets that had been torn from her mattress. The rooms were stark with few personal belongings if any. Moans and screams came from several of the chambers. Other rooms were soaked in a deadly silence.

At the end of the hall, they came to a door marked *private*. The doctor used a key to enter. From an office, they looked through a viewing window down onto a large room resembling an oversized living/dining room. There were various wooden tables strewn about, in no particular order. An entire wall held a display of mugs. They appeared to be handcrafted by the patients. A television set was switched on to cartoons. He saw Minnie Mouse on the screen. A woman with heavy makeup and colorful attire, not unlike Minnie Mouse, except the mouse was in black and white, sat on the couch watching. Her lipstick was all wrong, like a child not coloring within the lines. Two women folded laundry at one table. They looked back and forth at the other patients while engaging in a lively conversation. An elderly woman who still gave heed to her appearance sat on an overstuffed chair in front of a bookcase reading.

Mr. Harrison eyed every facet of the room and then saw her. She sat in the far corner, frantically writing in a notebook. He felt a stab to his heart. It was pity. She looked up and stared in his direction. His heart skipped a beat. Dr. Hoffman assured him their presence was hidden.

Her long, unruly hair was streaked with gray. Her almost translucent stick figures of arms and hand hung out of her loose, blue flowered hospital gown. Still, he recognized her. The essence of the young woman he had known in her twenties was still intact. Through the time-weathered, roughened exterior, he saw a childlike radiance. He remembered the original attraction he had to her. Not so long ago, she had been beautiful.

A young blonde went over to Jessie. She held a cup up to her mouth in an effort to get her to take some juice.

"That's Amy," said Dr. Hoffman. "She is our best nurse. She's an angel. All the patients love her. I'm afraid we are going to be losing her soon. She recently got engaged."

Through the glass, Malcolm could see the nurse gabbing away to Jessie. Jessie continued to write in her notebook. They watched a while longer and then returned to Dr. Hoffman's office.

The doctor asked if Mr. Harrison might still help if he could.

"Doctor, I don't know what I can do. My marriage to Jessie was so long ago. I'm remarried now and have grown children with my second wife. I don't know how I could possibly help. I lost track of Jessie years ago."

Dr. Hoffman looked disappointed.

"Well, I did see her once," he said trying to ease the look of disappointment on Dr. Hoffman's face. "It was maybe a decade ago or even longer. She was in Central Park. I didn't recognize her at first. She was feeding pigeons. I don't think she recognized me at all. I was relieved she didn't. I was with my family."

A younger doctor walked in. He was Asian and had a pronounced limp. Malcolm observed that he had an artificial leg. The young Asian doctor didn't seem to let his handicap bother him in the least. He was most enthusiastic in his job, and specifically, he wanted to help Jessica.

Dr. Hoffman introduced him as Dr. Linn, Young Ho Linn, a visiting psychiatrist from Korea. Dr. Linn spoke in fluent English. "Mr. Harrison, Jessica's case has particularly interested me." He continued in an earnest voice. "I do thank you for coming in and for your patience in this matter. I assure you that you are in no way responsible for Jessica. I only hoped that after searching for records on our patient and finding that you were once married to her that you might be able to shed some light on how we might best treat her condition."

"Dr. Linn, like I told Dr. Hoffman, I haven't seen her for years, but I will answer any questions I can."

"Well, let me give you a little back story," Dr. Linn said. "Jessica has been at Bellevue for nearly a month. She was brought in after complaints from a doorman on Park Avenue. She had tried to enter the apartment building on several occasions saying she lived there. She said she lived there with her husband and daughter. Mr. Harrison, have you ever lived at Park Avenue?"

Mr. Harrison laughed. "No, never. I'm a salesman. My sales aren't so good that I could ever live on Park Avenue."

"At first, Jessica didn't talk at all. But then slowly she began to open up, mostly through her writing. I believe you saw some of her writing or saw her writing in her journals. We only see bits and pieces. She guards it heavily. She has told us some rather fantastic things. When I say us, I mean Amy. She is one of our assistants here, excellent with the patients," Dr. Linn said.

"Yes, I saw her," Mr. Harrison said.

"So, if you don't mind," Dr. Linn continued, "Dr. Hoffman and I will run some of her story by you. If you could just tell us what you can about what she has said or written, we would most appreciate it.

"First of all, she never indicated that she was married to you at all. She gives her husband, or rather former husband's name, as Gino, who was from Italy."

"Gino, I don't know any Gino from Italy. If she married anyone after me, I'm not aware of it. As I said, I lost track of her after the divorce."

"Is there a daughter? Or any children for that matter?" Dr. Linn asked.

"No, we wanted children, but she couldn't have any. About a year into the marriage, I found she had an abortion before we married, maybe more than one. And then she gave up a child to adoption before we married. A little girl. Jessie never quite got over it."

"Were any of these your children?"

"No, this was from someone before we married. I only found out after we were married."

"Okay, she also mentioned an affair. Do you know anything about that?"

"Maybe that is who Gino is. Maybe that was a pet name for him. But he wasn't from Italy. His name was Eugene, and he was from Ireland. I saw him once. He was a big burly fellow, a dockworker. She was very young, her first love. I don't think she ever got over him. I know she got pregnant. He didn't want her after he found out. He married someone else. She told me she lost the baby. Later, she admitted to an abortion. Then she said a baby girl had been adopted. That all happened before we met. He was older. I think he had a son. I remember her saying something about it once."

"Hmm, this is indeed interesting. Was the son's name Joshua?" Dr. Linn asked.

"I have no idea."

"Do you know if this dockworker's mother liked Jessica?"

"I wouldn't have any idea about that either. My own mother protested against me marrying her."

"You are from Britain. Was Jessica also from Britain?"

"No, she's from New York."

"Was she ever wealthy?"

"No, never. There were lots of reasons we went our separate ways. Money was one of those reasons, although not the main one. You see, Doctor, I'm not a wealthy man, and I never will be. I don't think Jessie quite understood that. She lived in a fantasy world. Well, I guess you know that, don't you?

"Jessie loved hearing stories about where I came from. Before I came here, I lived with my parents who worked as caretakers on an estate. My brother, Jimmy, is still there working on the same estate. Both her parents died when she was young. She was too young to even know her mother. I think she particularly looked up to her father. From what I gather, he was a good man — that is if you can believe anything that Jessie says. That was the main reason we got a divorce. You never knew if anything she was telling you was true.

"Anyway, I do know her father was a storekeeper. His name was Carl. She used to tell me how she helped out in the store. She particularly liked working behind the counter. She said she could tell what people were like from their purchases. From that, she would make up stories about them. Carl, her father, died in some freak lightning accident, I don't know when exactly, several years after her mother died, I think. Jessie was always scared of storms after that. Her mother, Myra, had a weak heart I believe. That was what she died from.

"Jessie had an aunt that looked after her for a while, but she was getting old and died not too long after she took Jessie in. Jessie was on her own at a young age. She worked as a maid in various homes. She loved looking at their magazines and books. She loved to read. She was always about the latest fad that she would read about in magazines. She spent a good deal of her free time in the library. She became what she read.

"She should have been an actress. She was always getting these ideas in her head. Don't get me wrong. I think reading is a good thing. Jessie just couldn't seem to separate what she read from reality."

"What kinds of books did she read?" Dr. Linn asked.

"Hmm, just about anything. I think she liked mysteries. She read a lot of history, recent history, that is, this century. Once I remember her having a book about mafia figures checked out. She read a lot about the mafia, come to think of it."

"You said your mother didn't want you to marry her. Had your mother met her? Dr. Hoffman asked. "You said you were in Britain before coming here?"

"My brother, Jimmy, arrived in America with me but got homesick and went back to England. He wasn't too keen on Jessie. Thought she was cuckoo. He was right on the money."

Malcolm looked embarrassed. "Sorry, that was insensitive, wasn't it? Anyway, Jimmy expressed his concerns about Jessie to our family after going back. My mother wrote and begged me not to marry her. I wish I had listened."

"Why did you marry her?" Dr. Linn asked.

"Like I said, I was a salesman. I was traveling on my sales route one day in Brooklyn and came across her in a broken down car. I changed a flat for her. She said she was going to an island just to get away. She had a bag packed and a bunch of brochures in the seat and a rusty old bicycle strapped onto the roof. I knew she wasn't going anywhere in that broken down jalopy she was driving. I don't know, Doctor. I guess I felt sorry for her. She looked at life through the eyes of a child. Partly, it was lust. I found her attractive. I guess she found me the same. Before we knew it, we were having tea and pie in a diner. The next thing we knew, we were in a hotel room. Within a couple of months, we were married. After two years, we were divorced."

Dr. Linn looked over at Dr. Hoffman. Both shook their heads. Dr. Linn continued, "Things are beginning to make sense. Tell me, Mr. Harrison, you said you had a family now. I take it you have children."

Malcolm lit up. "Yes, my wife, Carol and I have four, all grown now."

"If you don't mind, what are their names?" asked Dr. Linn.

"We have a son, Michael, who is the oldest. He is a contractor on Long Island. The next is Clare, named after my mother. She married a minister. They live in Brooklyn. Then there are the twins, Gina, and Amelia, who are in college, both on scholarships. My wife and I wouldn't be able to afford college if it weren't for that." Malcolm removed his wallet and showed them pictures. "As you can see, Gina and Amy, we call her Amy, short for Amelia, aren't identical, far from it.

"Once, when they were small children, they came across Jessie. Carol was at the Macy's Day Parade with them. Carol, of course, knows about her, but the kids don't know that I was married before. Anyway, Jessie approached them trying to give them both candy bars. I don't think she meant any harm, but she scared Gina. Gina thought she was attempting to steal her doll. Amy went right up to her and took the candy bar. Carol told me about it. Carol just felt sorry for her. Amy was sympathetic. She takes after my wife in that respect."

"Mr. Harrison, it sounds like you have a wonderful family, and I wish the best for you. Dr. Hoffman and I thank you again for coming in."

Malcolm stood to shake their extended hands. "I don't want to seem heartless. It's just that Jessie was just so long ago. She wasn't right then. I know she had a hard life. Maybe now that she's got help, she'll do better?"

"Mr. Harrison, I don't want to lie to you," Dr. Hoffman said. "When she came in, she was confused. She didn't even know who she was. After a while, she began to tell us who she was or rather who she thought she was. Until we found you, the only thing we could confirm was that people in the park called her the pigeon lady. She has all but quit talking. She doesn't eat much. She drinks tea obsessively. She's wobbly. She can hardly stand. Wherever her mind is, she has built a happy world for herself. We've given her journals. She just writes. She did say once that she saw the world as a motion picture screen — that none of this was real — that we would all understand in the end."

EPILOGUE THREE

JESSICA PUT down her pen. Finished. She looked at the title, "Life is But a Dream." She thought to herself, a necessary dream.

Acknowledgements

This is my first novel. I completed it during the 2013 NaNoWriMo, otherwise known as National Novel Writing Month. It was a rather last minute decision, decided in October. NaNoWriMo takes place in November. But, a friend, Trish Ayers, mentioned she was doing it. Through her I made two other friends, Patricia Watkins and Pat Jennings. We formed a support group during the writing process. I would like to thank the ladies known as the three Pats and NaNoWriMo.

Since this was my first book I may have been a bit on the needy side asking anyone and everyone who would, to read my very rough draft and give me their opinion. Although the use of the word very is frowned upon, still I would have to say very, very, very rough draft. I would like to thank those who took the time to sift through it and comment back to me, my husband, my daughter, my mother-in-law Doris, Claudia Scholand, Marina Dannis, Bill Evans, Evelyn Knight, Anna and Tom Pekar, Brenda Ricker, Lisa Kramer, Susan Caldwell, and Mary Littleton. I appreciate everyone's constructive criticism. It was a learning process.

The Author

J. Schlenker, at seventeen, wrote a poem, which landed along with her picture on the front page of her small hometown newspaper. Instead of writing, though, she concentrated on art and made weaving her career. Upon retirement, with lots of encouragement from her husband, she began to write. In 2013, she completed her first novel draft while participating in NaNoWriMo (National Novel Writing Month). The first novel draft placed as a finalist for the William Faulkner - William Wisdom Creative Writing Competition. Schlenker entered a short story in the NYC Competition and received honorable mention on the first round.

Upcoming Works:

The Innkeeper on the Edge

The Missing Butler and Other Life Mysteries
(A Collection of Short Stories)

The Color of Cold and Ice

CPSIA information can be obtained at www.ICGtesting.com
Printed in the USA
BVOW06s1327020916

460987BV00022B/106/P